TOUCHED

Touched

SCOTT CAMPBELL

BANTAM BOOKS
New York • Toronto • London • Sydney • Auckland

TOUCHED

A Bantam Book/May 1996

Book design by Susan Hood

Library of Congress Cataloging-in-Publication Data
Campbell, Scott, 1945–
Touched / Scott Campbell.
p. cm.
ISBN 0-553-09996-5
I. Title.
PS3553.A4874T68 1996
813'.54—dc20 95-16172
CIP

Published simultaneously in the United States and Canada

Bantam Books are published by Bantam Books, a division of Bantam Doubleday Dell Publishing Group, Inc. Its trademark, consisting of the words "Bantam Books" and the portrayal of a rooster, is Registered in U.S. Patent and Trademark Office and in other countries. Marca Registrada. Bantam Books, 1540 Broadway, New York, New York 10036.

PRINTED IN THE UNITED STATES OF AMERICA

FFG 10 9 8 7 6 5 4 3 2 1

With love and thanks to my mother
And to the memory of my father

Part I

1

I am not an angry woman by nature. If anything, I've always gone too much in the other direction, being too friendly, too nice.

In high school, I was voted Sweetest Girl in my graduating class. Travis Dunlap and I had our picture taken for the yearbook at the Fanny Farmer on Michigan Avenue surrounded with heart-shaped boxes of candy, smiling sweetly at the camera. At least we were supposed to be smiling sweetly. But we got to goofing around and started feeding each other candies, then he smeared some chocolate on my face and I smeared some chocolate on his face and the photo that finally appeared in the yearbook showed us covered with chocolate, holding up fingers behind each other's heads as if giving each other horns. I hadn't looked at the photo since, until a couple of years ago, when I pulled out the yearbook to get ready for our fifteenth reunion. And there we were, Travis and me, looking like little devils. Somehow it seems appropriate now, this sweet-faced little angel/devil, in dotted *swiss,* of all things, smeared with what looks like mud. It seems almost prophetic.

Travis Dunlap was at the reunion. He's a hairdresser now in California. He has a dark tan and wears lots of gold chains, his shirt halfway unbuttoned. They took our picture again and posted it on the bulletin board at the Holiday Inn during the party. There he was in his chains and his tan, and there I was in my green silk dress, looking . . . well, I have to admit it, looking pretty good. A little wide in the hips, maybe, but looking good for thirty-three. Travis held his fingers up behind my head like horns again, but I couldn't do the same to him, I just didn't want to touch him. Somehow he didn't smell right to me. Maybe it was the bottle of Polo cologne he'd doused himself with.

It seemed like a measure of growth to me that I could choose to not like someone just because of the way he smelled, just on the basis of instinct. I'm not even sure I'd had instincts in high school. I'd always thought you had to find something to like about everybody, whether you wanted to or not. So it seemed like a step in the right direction that I could choose to dislike Travis Dunlap, or at least choose not to play games with him. I took it as a sign that I had developed a stronger sense of myself.

But when I think of those pictures now—the one of the innocent high school girl all dressed up and sullied with chocolate, and the one of the self-possessed mother of two with horns sticking out of her head—it makes me wonder about myself. What seemed like growth to me, I don't know . . . I'm not so sure anymore.

I am angry all the time these days. When a stoplight turns green, I lay on the horn before the person ahead of me even has a chance to move his foot from the brake to the gas. I can't get more than a few minutes into a television program before I get irritated and change the channel. And if anyone gives me grief at work because they've waited too long for a table, as likely as not I'll threaten to cross their name off the list and tell them to try their luck up the street at McDonald's.

I can't remember when I've felt so on edge. The closest thing I can compare it to was when I was carrying Danny, my oldest, but that was just being pregnant and scared. I wasn't even out of high school and there I was expecting a child. Well, no, I was not *expecting* a child. Ken and I were not *expecting* a child. It just happened, and I was upset all the time. First I was sick with morning sickness, then sick with fear about telling Ken, then sick with fear about telling my parents, my friends, the rest of the world. I wasn't the first in my class to get pregnant, but I was one of only two or three. In 1962, it wasn't the expected thing, the way it almost seems to be now.

Of course now in 1980 there are bigger things to fear for your children. I'd much prefer to have Danny come home and tell us Sharon is pregnant than to tell us he's doing drugs—or even worse, *not* to tell us he's doing drugs. It's scary to have a teenage son: You feel like you're watching them swim a channel full of sharks and swirling currents and all you can do is stand on the shore and knead your hands and worry whether they'll make it to the other side. But when they do . . . well, they've reached the other side. They're gone. No longer yours anymore. I think this is what they refer to as a no-win situation.

But here I am going on about Danny, when Robbie's the one who's in trouble.

I remember exactly what I was doing when Robbie came in and dropped his bomb. It was a Saturday evening in August, just about three months ago. It seems more like three years ago, so much has happened since then. It was about five-thirty or six. Ken was still at the hardware store and Danny was off with Sharon, as always. I'd been weeding my little vegetable patch and had just cleaned up and come in to fix dinner. I was standing at the kitchen sink, chopping onions for porcupine balls: meatballs with rice and onion and a can of tomato soup on top. It isn't anyone's favorite meal, but it's quick and easy and tastes pretty good, and I was too tired to do much more. I had a slice of bread in my mouth—a trick to keep you from crying, I read about it in the newspaper—and I was listening to the radio.

I was starting to wonder where Robbie was, when I heard the front door slam and he skulked into the room and took a cookie out of the jar. He was wearing an oversize tank top, gym shorts and sneaks, his skin nut-brown by then from being out in the sun all summer, and dusted with light blond fuzz. A sheaf of blond hair fell over one eye. I reminded myself to get him a haircut.

He parked himself in the corner of the counter by the oven and nibbled at the edge of the cookie, staring at the floor. I didn't really take note of it then, even though it was kind of odd for him to *nibble* a cookie—he usually just engulfs them—but I've played that scene in my mind so many times since, I can see it in VistaVision. I'm not sure if I spoke to him first—I might have said "You'll ruin your dinner" or "Don't slam the door" or something like that—but I'll never forget the first words that came out of his mouth. He nibbled on that cookie and stared at the floor—and I can see it now, even if I didn't see it then, I know it was there, I can see it now, his eyes were dark and furious, fixated—and he said "Jerry Houseman's been touching me."

You wonder how you'd react. When you see those people on *Donahue* talking about their messy lives, you wonder how you'd behave if your life all at once turned into a soap opera. I guess I'd always thought I'd know exactly what to say and do and I'd do it without a lot of fuss, crisp and confident as a nurse. But when it really happens to you . . .

What I did was, I got mad at Robbie. I didn't know it at the time, that that was what I was doing, but looking back on it since I see that I got angry at *him.* "What?" I said. I said "What?" and turned on him with the knife in my hand. I didn't remember I had the knife, I didn't remember to set it down. And even now I can see the horrified reaction on his face, the shock as he looked up at me to see me coming toward him. He tried to back away from me, but he was already lodged in that corner and he just shrank from me, as if he were melting inside his clothes.

I think I must have gone blind after that. I just remember those two things. Robbie staring at the floor, nibbling on that cookie, possessed. Then Robbie looking up at me, shrinking from me, terrified. After that the memory becomes white heat, as if we were both inside the sun, as if we didn't really have bodies. I think I knelt in front of him—I think I still had the knife in my hand, and holding him by the shoulders I held the knife right next to his face, his neck—and I think I shook him. *Spill,* I wanted to tell him. *Spill.* But I don't believe that's what I said. I probably said "What do you mean?" Or "Where?" Or "What do you mean?" again.

I've spent some late nights wondering since what made me quite so hysterical—I mean so *quickly* hysterical. Did I know before he told me? Had I suspected all along? Had I suspected and looked the other way? Even now I don't know, I really don't know. But it seems like I must have known, and maybe what made me so angry was that Robbie was making me see it.

I pulled him across the room and sat him at the kitchen table, set down the knife and squared myself, then looked straight into his eyes. "Now tell me," I said. "Exactly what happened."

He huddled in his chair as if he were cold, his shoulders drawn in toward his chin, his head scrunched down between them. He actually seemed to be shivering.

"Where did he touch you?" I said.

His eyes darted away from me.

I took a deep breath, swallowed hard. "Did he touch your penis?"

He grimaced and nodded.

"When?"

"Sometimes."

Sometimes? "What does that mean?"

He rolled his shoulders around the way he does when he's trying to ward me off, when I'm trying to groom him, or kiss him. "I don't know," he said.

"When did it start?"

He bent to tie his shoe.

"When did it start?"

"A while ago." His head was still hidden beneath the table.

"Robbie," I said. "Sit up."

When he did, his face was red. "I gotta go to the bathroom," he said. He started to get up. I grabbed his wrist. "I gotta go to the *bathroom,*" he whined, trying to twist himself free.

I realized I was holding his wrist like a handcuff. I let go of him and sat back. "OK," I said. "OK. Come back."

He shouldered out to the hall and thumped up the stairs.

I lay back my head. No thoughts would come to me, no words. I just sat there with my mouth open, looking at the little flap of paint hanging off the ceiling. I'd been meaning to scrape and repaint for months—no, it had probably been years by then—and there it was, still hanging.

2

Jerry Houseman had moved into our neighborhood a few years before. He and his wife bought a house at the other end of the street, near the corner of Francis. She was sort of mousy, I thought. I'd really only caught glimpses of her, watering her window boxes or getting out of her car. I guess they had three girls, one about Robbie's age, but they went to parochial school so Robbie didn't really know them.

The one he knew in the family was Jerry. I'd always thought there was something not quite right about Jerry Houseman. He seemed too eager to please, somehow. His eyes always looked like they were going to jump out of his head and glom onto you. I think he came from Napoleon, or maybe Michigan Center. One of those little towns around here that I've never even been to. There's no reason ever to go to them.

Robbie had started helping out with some of the yard work down there last year or the year before. I guess he helped rake leaves, or something. Helped put on the storm windows.

Shoveled the walk, carried in wood. I don't know, there were various things. I'm not sure how it started. He's always been a friendly kid. When he was small, he used to wander up and down the street by himself and just walk into people's houses, sit down and strike up a conversation. Just like that, no fears, no shyness. It always amazed me about him. By the time I found him there he would have told them all about Danny and Ken and the cat that lived in the woodpile. He didn't always get the facts right—once he'd told them we owned a horse—but he never left anything out.

Of course we knew everyone on the street, at least to nod and say hello, so it didn't worry me any. This has always been a nice neighborhood—friendly, quiet, safe. That's why we've stayed so many years. Especially the part about feeling safe. Safe is important in Jackson. There's a prison out on the north side of town, the State Prison of Southern Michigan—the largest in the world, they say, underneath one roof—and sometimes there are walkaways from the trustee farms, you hear it on the radio. It used to scare me as a kid and I'd bury my head beneath a pillow so I couldn't hear the report, even though my parents told me the escapees seldom come into town. They try to get out of the area as quick as they can, I guess. But still, there's this low-level sense of danger. There are signs along all the roads around here: DO NOT PICK UP HITCHHIKERS.

Where we are, though, has always felt safe. We're bordered on the south and west by a big municipal park, and on the east by a cemetery, so we're pretty much protected from any kind of development. We've always felt comfortable letting the kids hop on their bikes and take off for the day. So when Robbie started doing odd jobs for these friends he'd made up the street, I didn't give it another thought. Why should I? He'd helped out neighbors before.

And when he started hanging out with this friend he'd made, more and more . . . well, I wondered about it at first. Why this man, this grown adult, would want to spend so much time with a kid. He'd take Robbie to the stock car races, the movies, out for ice cream, the mall. They did a lot together. But Robbie seemed to like this man, they seemed to have fun together. And I figured, well, the man doesn't have any sons, he's surrounded by girls: Robbie is his substitute son.

My father had a friend like that when I was a girl. There was only me and my sister at home, there was this lone boy living next door, and my father befriended him. They worked in the garden together, built a birdhouse once, I think. Little Jimmy Southwick. He was sort of my father's pal, for a while. There was nothing wrong with it.

I keep trying to justify myself, as if this were all my fault.

It isn't my fault. I am a good mother.

When I heard Robbie flush the toilet upstairs, I grabbed the phone and called the store to tell Ken to close and come home early, but there wasn't any answer. He must have already been on his way. I hung up and composed myself at the table, straightened the salt and pepper shakers and slid the knife over to the corner. Then I knotted my hands in my lap so I wouldn't be tempted to grab my son again and waited for him to come through the door. When he did, he had a slingshot with him and was twisting the rubber sling in a coil, then twisting it the other way, pretending to be absorbed with it. The wart on his knuckle looked white against his tan.

"Robbie," I said. "Sit down here."

"I'm hungry," he said.

"Sit down."

He slouched into his chair, still absorbed in twisting the rubber sling.

"Now, honey," I said. I tried to sound calm. "Sweetheart, you've got to tell me. How long has this been going on?"

"What?"

"This thing with Jerry Houseman."

He twisted the sling. "I don't know. A while." He started to get up. "What's for dinner?"

I sat him back down. "Don't change the subject. What exactly is a while?"

He looked at the sling. "I don't know. A few months."

I grabbed his wrist. "You mean to tell me that man's been molesting you for *months*?"

His face screwed up into a knot and he jerked his hand away from me. "I don't know," he said. "Stop asking me questions!" Then all of a sudden he was crying, blubbering, leaking tears everywhere. His lower lip stretched out in a grimace. He put his head down on his arms.

I stroked his hair to calm him down. It was so strange to see him cry. My son was twelve years old and had become quite a tough little nut, I'd thought. He had cried as much as anyone else when he was a little boy, but as he'd gotten older and started to want to be like his older brother, he'd developed a sort of swaggering style.

He did it to win Danny's favor, I think. At least that was part of it, and it worked. Danny thinks Robbie is the best, a littler version of himself, a newer version, improved, and Robbie basks in Danny's affection. It always makes me smile to see it, and it also makes me a little sorry we didn't have Robbie sooner, so the two of them could have been closer. Five years is really too big a gap. But Robbie had picked up Danny's style so well, you found yourself believing that he was older than his years. "Oh, Robbie?" says Danny. "Hey, Robbie's OK." And you found yourself believing it: a happy, cocky little guy.

So to see him crying now, with his head on his arms, seemed almost artificial. It was as if the part he usually played, the swaggering little toughie, was real, and this child full of tears was the mask. Your children, they change before your eyes, from one thing to another. But I know this child like I know my insides. And in a way, as I watched him cry, I almost felt like my baby was being restored to me, returned to my care.

Returned, like damaged goods.

I lowered my head to the table to try to look into Robbie's eyes, but he kept his face turned away from me. I couldn't tell for sure, but it seemed like the actual crying had stopped and maybe now he was stalling for time. "Robbie," I said. "Honey . . ." I rubbed the plane between his shoulders where the dusting of fuzz swirls into a circle. "Hey baby," I said. "I'm sorry. I didn't mean to give you the third degree. It's just that I need to know exactly what happened. . . ."

Robbie sniffed and started to sit up, but then the gravel crackled in the drive, announcing that Ken was home. He threw me a panicked look. "Don't tell Dad!"

I stared at him for a second, trying to register what he'd said. "Robbie," I said. "I have to tell him."

"Don't tell him!" he cried. "You promise!"

"Robbie, no," I said. "I won't promise. I have to tell your father. He has a right to know."

"I don't want him to know!" Robbie cried. "I don't want him to know!"

I heard Ken's footsteps on the back porch. Robbie looked at me, horrified. "Don't tell!" he cried. "Don't you tell!" Then he lurched to the hall, bumped off the wall and ran up to his room. I heard the door slam, the lock turn.

Ken opened the kitchen door and stamped his feet, even

though it was dry outside. He started to smile, but as soon as he saw me the smile wilted on his face. "What's the matter?"

I stood in the doorway to the hall, torn which way to turn. I wanted to run up the stairs and hold Robbie, to comfort him if he would let me. It had been a while since he'd let me. But I needed to talk to Ken. I needed to know what to do.

And maybe I needed him to hold me. If he would, if I would let him.

I turned toward my husband. His face was open, ready for whatever I said.

"It's Robbie," I said.

"What is it?"

"He's all right," I said. "He isn't hurt. He isn't hurt physically."

"Is he in trouble?" said Ken. He came toward me. A part of me shrunk away, even then. I sat at the table. He pulled out a chair and sat on its edge, leaning toward me. "Linda," he pleaded. "What?"

I took a deep breath and looked at him, those deep brown eyes, those beautiful eyes, and then I started to cry.

He put his arms around me carefully, kind of awkwardly. "What is it?" he whispered. "Hey Lindee? What is it?" He hadn't called me that in months.

I drew back and looked at the ceiling. "He's been molested," I whispered.

"What?" He pulled away from me as if I were suddenly radioactive.

I closed my eyes. "Jerry Houseman."

"What?" he said. He started to stand.

I pressed my palm against his chest and pushed him back in his seat. "Stay quiet," I said. "Stay quiet." I glanced at the ceiling, at Robbie's room. "He didn't want me to tell you. He begged me not to tell you."

"Why?"

"I don't know. He's scared."

"Of *me*?"

"I don't know."

Ken fell against the back of his chair and let all the air out of him. He looked at me a moment, then shook his head and dropped his gaze. He stared at the corner of the floor by the refrigerator. "What do you mean, molested?" he said at last. His voice was tight and even.

"Jerry 'touched him,' he said. On his penis. It's been going on for months."

Ken shot me a look, and his cheeks flushed red. His eyes were glittering. Then the color drained out and his eyes seemed to darken as if he had fallen away from them, disappeared behind them. His shoulders lowered, he seemed to relax. And then, as if this day were just the same as any other day, my husband ambled to the refrigerator and poured himself some juice.

When I've thought of it since, I'm not even sure why I called Ken at the store that day. The truth is, my husband isn't much help in emergencies. He's a slow-moving, methodical man, as I suppose most hardware store people are. He believes that everything can be fixed, given the patience and the parts, and that belief gives him a quiet hum, like the hum of a furnace switching on and off automatically. It's comforting, reassuring. He seems to be on some inner track—some inner, balanced guideway—and so long as he's not disturbed, so long as he's left alone to travel that line, he's a smooth and easy man.

But give him a crisis to deal with and he fades into the wall. Like the time the neighbor's dog attacked Danny. I was in the bedroom upstairs when I heard the growling and screaming and I made it downstairs and out to the yard before Ken even got up from the table. I remember screaming at him that day, as he drove us to the hospital. I was holding Danny in my arms, covered with blood and slime, and I was screaming *Move it! Move faster! Are you dead? Get us to the hospital!* Later, after we knew that Danny was going to be OK, Ken broke down crying right there in the waiting room. I had been crying all morning, pacing, talking, while he just stood by me, with his steady hum. But once we knew that Danny was out of danger, he fell apart.

"Linda," he said. "When the dog attacked . . ." And then he just broke down crying. "I don't know what happened," he sobbed. "I froze. I don't know what happened to me . . ." I'd never seen him cry like that. I put my arm around him and turned him toward the window, so the nurses couldn't see.

But even though I knew this about him, even though I knew this problem with Robbie was going to be mine to fix, still my first thought was to call my husband.

I guess that speaks well for our marriage.

Maybe our marriage is OK.

I watched him as he laid back his head and drained the glass of apple juice, his Adam's apple bobbing. Then he put the empty bottle back into the refrigerator and turned to me, eyes watering. "I guess we'd better go talk to him?" He sounded like he would have preferred to do just about anything else.

I sighed and looked at the floor, then my hands, then nodded and pushed myself to my feet. "OK," I said. "Come on."

I turned into the hallway and he followed me up the stairs in silence. I knocked once lightly on Robbie's door. "Robbie," I said. "Can we come in?"

"No."

"We need to talk to you, hon." I looked at Ken, cocked my ear to the door.

"Robbie," said Ken. "Let us in."

It took almost a full minute for him to come to the door and open it. He looked tiny to me as the door revealed him, and from the way he glanced up at us, we must have looked huge to him, in the doorway. He turned away and flopped on his bed.

I followed him in and sat beside him.

"You told," he said into the bedspread.

"I had to, Robbie." I stroked his head. "I didn't know what else to do."

He didn't answer. I looked at Ken.

"I'm glad she told me, son," he said. He stepped forward. "Don't you worry about it. We'll take care of this."

Robbie squirmed away from us, turning his face to the wall.

"Robbie," said Ken. "Sit up. Look at me."

Robbie coiled himself tighter.

"Son," said Ken softly. "Sit up."

Slowly Robbie drew himself up and turned to look at us, shrinking from us at the same time. Ken knelt beside the bed. His face and neck were slick with sweat. He touched Robbie's arm as if he thought he were handling an explosive. "Now," he said. "Can you tell us about it? What. Exactly. Happened."

Robbie looked at him, then his lower lip began to quiver and his face fell in on itself. He lunged toward me and put his arms around me. It was so completely unlike him. He'd grown so squirmy in recent years, always pulling away from me, pushing my hands away when I tried to brush his hair out of his eyes, or to straighten his collar. He was like a bundle you couldn't pick up because its shape was too big and awkward. He made himself too awkward to hold whenever I came near him. But now here he was, clinging on to me. He turned his face into my belly.

Ken looked at me, helpless.

"Robbie," I said. I pulled back from him to look at him. But I couldn't do it either. I didn't know what question to ask. How do you respond to this news? Ask him to draw a picture? Give him a doll to play with? I'd heard that's what they did with children, very little children, but Robbie had the power of speech, he knew how to talk. The odd thing was that all of a sudden it seemed that *we* had forgotten how.

"Robbie?" I said again. But I knew as soon as I spoke that I couldn't wait for the answer. I didn't want to hear the answer. So when he didn't respond at once, I stroked his hair, pushed it out of his eyes. "How about some dinner?" I said. He sniffled, swallowed loudly. "I'm making porcupine balls," I said. "How about that? You want some?" He sniffed again and nodded, sat up, rubbing his nose with the heel of his hand. I stood and smoothed my hands on my hips. "I'll go get it ready," I said to Ken, then I tilted my head toward Robbie, suggesting to Ken he stay there with him.

It felt like leaving Ken with him now was like leaving the blind to lead the blind, but I thought maybe men had ways of talking about these things that women didn't. Maybe Ken would know what to ask, what words to use. Or not to use. I stopped outside the door and listened. I heard Ken's voice murmuring low, but I couldn't make out any words, so I finally went back down to the kitchen.

What I remember about that moment is the light in that kitchen. I'd worked in that room for fifteen years, but I'd never noticed how bright the light was. At least it never felt that bright before. It was a glare, a floodlight, leaving no shadows. It hurts my eyes just to think about it now.

At the dinner table, Robbie seemed better. He'd washed his face and combed his hair. His eyes were still a little red and his cheeks were still marbled a little, but he seemed much more composed. I glanced at Ken as they came in the room. He shrugged a little, as if to say he hadn't learned more. I brought in the plates and set them before them, then sat at my end of the table. I reached out and laid my hand on Robbie's.

"You feeling better?" I said. He nodded. "You look better," I said.

"We're going to let this thing lie for a bit," said Ken. "Just let things settle a bit." He reached over and wiggled Robbie's shoulder. "Right, Sport?" he said.

Robbie nodded again. He didn't look at either of us. "Can I have the cheese?" he said. I passed it to him, watched him sprinkle it over his meatballs. I looked at Ken. He was watching Robbie too. We were watching him like a zoo animal, like an alien: What will the stranger do next? It was the weirdest feeling. Ken glanced at me, then we both started eating. As we were chewing, our eyes met again, and I felt that old yearning I used to get when we first started dating, when I'd see him in the hallway at school, or mowing his parents' lawn, or driving by in his mother's car. It was a tangible ache.

"So what's on the tube tonight?" said Ken. He set both elbows on the table and leaned toward Robbie, overly interested.

Robbie shrugged.

"Maybe there's a good movie," said Ken. He chewed and looked at our son. Robbie just kept eating. "You want to go out to a movie?" said Ken.

I think I may have actually gasped. The thought of actually leaving the house, of going out into the world, seemed treacherous to me that night. My impulse was to huddle inside, stay sheltered and close for warmth. But Robbie perked up.

"*The Empire Strikes Back* is at Westwood," he said. He almost chirped it out.

Ken nodded methodically. "What's that about?" Of course he knew what it was about, we'd been hearing of nothing else all summer. But Robbie started to tell him about Darth Vader, Obi-wan Kenobi and Luke Skywalker. Ken kept urging him on, like a coach, just murmuring questions, nodding, rocking. And Robbie talked. My baby talked. My baby came back alive. He even began to poke his head in the air, the way he does when he gets excited. I sat there with a mouth full of food, so moved I forgot to swallow, and finally had to leave the room so my tears would not disturb them.

Most of what I remember about the movie was the three of us sitting there—Ken on one side, me on the other, and Robbie, protected, between us—but it was probably the worst possible film for me to see that night. It was all about good versus evil and giving youth the power and wisdom to protect themselves from those who would hurt them. It was horrible for me to watch, but Robbie seemed so completely absorbed that I was glad we went, in the end. By the time we got to Loud & Jackson's for our ice cream, after, we all seemed to be feeling better.

When we got home, Robbie went straight up to bed and

Ken and I stayed in the kitchen. I watched him from the table as he went through his homecoming ritual. He held up the juice to offer me some; I shook my head and he put it back, then came to the table and sat with me. We didn't speak for the first few moments—listening, I guess, to be sure that Robbie was safely upstairs, waiting for silence to settle around us. I watched Ken take two or three sips of his juice. He bent to meet the glass when he drank, like a little kid. Then he sat back. Finally we looked at each other.

"What are we going to do?" I said.

He held my gaze. "I don't know."

"Did you learn any more from him?"

"A little." He continued to hold my gaze as if he were assessing me, wondering how much he could tell me. "He said it's involved some hugging and kissing."

"What else?"

Ken glanced away, sipped some juice. "I don't know," he said. "He stopped talking."

"Well, didn't you ask him?"

"Of course I asked, Linda," he said, his voice taking on an edge. "You think I'm an idiot? I didn't see you asking any questions."

"I know," I said. "I know. I'm sorry. I just . . ."

Ken shifted his weight toward me, leaned his elbows on the table. "It's OK," he said quietly. "I think it's OK that you left. I think maybe it was easier for him to talk to just one person."

I folded my hands in my lap and nodded, glad for the benefit of that doubt. "What else did he tell you?" I said at last.

Ken's eyes flicked up at me. He considered me for a moment. "He said it's been going on for a year."

I fell toward him, my mouth gaping open, but Ken froze me

with a cautioning glance. I drew back into myself, squeezed my eyes shut and bit my lip.

He sat back, exhaled. "He clammed up after that," he said. "I didn't want to press him too much. I think we should wait and see . . ."

"How can you be so calm?" I snapped.

Ken's eyes shot up to me and hardened. "I'm trying not to panic," he said. "I think there's a danger of panicking here. I think we ought to wait and see . . ."

"You always want to wait," I said. "And look where it's gotten us!"

"You're blaming me for this?"

I stared at him, then hung my head. "No," I said. "I'm sorry. It's not your fault. I should have been home. I should have been here. I should have been paying attention. Robbie's alone so much of the time . . ."

"It's not your fault."

"Or we thought he was . . ."

"Linda, it's not your fault," he said. "It's nobody's fault. It's Houseman's fault." He spread his hands on the table. "Let's not get distracted with who's to blame. It's Jerry Houseman's fault."

I closed my eyes to compose myself, nodded again at his good sense. We sat in silence a moment. Then I stood up. "I'll call Lorraine," I said. Lorraine was a friend from work. "There's nothing she hasn't seen before. She might know what to do." I picked up the phone and started to dial but hung up before I finished.

"What's the matter?" said Ken.

"She's on vacation. In the Upper Peninsula somewhere."

He puffed out his cheeks, let the air out slowly.

I grabbed the phone and dialed again.

"Who are you calling?"

"Police."

Ken jumped up and took the phone from me. "No," he said flatly. "Not the police."

"Well, we have to talk to *someone,*" I said. "We can't just act like nothing's happened."

"I know. But not the police."

"Ken," I said. "This is a *crime.* It has to be reported."

He hung up the phone. "I'm not going to hit that kid first thing in the morning with the police," he whispered. He sat us down at the table again. "I think we should draw him out," he said. "I think we should let him lead us on this."

"Let him *lead* us? He's twelve years old! If he knew how to *lead* in this situation, he wouldn't be *in* this situation."

"Linda . . ."

"He's only twelve!"

"Calm down."

"I *won't* calm down. He's my *son.* He's been *hurt.*"

"It may have been only hugging and kissing. That may be all it amounted to. We have to wait and see."

All of a sudden I was sweating. "*Just* hugging and kissing? You can sit there and say to me it was *just* hugging and kissing? What's the matter with you? Your son has been molested and you're acting like Mister Rogers, here. 'This man has been hugging and kissing our son, isn't that nice, boys and girls?' "

Ken's eyes were suddenly on fire. "I'm *not* Mister Rogers, Linda. I'm Robbie's father and I'm damned upset. What do you want me to do to prove it? You want me to beat on my chest and scream? You want me to tear my hair out?" He jumped to his feet and started pacing, his voice for the first time rising. "Should I get a gun and go after Houseman? Or maybe torch his house?" He grabbed a butcher knife from the drawer. "Maybe we should go down there and dismember him right now!" He waved the knife at me a moment, his eyes all wide and wild, then he tossed it in the sink and stared out the window, shaking his head. A silence fell over us.

"If that man laid one hand on my son," I muttered, "I'll see him rot in prison."

"Fine." Ken turned toward me. "But don't accuse me of not caring because I don't do somersaults. I'm scared about this too, Linda. But that's exactly why I'm trying to keep a lid on it."

He took a step toward me and pointed at the ceiling. "That kid is terrified," he whispered. "I've never seen him so scared in my life. If we start bouncing off the walls, it's only going to make things worse." He rocked back on his heels and looked at me. "Now, you just go and get as hysterical as you need to get, but I'm going to work for sanity here." He stared at me a moment, then he pointed at me and shook his finger, sighting down the length of his arm as if he were aiming a rifle. His voice dropped to the tightest whisper. "And don't you ever suggest again that I don't care about my son." He stood quivering like he was going to explode, then slowly lowered his arm. "I'd lay down my life for that boy," he said.

I went to him, put my arm around him. "I know you would. I know."

He took me in his arms. "I love that boy."

"I know," I said. "I do too."

3

When Robbie was born, Ken and I had been married for six years.

For the first four years we'd lived in a rented apartment on South West Avenue, near the Frost Junior High. We lived above a party store. Ken worked at his uncle's hardware and went to junior college at night, and I took care of Danny. It wasn't what I'd expected. I'd thought I'd go to the junior college myself after high school, maybe get a business degree or diploma, maybe even go on to college. But then when Danny came along, suddenly all that changed.

It happened so fast. We were high school students, going to proms, and then we were our parents. Suddenly we had to think about security, the future, money. It was a switch, a real new tune. And even though we knew there was no turning back—once you have a kid, it's there—we both felt a little breathless at the sudden change in our lives and we wanted to stop and think a little bit about where we were going. Ken especially didn't want to have more kids until he had his feet beneath him financially. He was very responsible, dedicated. I remember coming upon him when I got up to quiet Danny, studying late in the kitchen with only the table light on, the rest of the apartment dark.

It took three years for Ken to get his degree at the junior college at night. And by that time he was too tired to want to go on to college. So he started his own hardware store out here on the south side of town—his uncle's is on the east side—and once the store was up and running, we moved out here and bought this house and decided to have a second child. It took a year after that for me to get pregnant. When you want one, you can't ever have one. It's the little surprise packages that come along so easy.

When Robbie arrived, it felt like our life was finally under way. Ken wasn't studying every night, or at the store all the time anymore. We had a decent place to live. And when Robbie came home from the hospital, all full of gurgles and smiles and charm, it seemed like we were becoming the family we'd always intended to become as soon as we had the time. We went on picnics together. Took Sunday drives in the car. It was just like it was supposed to be, and those were the happiest years of my life. Everything seemed to be flowing along just the way it was meant to, at last.

It lasted about five years, maybe six. Then there was the recession and the business wasn't doing so well. And after a while, with both boys in school, I decided to go to work. I got a job as a lunchtime hostess at Gilbert's Steak House, out by the intersection of 94 and 127, across from the Holiday Inn. Gilbert's had been there forever, as a kind of cushy dinner place—I remember my parents used to go there on special occasions—and as business had grown up around the interstate intersection, it had become a place for lunches too.

Going to work every day at a restaurant was an enormous change for me. In some way, it almost felt like I was reemerging into the world after more than a decade in hiding. Of course it wasn't true. I'd been out in the world all the time since Ken and I had gotten married. But I'd always been out as mother, and wife. I'd always had a child in tow, I'd always been Mrs. Young. I liked being Mrs. Young, and I loved my two boys, my three boys. But there was a different quality to the time I spent at the restaurant.

The restaurant is dark, even by day. It's relaxing, meant for lingering. Coming out at the end of a shift, you can't believe it's daylight outside, that people are trudging all around, running mundane errands. You feel like you've been in the movies, suspended in a dark dream, and the daytime world seems harsh and boring.

I liked the restaurant, the feeling it gave me. There was a seedy glamour in it, like the circus, or show business: The people there had a kind of weary knowledge I'd never encountered before. The weary part I could relate to, the knowledge part was new. It was already 1976. Somehow the sixties had come and gone while I was nursing my babies, all the sex and drugs and rock 'n' roll. But when I got to the restaurant, it felt like anything was possible.

I started dressing for work, a bit. Dangling earrings. Dramatic clothes. A little extra makeup.

I make it sound like some kind of party. It was work. And after work there was more work, taking care of the kids and Ken. But it was a stage, a platform, I guess that was the difference. I was meeting people, taking care of them, seeing to it that they had a good time. And I was meeting them as Linda, just Linda. Not as Danny's mother or Robbie's mother or Mrs. Young. Not even as Linda Young. Just Linda. There was a kind of thrill to it.

And people watched me, I knew it. I stood at my desk in my sleek black dress with the piano light shining up from below, and I knew I looked pretty good. I knew when I walked across the room to seat a party of businessmen that all the men were looking, or might be. I liked that feeling of being onstage. This was what I'd thought life was going to be like, when I got out of high school. A stage, a public event. An entering into the world, a time of being noticed.

And then I met Peter French. It didn't happen right away. I worked there two years, I think, maybe three, before Peter ever came in. And we must have flirted with each other for two or three months after that, over his lobster Newburg or his filet or Caesar salad. He wore shirts with starch-stiff collars and cuffs. I remember the cuffs of his shirts in particular. They were so crisp, so precise and clean, with a little monogram on them. When I noticed them, I looked up at him and found him looking at me, smiling, as if in noticing his cuffs I had revealed something about myself. He seemed to know something about me, to be able to see something in me that I didn't know was there. He was mysterious. You wanted to know what he knew.

Eventually the inevitable happened. It was a motel, I'm ashamed to admit it. The Quality Court, out toward the prison. The *Quality* Court, of all things. Three o'clock in the afternoon. Three till five or so, most often. Not that often. Maybe three or four times a month. Anticipation was nine-tenths of it. He had wonderful hands, and his breath smelled of mint. And even now, he seems knowing, to me.

The odd thing was, it actually improved my marriage in some ways. He said it improved his too. It gave me something to be excited about. It's pretty hard to be excited about making breakfasts and packing lunches and running errands and making dinner day after day after day. I loved my family, I loved my life, but this did add a thrill running through it. My little walks on the wild side made me appreciate my home still more.

But I also appreciated Peter. His knowingness. His sly, slow laugh. The way he'd pucker his lips sometimes as if he were sucking a lemon drop, and his eyes would sparkle with light. Ken began to seem rumpled, used. Like a pillow beyond its prime, kind of lumpy and shapeless. In fact, he's not out of shape so much. He's got a bit of a roll, but that's all. Peter was just something new, and forbidden. That's more of it than I'd like to admit. Peter was something forbidden. In all my life, in my thirty-five years, I'd never allowed myself the forbidden.

Except of course with Ken, in high school. But I couldn't really savor it then, it was such a desperate pawing. This was more sly, more willed. I'd never met this part of myself before, and I thought I liked what I saw.

After Peter, my contact with Ken became more friendly, almost formal. It wasn't because I didn't love him. It was just that if I'd been with Peter, I couldn't touch Ken without thinking of Peter, and being reminded of Peter in the presence of Ken made me nervous. But that night, that Saturday night last August after Robbie told, I wanted to be close to Ken, to be comforted and to comfort him. At least I thought that was what I wanted, especially after our fight. So when we got into bed that night I fit myself in under his arm like a chick crawling under its mother's wing and nuzzled against his neck. But as soon as he tried to put his other arm around me, I pulled away. I rolled on my back, then rolled on my side, then rolled around to try to cuddle up to him again, but flopped again on my back. It was like I had an animal in me, a big furry animal rummaging, circling for a place to sleep, and it couldn't find anyplace to rest, anyplace to get comfortable.

I finally gave up and went downstairs, made myself a mug of warm milk and sat in the kitchen in the dark. I kept trying to think how this could have happened to Robbie, kept trying to imagine it, kept trying *not* to imagine it. *When?* I kept asking myself. *When* could it have happened? But the answer was obvious. On the days I worked, I didn't get home until five or six, and Robbie was home from school by three-thirty. Often he would have come home and then left, charging off to play on his bike, to be home again for dinner at six-thirty or seven. And often—I knew it, I knew all about it—he spent that time with Jerry Houseman. Jerry had a bike of his own—a middle-aged man with a bike—and he and Robbie often went riding into the park together. He'd even given Robbie a bike, a brand-new bike, some kind of trickster thing that Robbie had begged for. We thought it was pretty extravagant, but then—well, again, he had no sons, and he'd given Robbie gifts before—what were we supposed to do, make him give it back?

We *should* have made him give it back, we shouldn't have let him take gifts from that man. Why wasn't I paying closer attention? Why didn't I know he was luring Robbie? So he could . . .

So he could what? When I thought about what he did to Robbie, my mind just stopped. I'd start to get a picture of it, a picture of his hand reaching out, a picture of Robbie there, unguarded—but my mind would just shut it out, go blank.

Then I'd see Peter French's hand reaching out for me beneath the sheets at the Quality Court.

I went into the living room, wandered into the dining room and back into the kitchen, then circled the rooms again, then again, trying to find a nook or shadow where my thoughts couldn't find me. But every corner I turned, there they were, like hands reaching out to grab me.

I finally decided to think about breakfast, about how I would feed my family in the morning, how I would stock my son full of warmth and substance and make him whole again. I circled back into the kitchen to see if I had any muffin mix, and heard Danny's car pull into the driveway. It came to a stop and idled awhile before he turned it off. Then I heard him step lightly onto the porch and let himself in the door.

I stood in the dark by the stove and watched him, a lanky shadow in the dark. I didn't mean to startle him but I was so deep in my thoughts, it didn't even occur to me to speak. He shut the door quietly and started to cross to the hall, then he jumped.

"Jesus!" he whispered. "You scared me."

"Sorry."

"What are you doing?"

"I couldn't sleep."

His body settled onto one hip. "You said you'd stop waiting up for me."

"I wasn't waiting up for you."

He lifted his chin like he'd caught me in a lie. "Then what are you doing up?"

I looked at him. I wanted to tell him. It seemed like maybe he could have helped me figure out what to do. He understood Robbie differently than I did, maybe he'd understand what to do. But what I saw when I looked at him was such a wall of attitude I didn't dare risk telling him anything, especially Robbie's secret.

"It's nothing," I said. "I just can't sleep."

"Oh." He seemed almost disappointed there wasn't going to be a fight.

"How's Sharon?"

"Fine."

"Did you have a good time?"

He shrugged. "It was OK. I'm tired."

"Me too."

He ran his fingers through his hair. "You going up?"

"I guess so," I sighed. "You go on up. I'll be along."

"Mmm-k," he said, turning to the door. " 'Night, Mom."

And there it was, in that quiet little phrase. 'Night, Mom. In there I heard that he loved me. The simpleness of it. The quietness of it. 'Night, Mom. Like he used to say as a boy after I'd tucked him in, snug and safe. 'Night, Mom. How had we strayed so far from that? How had our relationship become so complicated? Why was Sharon the only one in the world he'd admit he loved?

Sunday was the one day of the week we all had breakfast together. On the other days, my boys would parade through the kitchen—first Ken, then Robbie, then Danny—grabbing a doughnut or toast or cereal, coffee, juice, a piece of fruit, and pass out the door again, almost without sitting down. Occasionally there were three of us in the room all at once, but rarely were we all there together. And dinnertime was even worse, with Danny working after school at the grocery, with Ken staying late at the store and me not home until six or so myself. I used to joke that we ought to teach Robbie how to cook so he could have dinner waiting for us when we all got home, but it doesn't seem funny to me now.

I made waffles with sausages, and bacon. Scrambled eggs. Coffee and juice. I set the table in the dining room and folded the napkins on the plates like they do at Gilbert's, like a pleated fan, but it looked too fussy, too staged, and I didn't need to be reminded of Gilbert's, so I shook them out and folded them simple again, beneath the forks. I was worried that I was doing too much, that by going to such an extra effort I was making the morning even more awkward than it already was. But there wasn't any turning back, the food was all under way.

Ken came down first, then Robbie. Ken seemed quite expansive, robust. Boomed good morning, breathed deep of the smells. Robbie was subdued and distant, pretending to be still fogged with sleep. They had sat at the table and I was bringing in the first batch of waffles when Danny arrived. Danny, in a T-shirt and jeans, his hair sticking up in all different directions, his face still puffy, his eyes still bleary, sort of *hanging* in the doorway.

I don't know how to say this without just coming right out and saying it. There is something sexy about my son, about Danny. He is seventeen, and lean, and he has Ken's beautiful eyes. The way he holds himself, the way he moves—he's slow-moving, like his father. But Ken's slow motion is deliberateness, caution. Danny's is sullen and sensual. Like a cat. Standing there in the doorway, barefoot, his hair falling like a veil over his dark eyes—even swollen with sleep, maybe even especially swollen with sleep—there was something sexy about him. I still hadn't gotten used to it. He was now about the age that Ken was when I got pregnant with Danny.

He surveyed the spread, including the muffins I'd made, and the marmalade. He looked at it all through slitted eyes, then drew back as if from an odor.

"Who died?" he mumbled.

"What's that?" said Ken. He almost chirped it. He was never that cheerful in the morning.

Danny shrugged and slid into his chair, staring dumbly at his plate. "Looks like a funeral breakfast," he said.

"I felt like cooking," I said, setting a plate in front of him.

"What time you get home last night?" Ken asked.

Danny shrugged and drank some juice. "I don't know. Maybe one o'clock."

"Where were you?"

He shrugged again. "Went to a movie, hung out." He stared at his breakfast, sighed.

"We went to the movies too," said Ken. He was so *conversational* this morning. Usually he ate his food, then went off to read the paper. Or sometimes read it at the table.

Danny slid him a look. "The Flintstones Enter the Twentieth Century," he slurred. "Can I have the syrup?"

Ken held the syrup out to him on the palms of both hands, like on a tray. *"May the Force be with you,"* he said.

Danny stared at him, then looked at Robbie. "Any good?" he said.

Robbie nodded without looking up. He shoved a square of waffle around in the syrup.

Danny kicked him under the table. "Hey, mutant," he said. "Was it any good?"

Robbie squirmed to get away from his foot. "Cut it out," he whined.

Danny sat back and stared at his brother. "What's the matter with him?" he asked me.

"Robbie's feeling . . ."

"He's fine," said Ken.

Danny looked at his father, then at Robbie. "Hey, Pogo," he said. "What's up?"

"The movie was fine," said Robbie.

Danny set down his fork. "What does that mean, 'fine'? Does that mean funny? Does that mean good? Does that mean wonko-weird? Huh, Batman?"

Robbie shrugged. "It was good," he said. I could tell he was feeling uncomfortable with Danny's attention, with any kind of attention. I reached out to check his brow for a fever. I don't know why, it was instinctive: Your child is uncomfortable, you feel his brow. It's an automatic response. And I think I probably also thought the gesture would interrupt Danny.

Robbie pushed my hand away. "Leave me alone," he said.

Danny screeched a high soprano hoot that broke and became a kind of a grunt. "Touchy, touchy, touchy," he said. "The Rob's got a hair across his ass . . ."

"Watch your language," I said.

"Just leave him alone," said Ken.

Danny looked at us in turn. "I didn't do anything," he cried, suddenly all wrongly accused.

"Just eat your breakfast," said Ken.

"Jeesus!"

"Just do as your father says," I said.

Danny pushed back his chair. "What the fuck is going on here?"

"Danny!" said Ken.

"Why is everyone acting so fucking weird?"

"I told you to watch your language," I said.

"My *language*?" he said. "What the fuck is that? I'll say

whatever I fucking like. What the fuck is wrong with this fucking family . . . ?"

Robbie rammed back his chair and ran out of the room. The chair fell on the floor with a smack. The three of us froze and watched him go, then heard the front door slam. Ken jumped up and ran after him.

Danny turned to me. "What's going on?" he said, scared and defiant.

I didn't know what to say. I just didn't know what to say. I shook my head and looked down at my plate. My muffin and eggs were soaked with syrup.

Ken came back into the room. "Well, he's gone," he said. "He took off on his bike."

I started to get up to go after him.

Ken shook his head. "Just let him go. He'll come back when he's ready."

Danny slammed his hands on the table. "Will somebody please tell me what the fuck is going on?"

Ken sat down and planted his elbows on the table, clasped his hands in front of his mouth and blew, as if he were trying to warm them. He stared at the table, to steady himself. "Robbie's been molested," he said.

Danny turned to him, then to me. In all my days I'd never seen that expression on Danny's face. He'd become so guarded, so tough, protected. No one could get beyond the surface with him, no one except Sharon. But in that instant his guard was gone.

"What?" he whispered.

I nodded.

"Who?" said Danny, the toughness flowing back into his voice like a drug into his veins.

"Jerry Houseman," I said.

He looked at me, his dark eyes shining. Was this the look they saw in his eyes the moment just before he attacked, all the boys he'd gotten in fights with? He'd been a fighter ever since grade school, my Danny, always being sent to the principal's office, or being suspended from school. From the day he'd been born he'd had a kind of instability in him, a readiness to explode that erupted periodically like a volcano. I could see him ready to spew forth now.

"God*damm*it!" he cried. He slammed the table and turned to Ken. "What did he do?"

"We don't know," said Ken. "We don't know exactly. Robbie hasn't been willing to talk about it . . ."

"I'll go find him," said Danny.

"Just leave him for now."

"He'll talk to me," said Danny. "Robbie has always talked to me."

"Just wait till he comes back," said Ken.

"I wanna *talk* to him," cried Danny. "I can't just sit here and wait for him."

"You're not going to do him any good by getting all excited," said Ken.

"How can I *not* get excited about it? Some guy has fucked with my little brother and you want me to stay *calm* about it?"

"Danny," I said. "Now, just calm down." It was frightening to me to see him lose control of himself like this—the fear I thought I saw in his eyes, the knowledge he couldn't control it.

"What's the *matter* with you people?" he cried. "Don't you care what happens to him?"

"Of course we care . . ."

"Then *do* something!" He caught the edge of his plate on

his finger, lifted it and gave it a spin. Some of the eggs spilled off on the table. "You think a nice *breakfast* will fix him up?"

"Danny!" It was Ken. He was halfway out of his chair.

Danny shoved back his chair and started to rise.

That was when the doorbell rang. I wadded my napkin and jumped to my feet. "Now be quiet. Just be quiet," I whispered, and hurried to the door, almost grateful for the interruption.

It was Jerry Houseman.

Standing there on my porch, smiling through my screen.

" 'Morning," he said. "Is Robbie around?"

I believe I actually stopped breathing. My heart may have even stopped beating. The outrage of it, of him standing there actually smiling at me and asking to see my son. It left me dazed, a blank white sheet. But when I came to, I came to quickly. My stomach churned, turned over.

"Get out of here," I said.

The smile froze on his face, then fell.

"Get out of my sight. Get off my porch."

"Linda?" said Ken. He stood in the dining room, looking at me strangely.

"Get off my porch," I said again. "Get your . . ."

Ken hurried toward me. Jerry Houseman was backing away from me now. When Ken saw him, he burst through the screen door. "Get off this property," he ordered, grabbing his shoulders and steering him away.

Then Danny came out of the dining room. "Who is it?" he said. "What's going on . . . ?"

I tried to stop him, I knew what was going to happen, but I didn't try very hard. When he saw Houseman, he charged. "You *fuck*!" he shouted. "You miserable *fuck*!" He flew out the door and jumped on Houseman, knocking him down the steps to the ground. Danny tumbled down the steps after him and started pounding him. "You fucker!" he kept crying. "You *fucker*!" Danny's face turned purple, the veins on his neck were popping. Ken grabbed him and pulled him away long enough for Houseman to get to his feet, but Danny broke free and charged him again. I ran down the stairs and dove into the fray, not sure if I was pulling Danny off or clawing at Houseman, but between the two of us Ken and I got them separated. Ken held Danny's arms behind him.

Houseman just stood there, disoriented. Blood was streaming from near one eye. "No," he said. "No, no . . ."

I turned on him. I raised my hands and held them like claws facing toward me, like I was trying to hold the weight of all I wanted to say. "Molester," I growled. It was not my voice, it was some kind of guttural rasp. "You molested my child!" I growled at him. I could feel the power growing in me. "You molested my child!"

Houseman backed away from me.

"Child molester!" I cried. "Child molester! Get out of here! *Get out of here!*"

Houseman turned and started to walk, shaking his head, looking at the ground. The neighbors were all in their yards, on their porches. I could see them in my peripheral vision, stopping their mowing, looking up from their papers, coming to their windows. The entire street was watching us.

"Child molester!" I screamed.

Then I saw Robbie riding toward me from the direction Houseman was walking. He stopped in the middle of the street, straddling his bike, and stared.

"Robbie!" I cried. I held out my arms.

He spun his bike around and charged off.

4

I was raised to be polite. At one point, I concluded that that was the only thing my parents really cared about, that we be polite, me and Janet. Janet is my sister, two years older. We were taught to fold our napkins and slide them back into their rings after dinner. We were taught to stand whenever an adult came into the room, and to remain standing until they sat. We were taught to hold doors, to let others go first, to be considerate at all times. And we were taught to smile.

I got so good at it that in high school Roger Hatt was said to have said that he saw me smile at a drinking fountain. I believe the story is probably true. I smiled at everybody, every day, all day long. Sometimes my face would actually hurt by the end of the day because I'd been smiling so much. It wasn't artificial, really. I've always genuinely liked people, and was glad to see them. But it was, shall we say, *insistent.* I *insisted* on being pleasant, as my parents had taught me, and Janet did too.

For a while when Ken and I were first married, I found myself getting short-tempered a lot. Ken was working all day and studying all night and I got irritable with him because he was never around to help. Then when Danny started howling in the middle of the night, every night, Ken got irritable with me, especially when I couldn't do anything to quiet Danny. It was not an easy time. But we always smoothed it over. Ken was raised to be polite, like me. And in time we learned to lay our politeness over our differences like a blanket, until they settled down. It worked. There was goodwill in our house. Our parents had taught us well.

But with Peter French, things were different.

Peter French taught me to beg, to demand. To parade myself naked in front of him. To watch myself in a mirror with him. To make love all over the room, not just in the bed. He taught me to growl with pleasure, and he talked to me in my ear just above the threshold of hearing, so I could hear he was talking to me but didn't know what he was saying.

At first it was just a game, something I played at in the afternoons. But in time it became an itch in my skin, so I wanted to crawl out of my skin, to be bigger than I was, bigger than I had allowed myself to be. Then I'd go home to Ken and the boys, to the same little house on Palmer Street, to prepare the dinner and sort the mail and bake the cookies for the scout meeting. As I approached it, sometimes I thought the house looked just too small to contain me, this newfound full-blown version of me, but once I got inside its familiar walls and corners made me feel safe. My movements in the house were routine, predictable, like clockwork. I could slip inside them as if I were slipping into a coat, or dress. Glasses go here, forks go there. Now comes the news, now I load the dishwasher. Bedtime is at ten. Life was stable. I could experiment.

But when I saw Jerry Houseman standing on my porch and smiling, asking to see my son, that house could no longer contain me. The house itself was under siege, and I did crawl out of my skin for a moment. For a moment I was all rage. And I scalded that man with my venom.

And then, there in that poisonous state, I saw my son coming toward me.

It's not that I didn't have every right to denounce that man in public. It's not that I didn't have every right to be consumed with rage. It's not even that I didn't have a right to indulge my feelings. But to announce my son's most shameful secret to the entire neighborhood. To strew it across the landscape like trash. To do it in his presence. I know now what it's like to see the edge of the abyss. If I were religious, I think I would say that I had seen the face of Satan at that very moment. And judging by the look on his face, I would say my son had too.

Robbie was my baby. Danny was always in a hurry—to be conceived, to be born, to be weaned, to walk, to run, to get out of the house, to fall in love, to leave home. From the moment he was born, it seems he was trying to get away from me. But Robbie was exactly the opposite. A gurgling, gooing, happy pudge. There was a magnetism to him that made you want to love him, to hold him. And I held him all the time when he was a child. All the cooing and cuddling I didn't get with Danny, I lavished onto Robbie, on top of all the cooing and cuddling I wanted to do with him, himself.

He brought out the best in me, I thought. After he was born I found myself smiling differently. It wasn't the same as smiling in response to seeing somebody and saying hello to them. In a way, that kind of smile came to seem almost like a screen, a way of fuzzing my vision, distorting my face, so people couldn't see me, or so I couldn't see them.

But after Robbie was born I found myself smiling to myself

all the time. It came from a warmth inside me, a pleasure that went all through me. It was a tenderness I hadn't been allowed to feel before, an unguarded tenderness unlike I'd ever felt for Ken, and which with Danny had only been frustrated. It would come to me as I drove the car, as I walked, as I washed the dishes. A sense of utter peace and contentment as if the answer were here, inside. The answer to all the questions. Or the knowledge that the questions didn't really matter anymore, not in the face of this feeling. I felt like I had been introduced to a part of myself I'd only before dared to hope was there, a place I'd always strained to achieve, but here it was, just opened to me, opened as simply as a flower and just as soft and delicate.

It was all so different from Danny. Danny had such an irritable nature, did from the first day. When he learned to ride a tricycle, he rode it furiously fast, pumping, pumping, his eyes sort of fixed on some imaginary target. Sometimes he almost frightened me, the hysteria in his laughter. There is a darkness in him, a shadow, and he views the world through it—from behind it, or within it. I'd always thought that clouded people were products of their experience, that something had happened to them that made them see the world so darkly. But Danny seemed to be that way from the very start. Fearful, nervous, a crier. And the fact that he wouldn't take comforting well made it especially hard. It made me feel so helpless. Of course I was sure it was all my fault, and the pediatrician shared that view. He kept telling me to relax, not to be nervous around him, to drink warm tea, think kind thoughts. Which only made things worse because it fed my fear that I was at fault, which made me more nervous than ever with Danny, which made me handle him badly, maybe, which made him more irritable. Who knows? Was it the chicken or the egg? All

I know is, Danny has always made me worry. About him, and about my worth as a mother.

But when Robbie was born it seemed like even Danny was happy, for a while. He was totally taken with Robbie, and a little jealous too, and he became a part of the family in a way he'd seemed unwilling to before. There is a photo from that era that captures it for me. We were at the Cascades, this man-made waterfall in town. It was built by one of the city fathers as a tourist attraction, and I guess it is one, of sorts. It's as wide as three or four car-lengths, I'd say, and a couple of stories tall, built into the side of a hill in the park near where we used to live. It's built in maybe a dozen steps with fountains spraying up on the sides, and the lights in the water change color in time to music broadcast over loudspeakers. "The Battle Hymn of the Republic." "Blue Hawaii." "Nearer My God to Thee." Very corny. A lot of fun.

This photo was taken by a friend, on the steps that go up the side of the falls. It was a summer evening at twilight, we had brought the kids on an outing. I am holding Robbie's hand, Ken has one arm around me and is holding Danny's hand. Robbie is two and Danny is seven. We're all in shorts, all tan and relaxed. And just as Sandy snapped the picture, the fountain on the side of the falls, above us, sprayed up into the air, caught the breeze and showered down on us. The picture captured us just as the spray was drifting over us. I have huddled into the nook of Ken's arm, he has raised his shoulder to protect me, Danny has one hand over his mouth and is looking up at us, giggling, and Robbie has thrown both arms open wide, as if to receive this gift from the heavens. We are all of us laughing, happy, healthy. The family we always meant to be.

For years I kept that photo on my dresser like a little shrine and sort of paid my respects to it every time I dusted. But at some point, after some years had passed, I'd sometimes find myself picking it up and actually almost studying it, as if I were looking in a mirror searching for a blemish. Was there something in Ken's attitude, or in mine, that should have warned me? Was there a perceivable flaw? But the photo didn't show anything except what it appeared to show—a perfectly happy family.

Sometimes I thought if I stared long enough I could bring that perfection back again just by looking at it, just by concentrating on it. But the more I looked, the more it was clear that reality had faded. The photograph was still vivid and clear, but Ken and I had grown pale. Our sexual life was going along as well as could be expected for two people in their mid-thirties who had two kids in the house, and who had been sleeping together every night for God knows how many years. And we were getting along OK. But we weren't in love anymore, or I wasn't. I didn't expect violins and roses, I knew that love evolves. But what I was feeling was not evolution.

I'd had doubts when I married Ken. We'd been dating only about a year, since the spring of our junior year. Our first date, in fact, was the junior prom. We'd never even gone out before, and there we were at the junior prom. It was one of those situations. I had just broken up with the boy I'd been dating for several months, and he had just broken up with the girl he'd been dating since we started high school, so some friends arranged the date for us. I'd known him before, and I thought he was cute, but I'd never really considered him a possibility because he'd always been involved with Kathy. He'd seemed nice, but somehow not quite there. Distracted. Otherwise engaged. Maybe a little dreamy.

He did have dreamy eyes. Lashes as long and thick as mink.

So we went to the junior prom, and I liked him. When he focused those eyes upon you, when he really was there, all of him, all at once, he created tremendous warmth around him, a relaxing warmth, like a bath. He wasn't especially witty, or funny. But the boy I'd just finished dating considered himself a real cutup, and I'd grown tired of his red-faced giggling. Ken seemed serious, quiet, with a simmering intensity that you saw only when you got close. I was feeling a little lonely after breaking up with David, even though I broke up with him, and Ken was always standing by. He made me feel special, wanted. He was almost like a house that had been built especially for me, and all I had to do was move in.

It was actually pretty much the way Danny is with Sharon.

But I didn't think that Ken was necessarily the end of the line for me, the last man I'd ever date. He was a great companion for senior year, and after that none of us knew what was going to happen. But then I got pregnant. I never considered an abortion, my parents would not have allowed it. So I planned a big wedding instead. A dozen bridesmaids, a dozen ushers. In June, just after graduation. And we stayed at the party till two.

I loved my husband, I did. But after a while he began to feel to me the way he used to feel before we started dating, when I just witnessed him from a distance. He always seemed to be thinking of something else, usually the store. I wondered at first if maybe he was having an affair, but I couldn't make the story fly. He just is not the type.

So I finally reached the conclusion that this was just the way it was. That after a while things get ordinary. And it was up to me to deal with it. If my husband was preoccupied, well, at least he was preoccupied with the thing that was keeping our table set. He was good to me, and good to the boys. What more was there to ask for, really? Those were the things that mattered.

So I decided to adjust, to find something else to engage my interest, and that was when I started working. I could have gone to work at the store, helping Ken at the register. It might have brought us closer together. But I didn't even consider it, not for any longer than it took to think of it. That would have made my life too much a closed circle. That would have made it feel like a prison, a room without any doors. I wanted something fresh and new to bring to the dinner table. Well, I got something fresh and new. But it wasn't exactly anything I could bring to the dinner table.

What can I say about Peter French? I could say he made me shiver, he made me giggle, he made me feel like a schoolgirl, all that trite baloney. I could say that he had money, and that impressed me. I'm not much proud of that, but I did love the fineness of his things. The big plush car, the tailored suits, the perfection of his fingernails.

But the thing I really liked about him was his selfishness. I'd never met anybody before who was so guiltlessly selfish. Not that he was out to advance himself at other people's expense. It was just that he took what he wanted from life. What *he* wanted. Not what others told him to want.

He owned real estate here and there around town: He bought things that interested him, then sold them when he got bored with them. He went to New York to buy his clothes, then sent half of them back. He ate whatever he wanted, whenever he wanted, day or night, and would sometimes leave half the meal on his plate. He took only what he really wanted.

And when he saw me, he wanted me. It was that simple to him. He didn't see it as any kind of reflection on his love for his wife. He loved his wife, but he wanted me too.

"But if you really love her," I said, "how can you do this to her?"

"I'm not doing anything to her," he said, twirling a silver fork in his hands. "What I want is to do something to you."

I found it strangely exciting to be wanted in such an arbitrary way. He wanted to use me for his pleasure and the thought of that pleased me. It pleased me that he wanted me and it pleased me that he made it so simple. It was something just between him and me. It had nothing to do with anyone else. It was something that we would give to each other. Or, rather, something we'd both give to ourselves. We would pluck this piece of life and slowly savor it together.

And I must say that yes, I did savor it. I enjoyed every minute of it. It was mine. In some way, this was the first and only thing in my life that was totally mine. Done because I wanted it. Done for no other reason than to gather pleasure for myself. And no one was getting hurt.

Except, while I was busy, my son.

Jerry Houseman's been touching me.

I remember watching Robbie at Clark Lake one afternoon. We had gone to visit friends who have a summer house out there. He was playing on the raft with their son, the same age, playing king of the mountain. He was stronger than the other boy, slick and shiny in the sun, the curves and lines of his body just suggesting the bulk of the man to come. They swam back in and he hoisted himself from the water and stretched himself on the dock. I watched him dry in the sun—sleek at first, then pebbled with drops. And I remember being struck by how beautiful he was. For a moment he wasn't my son, he was just this beautiful object that you might want to own, to possess. It was a hot summer afternoon—I'd had a beer or two, I was lying in the sun—and I remember coming to and being chilled by the thought of having those feelings find their way into the wrong person. Had I taught him? Did he know? The world was full of crazy people. People who destroy things just because they're beautiful. Did he know about evil in the world? We'd talked about war and murder, we'd told him to be careful of strangers. But had we taught him to be careful of friends?

Jerry Houseman's been touching me.

From the moment Robbie was born, I touched him and kissed him all over his body, everywhere, fascinated with every mound and crevice. His body itself was a miracle—the fact that it existed, the fact it came out of me, the fact that it was perfect. I touched him and touched him and touched him, to be sure he was real, to make him real. And I did feel stirrings in me. Not sexual stirrings exactly, but stirrings so deep and powerful, that tugged so hard on me that they were almost indistinguishable from sexual stirrings.

But then, as he grew older, I got to feel self-conscious about those feelings. As he developed into more of a separate person, I touched him less often, in fewer places. Then he began to want privacy, became protective of it. Shutting the door to the bathroom and not wanting me to come in. Later, shutting the door to his bedroom. It was hard to accept his withdrawal from me, but I did it gladly, proudly, because I knew it was the right thing to do and I was pleased to see him developing just the way he should. I ached for him, but I let him go.

It was hard from the very first moment. I remember how sad it made me when I had to let him stop breastfeeding. Danny had chewed me raw, it hadn't been a pleasant experience. But with Robbie I was wrapped in this wonderful soft and warm cocoon that I didn't ever want to leave. At some point, though, he was ready to stop. And the doctor told me if I didn't let him, I'd never get rid of him, so I stopped. But I remember how sad I was. I remember I curled up with Ken in bed and laughed, because I was crying.

And that was just the first step in a never-ending succession of steps away from each other. Almost as if we were on separate ships headed in different directions. But you let go of your children. You let them go. Sometimes you want to hurry the process, to get them out of your hair for good. Grow up, get married, go raise your own kids, just leave me alone. It's a thicket of feelings, always. But somehow through it all you're trying to steer them to a place where they can stand free of you. You let them out in little bits to see what they can handle. You follow one step behind, then two steps behind, then four steps, then you watch from a distance, and finally you let them out of your sight for a minute, two minutes, ten, an hour, a morning, an afternoon, a day. You watch, to see they can handle it, then you say your prayers and go on your way.

Jerry Houseman's been touching me.

When I was a girl, my mother gave me a brooch to take to school. It was a cameo, a profile of a woman's head on an ivory oval, ringed with gold filigree. It had belonged to her mother's mother. I thought it was the most beautiful thing I had ever seen, and I begged my mother to let me take it to school for show-and-tell. She said no and no and no again, and offered me all kinds of other choices, but finally I was so insistent, she gave in and let me take it. She wrapped it in cotton, then tissue paper, then put it in a box. And when I got home the brooch was gone, just disappeared from my bag. My mother was painfully kind to me, but the horror I felt was unspeakable. To have something given to your care, so precious, so much not yours to keep, and to fail that responsibility. I don't know that I've ever really gotten over it. To think of it now makes me wince inside. A little. Still, a little.

5

I finally went searching for Robbie at one o'clock. Ken still thought we ought to just let him come back when he was ready, but he'd been gone for almost an hour and a half and Ken could see it was making me crazy, so he agreed to let me go look. He stayed at home in case Robbie returned and Danny went in to work at the market.

I drove out Francis toward Vandercook Lake, then turned on Probert toward the park, which was where I was sure he had gone. He always hung out in the park, riding his bike up and down the hill, exploring around the old zoo. The back of the park by the stream was overgrown and utterly empty, not a sign of life in sight. You could have been way out in the country or on the plains of Africa for all the sense you had that there was any civilization around. The only sound was the buzz of the beetles and the swish of the breeze through the grass. I drove slowly, peering down the few paths that led into the grass and trees. It felt like there might be wild animals in there, a lion or boar that might charge any minute.

I followed the curving lane up past the baseball diamonds, mostly deserted, and over toward the old zoo. It was a spitefully beautiful day. Some families had come out after church to walk in the rose garden. There was one black family, especially dressed up, the woman in a wide-brimmed straw hat and a kind of forties flowered dress. The man was wearing a straw hat too, a panama, and an ivory suit. And the children, a boy and girl about four and six, were dressed to the nines, he in a little short-legged suit and the girl in a stiff little pinafore. There was no sign of Robbie.

I drove up to the sledding hill, then back down past the zoo again and over to the picnic pavilion, the golf course and the tennis courts. I prowled the neighborhoods beyond, where the houses get bigger and more expensive, cruising slowly up one street, down another and back again. There were no people mowing their lawns or washing their cars or sitting on porches. It was so still it would have been easy to spot a boy on a bicycle, but there were so many streets, so many curving lanes and cul-de-sacs and mazes turning back on themselves that my search began to feel like the empty effort it probably was.

I searched all the way to Brown's Lake and after that to the Wickwire Farm, where Robbie's friend Buzzy lived. He almost never rode out there, it's so far, but I figured I'd give it a try. Mrs. Kaser was working in her garden. She said she hadn't seen him, that Buzzy and his father had gone to the lake, but she let me use her phone. Ken said that Robbie hadn't come back. I almost asked him if it wasn't time we called the police now—maybe at least they could *find* him—but I knew he wouldn't agree. So I drove back to town and checked Robbie's school, and the junior high where he'd go next month, then canvassed the park again.

Finally, after two, I went home. Ken was on the porch with the paper, by all appearances reigning over a tidy, peaceful household.

I dragged myself up the steps, defeated.

"No luck?" he said.

I shook my head.

He held out his hand. "Come here." I slumped on the glider beside him and he put his arm around me. "He's all right," Ken murmured. "Don't worry."

I wanted to believe him but I'd believed that Robbie had been all right all along and I couldn't have been more wrong. How could I go on good faith now?

"Just take care of yourself," Ken murmured. "So you'll be ready when he comes back."

It seemed to make so much sense. He always seemed to make so much sense. How had I come to resent that? I nodded and patted his knee, forced a smile, then pushed myself to my feet and went to the kitchen for a glass of juice. The breakfast dishes were all cleaned up, everything put away. I felt so grateful for Ken at that moment. I couldn't have washed a fork just then, I was so exhausted.

I went upstairs and took a shower, letting the water rush over me, pummeling my face and neck. For a moment I lost myself in the waves of heat, the drum of the water, the billows of steam intermingling with the afternoon breeze through the window. It felt decadent taking a shower at this time of day, like sneaking a nap on a weekday. I let it wash me clean and limp. Then I pulled on some shorts and a tank top, tied my hair back in a ponytail, and went downstairs to keep vigil with Ken.

I couldn't remember the last time I went downstairs for the

purpose of sitting with Ken. I could remember a time when I always approached him with anticipation, when every meeting was an event, even after we were married. Having dinner together, or breakfast. Hearing him come home from work. Stopping at the store to give him his keys. Even after we'd had two kids, there was still a little thrill to it, knowing he was mine. I wasn't sure when I'd stopped feeling that way. But walking down the stairs in wet hair, barefoot in my tank top and shorts, I felt almost like I was coming downstairs for our first date. Not the sexiness and excitement of it, but the sense of being focused on him, of having my whole sense of future narrowed to this meeting.

I dropped down onto the glider beside him and fell against his shoulder. "What's in the paper?"

"Not much," he said. "Khomeini's spouting off again. Carter and Reagan are grandstanding. Kenny Rogers is at the Fairgrounds."

I let my head rest on his shoulder and gazed across the street.

"Mrs. VanderVelt came by," he said. "Just out for a stroll down the street, don't you know . . ."

I snickered. "What did she have to say?"

Ken put on a falsetto voice. "Is everything all right?" he mimicked. "I heard some commotion down here . . ."

"What did you say?"

"I told her everything was fine and that we were sorry we'd bothered her. 'Oh, no bother,' she said. Then she looks up and down the street. 'You know I've been suspicious of that man ever since he moved in here,' she said. 'His eyes are too close-set. You know, you can *tell* a criminal by the structure of his face. I saw it in the *Free Press*. And close-set eyes are a give-away. Lee Harvey Oswald had close-set eyes.' "

I actually found myself laughing a kind of helpless, exhausted laugh. "What did you say?"

He put his arm around me. "I told her I'd always admired her eyes," he whispered. "Because they see so much."

I set my heels on the edge of the seat and rested my chin on my knee. As sick to my stomach as I felt, he was making me feel better. "What did she say?"

" 'Well, thank you. Yes, I'm very observant.' And then she went on her way."

I smiled and laid my hand on his thigh, rubbed my thumb across the raised mole. He's not an entertainer by nature, but he comes through when it matters. I sat there a moment, just swinging with him, then looked up and saw Robbie riding toward us. He was riding slow, letting his bicycle weave from side to side, steering with just one hand. He didn't look at us, just turned in the drive and rode up beside the house, headed toward the garage. I sighed and looked at Ken; he raised his brows and pursed his lips.

I heard Robbie go in the back door, then pushed myself to my feet and saw him through the front door screen, rummaging in the kitchen. I glanced at Ken, slipped into the house and padded quietly to the kitchen, propping myself in the doorway. Robbie had pulled out some bread and peanut butter and was rifling the drawer for a knife.

"You want me to make you something?" I said.

He didn't acknowledge my presence.

"I could make you some breakfast. You haven't had breakfast."

He began to spread the bread with peanut butter.

"How about some ham salad? I think I've got some ham in the—"

"I don't *want* anything!" he snapped.

I nodded, looked at the floor while he made his sandwich and started to eat. The instep of my foot was tan; my toenail polish was chipped, red. Ken moved in behind me. I could feel his warmth enveloping me.

I looked up at Robbie. He was still at the counter eating with his back to me. "Robbie," I said. "I'm sorry. I didn't mean—"

"Why did you *do* that?" he cried. He turned to me. There were tears in his eyes.

"I didn't mean to. I lost my head. But he came to the house, he was looking for you . . ."

"You didn't have to shout. You didn't have to tell everybody."

"I'm sorry. You're right. I shouldn't have done that."

The tears began to spill down his cheeks. "Everybody knows . . ."

I went to him, knelt next to him. "Oh, Robbie," I said. "I'm sorry, baby. It's just . . . When I saw him standing there, it made me so angry, I wanted to kill him. I just wanted to kill him for what he did."

"You're not supposed to kill people."

"I know, but I wanted to punish him." I brushed the hair away from his face. "What was I supposed to do? Invite him in for breakfast?"

"You didn't have to shout."

"I know. But it's done. I'm sorry. I'm really so sorry."

He kept his eyes cast down at the floor, refusing to look at me. I studied the shiny brown whorl of his ear, the streak of blond fuzz on his cheek, the faintly freckled, sunburned nose. For a moment, the smell of his peanut butter mingled in my memory with the smell of baby oil and powder.

"Where did you go?" I said at last.

He shrugged. Why should he tell me? Why should he ever tell me anything again? It would be a long road to win him back.

I glanced at Ken. His eyes were wide, just drinking me in. I looked back at Robbie, the wall between us. I felt some lock in me turn. "I think we should call the police," I said.

Robbie looked at me, scared.

"Robbie, it's a crime," I said. "What that man did to you is a crime." His face continued to grow more distorted, like it was twisting into a knot. "He deserves to be punished for it," I said. I felt myself getting stronger.

Ken crossed the room and stood behind me. I don't know why he backed me up except that he loved me, I guess. I had taken the plunge and he would not let me swim those waters alone.

Robbie looked up at him.

"It's up to you," Ken told him.

He glanced at me, then back at his dad. "What'll happen?"

"I don't know," said Ken. "The first thing they'll do is send someone out to talk to you, probably. That's all. Just a private talk."

I watched Robbie swallow. "What'll happen then?"

"They'll arrest him," said Danny flatly. I looked up to see him in the doorway to the dining room. None of us had heard him come in. He was wearing his bag boy's apron.

Robbie turned to him. "And then?"

"They'll put him in jail," said Danny. "Exactly where he belongs." He held his brother in place with his gaze, then crossed the room and squatted down beside him like a coach, so the two of us were flanking Robbie, looking slightly up at him. Danny put his hands on Robbie's shoulders, turned him to face him squarely. "There may have to be a trial," he said. His eyes were dark, intent. "But I'll be there with you," he whispered. "OK? I'll be there the whole time, OK?"

Robbie didn't answer.

"I'll be there the whole time."

I placed my hands on top of Danny's, both of us holding Robbie's shoulders, and pressed my head to Robbie's back. Ken moved around beside us and knelt with one arm around me and one arm around Danny. The four of us huddled together there, all of us touching, a family.

Part II

1

When I woke up that Sunday morning, the first thing on my mind was Robbie. I was used to that. In the eighteen months or so since I'd met him, I'd come awake more and more with him the first thing on my mind. The way he grinned after telling a whopper, waiting for you to figure out he was just putting you on again. The way his hair stuck up in the back, like a flame burning in the light. His interest in bugs and birds and furry things, how they lived, what they did with their days. I never knew much about that myself: In a way I was learning more from him than he was learning from me. He explained to me about ants, this fancy communication they have. About bees, and the way they dance. I'd heard some of this stuff before but I'd forgotten most of it, so being with him was like being reeducated in the world, getting reacquainted with life.

On mornings when I woke early enough so I had some time to spare, I'd lie there in bed and think about him and watch the light creep across the ceiling toward the crack above the dresser. I think if I made a chart of it, I'd find out I was waking up earlier and earlier during those months in order to get that time for myself. Jeanette would be up and at her day—she's always been an early riser; you can't raise three kids and not be—and while she was in the shower, I'd think. Just stare at the ceiling and think. Then I'd have to think about something else in order to bring myself down to normal so I could get up and start my day too. But it sure did make the mornings bright, to wake up thinking of Robbie. I think me waking up happy improved the mood of the whole house.

I remember one morning last winter coming down to breakfast smiling and whistling, and my oldest, June Marie, rolling her eyes. "Daddy's lost touch with reality again," she said.

I stopped and parked my hands on my hips. "And what's wrong with being happy?" I said. I tweaked her on the cheek. Then Karen, her sister, pushed the newspaper across the table—still folded, she didn't read it, she just stared at the headlines while she ate—and there was murder and war and all that stuff. She cocked her head at me, like she'd just proved that being happy was an impossibility. So I tore off the top half of the first page and folded it into a paper airplane and sailed it across the kitchen. It looped over the window and nearly hit Jeanette in the head, by the toaster—she ducked and hooted at it, bugging her eyes in exaggerated surprise—then it landed on the floor by the fridge.

Lynnie, the little one, dropped her mouth open, forgetting for a minute the two huge teeth she was always trying to hide. Karen slouched down and stirred her cereal, too bored by us all to show a reaction but kind of amused, I could tell. Then June Marie gave me a kiss and started putting on her coat. "Gee,

Dad," she said. "I didn't know you were so sophisticated. Aerodynamically speaking, I mean." She was already at the door by the time Sally honked for her. Somehow she always knew in advance just when Sally would arrive, and was on her way out to meet her. "Cheerleading tonight," she said to Jeanette. "I'll be late." And then she was out the door.

I stood there a minute, feeling the rush of cold air she'd let in the room, then feeling the warmth of the kitchen again, the smell of toast and coffee and eggs. I drew a happy face in the condensation on the window, then picked up my paper airplane, unfolded it and spread it back in place on top of the newspaper.

"Thank you," said Jeanette, scraping the burned part off the toast in the sink. She turned to the girls. "Did all of us see that? That's called 'picking up after ourselves.' It's a whole new concept in living." I slipped my arms around her waist and nibbled on her earlobe. "*You* are a whole new concept in living," I whispered, and Karen groaned at the sight of her parents acting romantic and happy.

That was the way it often was on the mornings I woke up thinking of Robbie. But that Sunday morning last August, the thought of Robbie didn't fill me up with quite so much happiness. I woke up thinking about the way we'd left it the day before, the pissy mood he was in. We'd been out to the mall in the afternoon. We'd just finished washing my car, and I told him to come with me to the mall and we'd get some ice cream.

On the way in, we went through Montgomery Ward and looked at all the TVs—dozens of them all lined up and stacked on top of each other, all of them playing the same show, a golfing match, I think it was. I remember I knelt down next to him, squatted, and said something about how that was how the world looked through an insect's eye, the same image, over and over. He curled his shoulder away from me—"I know that," he said—and wandered off. I figured he was just in a mood, and that he didn't like me assuming he didn't know about insects' eyes. He was the nature expert, after all. If I'd thought about it, I would have known he knew about insects' eyes, but I didn't really think. I just wanted to stay close to him. We'd been having so much fun before, squirting each other with the hose. It had been exactly the kind of time I always loved with him: no second thoughts, just fun. And then all of a sudden there we were in this buzzing public place, surrounded by all these *machines* and, I don't know, I felt like I was losing touch with him. I guess I just wanted to have an excuse to smell his bubble-gum smell. So I hunkered down and said that to him.

But he didn't want me that close. Kids. They're really a cruel joke. God makes you love them so goddamn much, then He makes them want to become adult and go away from you. But that's God's lesson, isn't it? That loving is letting go. Isn't that what they say? So I let him go. I let him wander off down the aisle and I hung around behind.

I spent some time looking at little televisions, those little jobs that hang on the bottom of kitchen cupboards. I was thinking Jeanette might like one of those for her birthday, or for Christmas, she spends so much time in the kitchen. But they're really pretty expensive and her birthday wasn't until the next April. So after a while I ambled down the aisle, looking for Robbie.

I don't know what got into him that afternoon. It's not like I did anything to him. But he really got into a mood. Of course, I'd seen him in moods before. He could be as pouty as any kid, and he could be as on-purpose about it as any other kid too. That's one of the things about kids. They're always trying to play the angles but they haven't got it down yet. They're not as good at it as adults, so you can see them working at it. You can see the wheels turning in their minds, the calculations clicking. Like the Invisible Man, this toy I gave Robbie that shows all the human organs. You can see what's going on inside. It makes them easier to handle sometimes.

As if a kid could be easy to handle.

I found him in this soundproofed room, all glass, with a couple of other kids, fooling around with this demonstration of different kinds of speakers. They were laughing and punching each other's shoulders, cracking jokes, just being kids. The others must have been friends from school. One was wearing a too-big letter jacket that probably belonged to an older brother; the other had this spiked-up haircut sort of like a mohawk. They were like a picture of something, like something out of Norman Rockwell, but updated to 1980. I don't know. There was some sort of balance there.

I slid up to the door—it was open—and watched them, leaning against the jamb. At one point Robbie turned and ran his hand across the other kid's mohawk, pretending like it was cutting him, and he saw me standing there, grinning. He didn't smile or say hi. He just looked away.

"Who's that?" said the kid in the jacket.

Robbie shrugged. "Hey, look at this!" he said, fiddling with some machine.

It wasn't like I was in a big hurry, but I didn't like him ignoring me. So I straightened up and tightened my voice. "Robbie," I said. "It's time to go." He kept on mucking around though, trying to ignore me like he was hoping I'd just go away. It was more than just defiance. It was like that time we'd spent washing the car hadn't even happened. Like none of what we'd ever done together had ever happened. All of a sudden he was this other kid, this angry, defiant kid who didn't need anybody. I knew he was just putting on a display for his friends of how independent he was, how no adult could tell him when it was time to go, but that was no excuse. I resented him treating me that way just so he could show off. I resented him treating me like I didn't really matter to him.

I had to say it three or four times, but he finally gave up and came with me. He didn't have any choice and he knew it. There was no way for him to get out of that room without going past me, and I wasn't going to just wander off and let him get away with this. In some ways, I think when he acted like that, he *wanted* me to draw the line, to show him that I cared. So I drew the line, and we left. But he wasn't happy about it at all. He pouted all the way home, glowering out the window. When I asked him what was the matter, he wouldn't answer.

"You know, it's not funny when you act like that," I said.

"It's time you learned some manners," I said.

"You want to go swimming tomorrow?" I said.

But he never answered, not once. Just kept glowering out the window. And when I pulled up in front of his house, he shouldered his way out the door almost before I came to a stop. I watched him walk up the walk, up onto his porch and in the door. He didn't walk fast or slow, there wasn't a swagger or slump. But he slammed the door when he went in.

I figured he'd get over it. But the next morning I woke up thinking about that little scene we'd had. I played it over in my mind, trying to figure out what I'd done wrong, to figure where Robbie was coming from and how I could work him around. It takes time and effort to deal with kids, you have to give it a lot of thought. You want to give them guidance and you want to give them freedom, as much freedom as they can take. It's a real balancing act, and you've got to concentrate.

But I was also feeling like he'd left me in the lurch. I kept playing that picture in my mind, that picture of him walking up the walk and into the house and slamming the door without even saying so long, like he was just walking out of my life without even turning to wave good-bye. The sight of him moving away like that in the early twilight . . . I felt lonely, that's what it was. I woke up feeling lonely. I couldn't stand it, having my last sight of him be his back, moving away from me. I wanted to see his face, see him laugh, to have things like they were before.

So I decided when Jeanette and the girls went to church, I'd walk over to Robbie's house. When Jeanette and I got married, I agreed to raise the kids Catholic, but I never agreed to be Catholic myself, so I never went to church with them except on holidays. I'd go down in my robe and have coffee with them while they were having their breakfast, then I'd send them on their way and read the paper while I ate.

It always made me feel proud to see them, the four of them setting off together in the Pontiac station wagon we'd inherited from Jeanette's mother. That morning Jeanette was wearing a suit she'd made and the girls were in summer dresses. Karen didn't want to go; she slumped in the back seat and stared out the window. But June Marie sat in front with her mother, being adult and responsible. And Lynnie had her Bible with her; she was into it.

I watched them out the kitchen window while I was sipping

coffee. I thought they looked cute in that big fat car, like the little peglike people in one of those Fisher-Price toys the kids used to have. They looked like a nifty little package, like they'd get along fine without me that morning.

I watched them back out of the driveway and head up the street toward Francis, then went about cleaning up their dishes. It felt like taking off a tight shoe, watching them pull out. All the time they'd been getting ready, I'd been feeling antsy for them to leave. I wanted them to get on with their business so I could get on with mine. Of course I couldn't say that to them. As far as they knew, I had nothing to do but read the Sunday paper. But privately I was in a hurry, I wanted to see my boy. So after they left, I grabbed a quick shower, then jumped into some shorts and a T-shirt and headed down to Robbie's.

It was a beautiful Sunday morning. The sky was this electric blue, I don't think there was a single cloud, and the temperature was eighty or so. A spectacular Sunday, ripe for the plucking. And Sundays were a great day for Robbie and me, or they had been, sometimes. Sometimes he was busy with his family, sometimes I was busy with mine. But sometimes we managed to go off on an outing on a Sunday together, and it was really something. To have such a long stretch of time instead of only an hour or two. To go off on an adventure together. Once we drove into Detroit to a baseball game. Once we went to Lake Michigan and spent the day on the beach. I wanted to take him to Chicago sometime, maybe for a whole weekend. We'd talked about it; he was excited about it. He wanted to go to the zoo. So as I was walking over there, I was thinking about those times—the good times we'd had, the times we had planned—and I was thinking maybe he'd be into going swimming that day.

All up and down the street the neighbors were mowing their lawns and working their gardens and hanging out on their porches. I nodded and waved as I walked by—I felt like I was on my route, felt like I should have had my mailbag and my spray can of *Halt!* for the dogs—and Mrs. VanderVelt stepped toward me to chat about what a nice day it was. I just kept moving and nodding and smiling. "Yep. Sure is. You bet." Like that. She was always an obstacle on this walk—Robbie and I used to joke about it: If you got too close to her, she started talking and you never got free. Once, just to keep her from talking to him, Robbie told her he'd gotten hit with a wild pitch and had lost his hearing. He said it real loud, like he couldn't tell how loud he was talking, and he had her believing it too. Until she saw him look around when the ice cream truck came up the street behind him, ringing its chimes.

I was laughing about that time as I was climbing Robbie's steps, planning on reminding him of it as a way to break the ice between us. To make it easy for him to be friendly instead of feeling like he had to play out the mood he was playing the night before. Sometimes kids get stuck in a mood and don't know how to get out of it; you kind of have to help them.

I rang the bell and shoved my hands in my pockets and looked around, bouncing on my toes. I was really feeling excited about getting this problem ironed out and getting on with this beautiful day. I felt like I used to feel at the start of a race—I was on the track team in school—all anticipation.

The door swung open and I turned around. There was Mrs. Young, Robbie's mother, hazy behind the screen, in the shadow. I nodded and smiled. "Good morning!" I said. But then I saw her face just crumble. It just turned into a different face. Linda Young is a good-looking woman—blond, very pretty, pleasant-looking—and she was always nice to me. But in that moment her face melted and turned into something else. It was the strangest thing ever happened to me. The only thing I can compare it to is some experiences I've had with dogs on my route. They look all fuzzy and warm one minute and all of a sudden they turn on you.

She pushed her way out onto the porch, backing me toward the steps, and I knew immediately what had happened. I'd been dreading this all along, but I couldn't believe it was happening, that it was actually happening.

"Get out!" she kept saying. "Get out! Get out!"

I didn't know what to do. This woman was coming at me. Then Danny burst out the door, Robbie's brother, and jumped on me and knocked me down and started pounding on me, yelling. All I could do was curl up and hold up my arms to try to protect my face. I was taken so off guard, I couldn't even get to my feet, never mind fight back. Robbie's father finally pulled him away and held him with his arms behind his back, but he kept on yelling at me.

I got myself to my feet. I was bleeding over my eye. Then Robbie's mother started again. "Child molester!" she was screaming. "Child molester! MOLESTER!" I backed away down the sidewalk, stumbling. I wanted to defend myself but I couldn't find any words. I couldn't even find my voice. I stumbled backward down the street, then turned and started to walk away, mopping my eye with my hand, wondering where else I was cut. There was blood dripping on the sidewalk, there was quite a lot of blood. I knew I had to get out of there, whatever it took I had to get out, to get away and tend to myself and figure out what to do next.

I started moving more on-purpose, heading back toward

home. Then I looked up and saw Robbie on his bike, riding down the street toward me. I felt like I'd seen my savior, that he was coming to rescue me, to tell them it was all a lie, there was nothing wrong, there was nothing wrong, but he stopped and straddled his bike in the middle of the street, and stared. I think I reached out toward him. I think I tried to say his name. But he turned his bike and rode away.

I started walking again. I passed by Mrs. VanderVelt's house and she stepped out in front of me. "Mr. Houseman," she said. "Are you all right?"

I waved her away. "It's OK."

"That looks like a nasty cut," she said. "What would make a body just attack you in such fashion? That boy has always been a surly one, ever since he was a lad. But I never thought I'd see him just attack someone for no reason . . ."

The way she said "for no reason." I don't know. Was it my imagination, or was she accusing me? Was she asking me a question or was she enjoying saying those words? Testing out the story, toying with how she was going to retell it? And retell it, and retell it.

I left her there, still talking, staggered off toward home and went up to the bathroom to wash. It wasn't an especially deep wound; he just got me in one of those places that really gushes when it's cut. So I washed it out and put on a Band-Aid, then stood there and stared at myself. The Band-Aid hung over the edge of my eye and I had a scrape on my cheek—from falling against the sidewalk, I guess. I looked like a boxer after a prizefight.

I don't know if I had any clear thoughts. I was probably still in shock that all this had happened. I looked at my reflection like I was looking at another person, waiting for that person to tell me what I should do next. I felt like a terrified little kid, looking up to an adult. And I felt like a really mad adult, looking down on a bad little kid. I don't know what I felt like. Scared. Just scared, to the insides of my bones.

I started whispering to myself. "Oh my God, oh my God, oh my God." Over and over again, almost with every breath. It was the only thing I could say. It was almost like I was praying, but I wasn't praying at all. I was just making noise, just trying to keep myself tied to this moment, this room, this pain, so I wouldn't just fall apart. I paced around the room in circles, coming back to the mirror over and over to see if I had changed, to see if all this had disappeared.

It came to me I had to clean up, to remove all traces of blood. I washed the sink, then washed it again, then wiped the floor with the towel. I pulled off my T-shirt and my cutoffs and took them down to the laundry room. Then I thought, Well that will look odd, that I did a whole laundry for those two things. So I went upstairs and got the hamper and hauled it down to the basement and did a whole white load, with bleach, lots of bleach, in cold water. It came to me that Jeanette would be pleased that I had done the laundry while she and the girls were at church. I felt relieved at that thought at the same time I felt disgusted by it, that I could get credit for this. I went back upstairs and retraced my steps to see if I'd spilled any blood anywhere, but there didn't seem to be any. I started to go out to the porch to see if there was blood on the steps, but then I realized I was naked, I was wearing only my sneakers, so I charged upstairs and pulled on some shorts and another T-shirt.

Then I sat on the edge of the bed and took a few deep breaths. "OK," I said out loud. "OK. Now we've got to figure out what to do." I looked around the room. It was quiet as a cemetery and eerie dark for the middle of the day. The only sound was the whirr of the old alarm clock. It seemed sort of like a sickroom. And all of a sudden I knew I had to get out of the house. It was too quiet there, too organized, too small to hold all the things that were racing around in me. Like what was I going to tell Jeanette? What was I going to tell the girls? Was I ever going to see Robbie again? I was swamped by all these thoughts, these feelings, and I knew if I sat still I'd explode or disintegrate from the pressure. What were the neighbors saying now? What were the Youngs going to do? I grabbed my wallet and keys and charged back down the stairs.

I made it from the kitchen to the garage with no one seeing me. But as I was backing out, it came to me I should check the front steps, so I threw the car into park and jumped out. There was some blood, a few little drops on the cement steps to the porch, but I would have had to scrub them out and I wasn't about to pull out the hose and a brush and go to work in public, where the whole world could stare at me, so I just got back in the car.

I didn't look up once the whole time. I kept my eyes focused on whatever was right in front of me. The hood of the car, the sidewalk, the grass, the steps, the porch, the sidewalk, the car, the steering wheel, the gearshift lever, the view of the street in the back window. It was only when I got down to Francis, at the end of the street, and had to stop, that I looked up. I looked up into the rearview mirror and looked at my neighborhood. Everything had returned to normal. The neighbors were mowing their lawns again, reading their papers, tending their gardens. It looked like the same spectacular Sunday it had been a few minutes ago. A Norman Rockwell painting of Sunday morning in America. I gunned the motor and pulled onto Francis.

I drove out Francis toward Vandercook Lake, the direction Robbie had taken when he rode away on his bike. I knew he'd gone into the park. He always rode around in there. I pulled off onto Probert Road and went into the park from the rear. I drove around the baseball diamonds, the sledding hill, the abandoned zoo, the picnic pavilion, the tennis courts, but I couldn't find him anywhere. He was gone, just gone, just disappeared.

I ended up at the brook where Robbie and I used to go, next to the dirt bike hill. I thought that maybe he'd be drawn to that spot. We'd spent a lot of time there, especially after I bought him the DynoSlammer. We'd ride out there together after I got home from my route and I'd watch him charge up and down the hill, and turn wheelies, and show off the new tricks he'd learned and the newer ones he was practicing. Then we'd cool off in the brook, just sit on the rocks with our feet in the water and talk. About life. About things we wanted to do. And later, about how I loved him.

The brook was where it got started. The physical stuff, I mean. He'd been showing me some new tricks he'd learned and I'd been watching, encouraging him. And it was like he was in slow motion that day. When he leapt in the air on his bike, he seemed to float free of gravity. Like he was lighter than the air, or actually made of the air itself. He was so beautiful in the light. His straight blond hair flying up and falling over one eye. His sun-brown back gleaming with sweat. The silver-bright smile he flashed me. He was happiness, pure happiness. He was like this perfect Sunday morning—a clear blue sky, a bright hot sun. Nature at its most perfect. He was.

Watching him that day, I felt the way I felt when I saw the sun rise over the Grand Canyon. I know it's a weird comparison, but the feeling of awe was the same. Like I was being given the chance to peek inside the world. I stood at the edge of that canyon that morning and God brought up the sun and the world just opened up in front of me. There it was, just laid out for me, like He was saying Take it, it's yours. And I wanted to take it, to make it mine, to be worthy of it somehow. Now here was Robbie, before me, perfect. A sliver of sunlight on a bike. As if God were saying to me, Look what I have created.

Those feelings were all going on in me that day, even though I was acting perfectly normal on the surface. Laughing with him, calling out to him, cheering him on. And when he finally came over and sat with me in the brook, sat next to me . . .

He sat on a rock in the water, then leaned back and let the water rush over him. And it was like he was *part* of the stream, like the stream was actually rushing through him. I sat on a rock right next to him and dangled my feet in the water and watched him. We talked, but less and less. More and more there were just the birds, and the sound of the breeze in the trees, and the brook, bubbling, gurgling, urging me on. I just sat there and stared at him. And I loved him so much at that moment. I ached for him at that moment. I was trembling over what that meant. But there he was, perfection, right there. I could reach out and touch it. I could reach out and be part of it.

I don't know what made me do it. I had a touch of a summer cold, my head was a little woozy. I don't know, I was just off kilter enough . . .

I stood in the water and lifted him up so he was standing in front of me. Then I knelt in front of him. "Robbie," I told him. "I love you."

He just stared at me. A totally blank stare.

His mouth hung a little open.

"I love you," I said again. I couldn't believe I was saying it, that I was actually saying it. I wanted to take the words back, I didn't want to make him deal with this. But the words were out, it was done. I thought I was going to pass out. I pulled him to me and hugged him to steady myself with his strong, straight body. Then I pulled back and looked at him. And he was looking at me with such wonder. Not fear, I thought, but wonder. The way I'd looked at the Grand Canyon. I bent my face to his and kissed him on the lips. It was just the tenderest touch, the sweetest taste. He didn't kiss me back. Then I kissed his cheek and hugged him again. "I love you," I told him again. And the words didn't scare me so much that time, they sounded better that time. I pulled away from him again. "Do you understand what that means?" He swallowed deep and nodded a little. Then this look of concern came over his face, like a shadow flickering in his eyes, and slowly he shook his head no.

I pulled him to me and hugged him again.

"I don't either," I said. "I don't either."

We left the brook shortly after that. He asked if we could go. And we rode toward home in silence. I was so scared, so worried. I was afraid he'd want to get away from me and never see me again. I was afraid he'd tell his parents. I pulled up next to him. "How you doing?" I said.

He shrugged. "OK."

"Are you mad about what happened?"

"No," he said. His answer was flat.

I stopped my bike. "Are you sure?" I called as he rode on ahead.

He stopped his bike and looked back at me. *"Yeah,"* he said. "I'm *OK.*"

I walked my bike toward him slowly, trying to find the way in. Then he flashed that brilliant smile at me. "Race you to the playground!" he yelled. Then he took off, pedaling like mad, the bike rocking left and right underneath him. I hopped on my bike and rode after him, timing it so I would reach the playground just after he did, so he would win by a hair. He skidded to a stop in the dirt, leapt off his bike and ran in a circle, pumping his arms in the air. "I am victorious!" he cried. "I am the Excellent Best!" Then he climbed to the top of the monkey bars and sat there, smiling down on me.

I looked at him sitting on top of his mountain, and laughed. He was all right. He was really fine. He *was* the Excellent Best. I should have known he could handle this, because he was who he was.

And because he loved me too.

I knew from his smile he loved me too.

I sat at the brook for quite a while. I don't know how long. I think I was expecting Robbie to come there, trying to find me. At any moment I thought I'd see him come coasting down the hill, no hands, or pumping wildly, searching for me, and when he saw me he'd wave and pedal as hard as he could to get to my side. I thought he'd run into my arms and I'd hold him and brush the hair from his eyes and tell him it was OK, OK, it was all going to be OK. That was what was keeping me sane, the thought that he'd come to me and I'd comfort him and together we'd solve this problem, together we'd figure it out. We'd explain to people. Or maybe run off together. I didn't know, I couldn't even think. I just needed first to see Robbie. Until I saw Robbie, my life was stopped, my brain was stopped, my heart.

I sat in the car and waited. I stared at the rise where he'd appear. I smoked one cigarette after another. My eye was pounding with pain. Jeanette would be home by now, or getting there any minute. She'd figure I had gone to the store, or maybe out with Robbie. Maybe I'd even mentioned to her that I might go swimming with him. What if she went there, looking for me? She'd never done it before. But what if they came to her, looking for me? Or if Robbie came there looking for me? What if he'd gone to the house instead of the brook? Would he think to look for me here?

I could leave him a note, or a sign of some sort, then go back home and wait for him there. What kind of a note? Where would I leave it? If I stacked up some stones, like the Indians did, would he get the message? What was the message? Come find me. Come find me. I'm home.

But what was I going to tell the girls? What would I tell them had happened to me? That I'd walked into a door? Fallen down the stairs? Did they know already what really had happened? Had Mrs. VanderVelt come over "to see if I was OK" and told them the whole story? I could see her mincing toward the house, taking quick little baby steps like that would get her there faster, I could see her going over there the minute she saw them come home from church. I could see her all puckered up with concern, then surprised that I wasn't there—even though I'm sure she saw me leave—and telling the whole gruesome story. I couldn't let that happen. I couldn't let someone else tell this story. I had to go home and tell it myself.

But how could I say this to my girls? How could I line them up in the kitchen and tell them their daddy just got beat up for being a child molester? And what would I say to them after that?

How could I help them make sense of that?

Maybe they'd help *me* make sense of it. June Marie might. June Marie was so grown-up, so adult. Jeanette and I just marveled at her. But she was only sixteen. And Lynnie was only ten.

Robbie was only twelve.

I could see Karen, my dark daughter, just stare. Just stare at me with her accusing eyes. Karen was at that stage in life where she was accusing everyone of absolutely everything, and especially Jeanette and me. I couldn't bear to look at those eyes, to fulfill her worst expectations of me.

I couldn't go home. Not now. Not yet.

I'd call Jeanette. I'd call Jeanette and have her meet me in Vandercook Lake. I'd drive to Vandercook Lake and call her. I'd tell her it was important.

What if she already knew?

I'd call her.

What if Robbie came here after I left?

He wasn't coming. It was half past twelve. He'd had plenty of time. He wasn't going to come.

Unless he was just confused and scared, or didn't think to look for me here. Unless he had gone to the house instead.

I had to call home. I had to call home.

I had to talk to Jeanette.

2

I met Jeanette when I moved to Jackson, right after I got out of the navy. When I first got discharged I went back to my mom and dad's house in Napoleon, but I knew within a day I wasn't going to be able to stay there long. For one thing, the house is tiny, tiny—barely big enough for a gerbil. And when you add my mother *hovering* over me the way she did, standing there in the doorway with her hands in a ball at her waist, and my dad leaning back in his recliner, going on about World War II and all the buddies he lost there . . . Well, I started looking right away for a place in town and found one and moved, even before I found a job. I had a little money saved up and I needed some space to move around.

I've always had a tendency to feel crowded in small places. I've always hated elevators, and tunnels make me nervous. I feel like I'm just too big to be confined in those little spaces. I'm not—not literally, I mean. I'm only five foot eight and weigh only 145, so it's not about physical size. I just like to have space around me. I've been that way as long as I can remember. I feel so cramped in myself, I guess, that I just need room for all this stuff in me to get out and get away.

I got a place on Greenwood Avenue, the second floor of a two-family with three big yellow air-filled rooms, and started looking for a job. Jeanette worked in this coffee shop I went to every morning for breakfast. She was the counter waitress. It was the summer of 1962 and she was just out of high school, working until she started junior college in the fall. She brought me my coffee and eggs and toast.

I loved that coffee shop. It was just a couple of blocks from my place in this little stand of storefronts—a grocery, a drugstore, a card shop, a barber. I liked the scale of those little buildings. They seemed kind of neat and tidy. I guess it's only crowded spaces indoors that make me crazy; maybe it's the flip side of that that draws me to little places outdoors. I don't know. Anyway, I liked it. I'd wake up in the morning and listen to the birds outside, then roll off my mattress—I had no bed—shower and pull on some jeans, then walk over to this block of stores, get the paper and have my breakfast.

Remembering that time of my life always makes me happy now. Walking to the Busy Bee down those shady streets in the early summer, just enjoying the fact that I had the time to stroll along in the morning without anybody shouting at me, Do this or Do that. I remember going out with my hair still wet and getting the paper at the drugstore, that air-conditioned hospital smell, and ambling into the coffee shop. I remember the smell of the coffee, the toast, the smell of the eggs on the griddle. I remember the friendly hubbub of it. The grill cook was a showoff, loved making a production of breaking the eggs and dumping them on the grill, like he was doing magic tricks, then serving them up in a pool of grease. It didn't take long for him to learn my name and start greeting me every morning as soon as I walked in the door. He always did it with the "name game." "Hey, Jerry!" he'd call out. Then he'd start sashaying back and forth in this funny bump-and-grind way, singing "Jerry-Jerry-Bo-Berry, Banana-Fana-Fo-Ferry, Fee-Fie-Mo-Merry, Jerry!" It was a little family in there, I got to know other regulars. It was like the navy was at its best: close-knit. But it was better. You could get away from them.

To tell the truth, I didn't especially notice Jeanette at first. She took my order and brought me my food and she was very pleasant, but I didn't take an interest at first. I was too preoccupied, I guess. As much as I like to remember that time, I was really not in a good way then. I was pretty confused about what to do. Now that I was out of the service, I felt completely cut adrift. I hadn't really thought about what I'd do when I got out—I guess I thought I'd re-up, maybe—but by the time I got out, there was no way I was going back. So there I was on the streets. No job, no plans, no future.

I spent every morning reading the paper, start to finish, all the way through, and then I read the want ads. By the time I got to the want ads I was on my fourth or fifth cup of coffee, and most of the customers had moved along, and the Busy Bee settled into a lull before the lunch rush. That was when I got to know Jeanette. When she'd bring me another refill and watch me circling ads in the paper. "Anything this morning?" she'd say, and I'd shrug and tell her what I'd found, the way I felt my luck was going.

She took a real interest in it. She remembered what ads I'd circled before and asked how the interviews had gone, then she remembered what I told her and later asked about the follow-through, whether Mr. Smithers at Consumers had ever called me back, or like that. It had been a while since anybody had taken an interest in me. And it was different from the joking kind of friendship I had with the others there—when she spoke to you she looked right at you and waited for you to answer. Even though she was a waitress and always busy with something, you never felt like she was really busy with anything but you. Like until you answered her question, she didn't have anyplace else to go, she could wait. There was a stillness about her. She reminded me of a deer, a doe. She would stand there and look at you, all interest, but she had no desire to move in on you. She'd keep her distance. She wouldn't crowd you. But she was very interested.

Well, your eye gets drawn to a stillness like that. And I started to notice how really very pretty she was, if you bothered to look. Her nose was this tiny little thing, just a perfectly shaped little button. Later I learned to watch her nose for signs of a temper fit—when Jeanette got mad, her nostrils flared. That's all that happened: Her nostrils flared. It made me laugh, it was so cute. And her eyes were a pale gray. It wasn't a color I'd seen before or since in a person's eyes. The color of mouse fur. It doesn't sound so pretty, but it is, in eyes. And her chin was strong, determined.

So I started getting to know her. Started hanging out at the restaurant even longer than usual, and she'd take her coffee break with me. She helped me get adjusted to life in the world again. I wanted to have a life, a good life. I wanted to be happy, but I didn't know how to be. And Jeanette seemed to be happy, in a quiet way. She had a serenity to her. She wasn't troubled by anything. The way I felt when I walked to the restaurant, that sense of total calmness—she seemed to feel that way all the time. She took life as it came to her, absorbed it like a sponge absorbs water. I had the feeling I could say anything to her and she would just take it in. It would disappear inside of her, almost without a ripple. But it wasn't lost, it was registered, there. And it would come back in a few days' time, preserved, offered up.

She got off work at three, and by then I'd done whatever I was going to do that day in the job hunt, so we started going out to the lake almost every afternoon. Her folks had a cottage at Clark Lake, and we hung out on their dock. It's beautiful, late afternoon in the summer. It stretches on forever and there's this feeling there's nothing to be done. It's like that time between sleeping and waking, when you're aware that you're just hanging in this dreamlike state, and you can savor every second of it. Sleeping, listening to the radio, swimming out to the raft and back.

Her little brother, Stevie—the one who died—was ten that summer, and really into water-skiing, so we took him skiing a lot, and I got pretty good at it myself. I realized that this was what I wanted in my life—this relaxation, this sense of family. I got along great with Frank and Dot, her parents, and with her sister Sherry. And Stevie and I had a great time fooling around—he was always there, being a pest, knowing he was being a pest and making a joke of it, showing up whenever Jeanette and I were getting romantic.

And I was fascinated with Jeanette. The way she tied her hair back and wrapped a rubber band around it. The fluttering way she laughed when I teased her. The way I could make her blush by nibbling her ear in front of her parents. She was always reading a book, always. Sometimes a really serious book. Dickens, like. Or George Orwell. She was smart. I knew she was smarter than me. That was part of what I liked about her, that being with her I learned things. And hanging out with her that summer was the happiest summer of my life.

So when fall came around, I asked her to marry me. It was the day we pulled in the dock. Columbus Day weekend, a brisk fall day. Frank and Stevie and I spent the morning dismantling the dock and storing it in the garage while Jeanette and Sherry and Dot cleaned the house. Then we put the shutters on, eventually closing the girls in darkness, like we were shutting them in a box. We left the shutters off the front windows so they could still see enough to cover the furniture with sheets. Then Stevie and Frank and Dot and Sherry all went back into town, and Jeanette and I stayed to finish up the shutters.

It was an invigorating day—you could feel the nip of winter in it, that brittle edge to the air. Soon enough it was going to be time to be indoors again. We closed up the house, then took a walk down to the shore and just stood there, our arms around each other, looking at the day, and I felt this ache in my heart, this yearning not to let go of the happiness I'd found that summer. I'd been thinking about asking her—we'd said that was what we both wanted: marriage, a house, a family—but I didn't know I was going to ask her then. I thought my heart would break open though, from the yearning that day. So I asked her, and she said yes. Then she turned from me and looked across the lake and let out one of those little fluttering laughs of hers, like a flag run up in the breeze. "Oh my God," she gasped, half in fear, half in excitement. I wrapped my arms around her from behind and nibbled her ear. "Mrs. Houseman," I said.

So we got married, bingo, on New Year's Eve. And June Marie was born on Columbus Day—a nifty little piece of timing, we thought. Karen came two years later, in the midst of a summer thunderstorm. And then Lynette toddled along five years after that.

I started out working at Aeroquip, but it didn't take me long to figure out that wasn't for me. I couldn't stand being indoors all the time, cooped up in a factory. So then I sold tools for Kent-Moore for a while, which was better. At least I was outdoors, driving from place to place. But I didn't like selling things to people, pushing things on people. And finally I got a job at the post office, doing route delivery, and stayed. I liked it. I liked it a lot. Even in winter I liked it. I got to be outdoors, walking up and down the streets. I talked to people, got to know their kids and pets. It couldn't have suited me better, really.

And Jeanette and I never had problems. Our biggest arguments were always about who was going to take out the trash or how we were going to pay the bills. You don't exactly get rich delivering mail for the U.S. Postal Service. But Jeanette had a pretty good job at the bank: She started out as a teller after Lynnie started school and then became a drive-in branch manager. I was handy around the house, and Jeanette made all her own clothes, so we kept our expenses down. We got by. We had a good life.

There was just this one time.

There was this boy I met on my route.

This thing I have about boys. I don't know. I like kids. I've always liked kids, all sizes and shapes of kids. And there's nothing funny about it, nothing unusual about it. But there's something about a boy, some boys, when they reach the edge of puberty, when they're sitting right on the edge of it, part boy, part man, or not even part man, more like just containing a hint of the man that's going to come—the way the air in the fall carries a hint of the winter to come—there's something about a boy at that age that touches me in some way, some really deep-seated way. I don't understand it. I've never understood it. But it fills me with desire, desire is the only word to use. I want to be near them, to be around them. I want to hear their voices, their laughter, I want to see them run. And I don't just want to watch them. I want to laugh along with them, I want to run with them. There's so much freedom in a boy that age. And so much sense the freedom is soon to be lost, absorbed into manhood. It feels like a loss, but it's also a promise, their adulthood. You can see it in their bodies. The shoulders are starting to square. The torso is sharpening into four quarters. There's a looseness, a jangle in the limbs. It's like they're perfectly balanced in time. Not boys and not yet men. They're perfect.

I understood this desire as a sexual desire only after I was in the navy. Up until then I understood it only as an interest, even an obsession. I mean, I was certainly aware that I got a strange tingle around these boys, some of these boys. It was exciting, really thrilling. It made my breath come faster, made me pitch forward slightly when I was near them, so I could be that much nearer to them. This was when I was an eagle scout, working with younger scouts. But I never understood that excitement as sexual. It made me goofy, it made me embarrassed, but it felt different from how I felt about girls. It came from a different part of me.

But while I was stationed at Subic Bay, I went into Manila on leave and went out on my own to the bars. Mabini Street. M.H. del Pilar. I'd been to the bars in Olangapo with the guys from the base, and had spent some time with the Philippine girls. But in Manila there were boys as well. Ten-year-old boys, eleven, twelve. I almost couldn't breathe. All I could hear was the pound of my heart. I went back a couple of nights in a row and stood in a corner just watching—listening to Elvis and smoking Winstons and sucking down San Miguels—and finally dared talk to one of them.

There are depths you just don't know of. You go about your daily life, you eat your breakfast, you read your paper, you watch your television. You say please and thank you. You parallel park. You line up your shoes in the closet. You go through your whole life like that and you never know what life tastes like. But if you're lucky—or maybe unlucky, I really don't know which—someday you experience something that reaches down inside to the bottom of you and scoops you out clean, then leaves you there like a rag on the floor. You're not the person you thought you were, or the person you'd hoped you'd be. You're something bigger, more complicated. Something smaller, simpler. It twists you all around and you walk with your head on backward. But at the same time you feel like you've found the center. The center is there, and it glows.

His name was Nestor. He was eleven. I still have dreams about him.

But that was in Manila, during the Navy. All of life was sweaty and wet and filled with this drumming boredom. And when I got back home again, everything was different. I could walk down the street in the morning. I could eat my breakfast and read my paper. There was Jeanette, and our life together.

But then, ten years later, there was this boy on my route.

I thought I was over all of that after I got back from the navy. Over there, all the rules were different and it was possible to slip into a different corner of life. We experimented with all kinds of things over there, all kinds of sex and drugs. But when we got back to the States, I thought I was clean again. I thought I could just return to who I'd been before, that I could leave that version of me in Manila.

And for a long time I did. I still felt that interest about boys, but I wasn't about to act on it. I had a wife, then a daughter, then two. I was a family man, I wasn't going to mess with that. But then, when I started working for the post office, I started spending a lot more time outdoors on foot, started seeing these boys more often. On the streets. In school yards, as I passed. There was a school on my route, a grade school, and I used to time my route so I'd go by there at recess, just so I could watch them, the boys. Goofing around on the monkey bars. Playing baseball, sometimes. Or tag. Or fooling around with a basketball.

There was one boy in particular. Dark-haired with a high, sloped head. Incredibly dark, long lashes. He was popular with the kids, you could tell; he was always leading the games. Such a sure, strong swagger, such a little rooster. Sometimes during a break in a game he'd plant his hands on his hips and look around at all the other kids like he was looking over his kingdom, like all of this was his, his making, and they were all his subjects. He wasn't arrogant, not a brat. He was just filled up with himself, to the brim.

I used to love watching him. I'd hang out by the fence with my fingers hooked in the chain links and watch. I kept an eye to see who was noticing, if anybody was thinking it was strange I was hanging around like that. But nobody seemed to care. I was doing my job, after all. I was just taking a break as I went. And I was careful to stop by only two or three times a week. But on those days I didn't go, I was thinking about him.

His name was Tony. I heard the kids calling his name. Tony.

I started dreaming of him, daydreaming, while I was doing my route. I'd see his face in my mind, see him smile. I imagined us getting an ice cream together after he got out of school, imagined I'd run into him "accidentally" just as he was getting out, and we'd start talking. He'd ask me, "Hey, Mr. Mailman, you got any money for me?" Or maybe he'd sing out: "Hey, Mr. Postman, Wait and see, Is there a letter, A letter for me?" He'd do that kind of thing, I knew, partly to show off for his friends and partly just to exercise himself. So I'd reach into my bag and pretend to search around for his letter, then come up with a comic book or something. Or maybe I'd just say, "Nope, no mail today." And maybe he'd say, "Aw, shit," and pretend to cry and then I'd say, "Come on, I'll get you an ice cream cone."

Something like that. I worked on it. I polished the story in my mind, working out the details of it, how we'd meet, what we'd say, how our friendship would grow. It became an entertainment for me, a movie in my mind that I could run whenever I got bored. And over a period of weeks I found myself thinking about him all the time, constantly, even at home, even at dinner, even in bed with Jeanette.

Then I met him. School was out for the summer, but he still went down to the school yard every day to shoot baskets and muck around. Sometimes he had friends with him, sometimes he didn't. And one day I found him there, shooting baskets alone. My heart jumped into my throat. My fingers started tingling, then my whole body started tingling. It was like a fever waiting to break. Finally I couldn't stand it anymore. So I called out to him, "Hey! I'll match you best out of seven!" And he took me on, and I beat him. So I told him, "OK, winner buys the Cokes." And by God, he said OK.

I started going there every day, to see if I could spend time with him. On the days when he was alone, I shot baskets with him, or just hung out. On the days he had other kids there with him, I just watched and waved. Sometimes, when he was with the other kids and I came by, he'd turn to them and say something and then they'd turn and look at me. But I didn't think anything of it. I should have thought something of it, I should have been paying more attention. But I'd taken our friendship so far in my mind . . .

I don't know. I got confused, I guess. About what was real and what was not. I lost track of what had really happened between us and what I'd only daydreamed. So when I finally touched him—in my car, after driving him home; we were actually sitting in front of his house, I can't believe I was so stupid . . . I didn't do anything so bad. I just laid my hand on the back of his neck. He went still. Then I started to pull him toward me and started to bend my face to his. That was when he shrieked, and hit me. He hit me hard, right in the nose, and yelled, "Keep your hands off me, you pervert! You leave me the fuck alone!" Then he burst out of the car and took off running into his house.

I called in sick the next day and the next day after that. I was scared to walk my route. I was scared I'd find a cop waiting for me when I got to the playground, a squad car with its motor running just waiting there in the shadows. I told Jeanette I felt queasy, then stayed home and watched TV all day, trying not to think. But I was burning the whole time, burning around my edges. My ears were hot, my neck was hot, my shoulders, my arms, the backs of my knees. It was like I had a fever but I didn't, my temperature was normal. It was just that I was embarrassed, I think. More than embarrassed. Humiliated. But humiliated Big-Time. Like I'd been publicly disgraced in front of the whole town, the whole state, the whole human race.

What it was, I think, was that I'd been humiliated in front of myself. I'd come right up against someone else's idea of what they thought of me, me and my strange little secret. In the Philippines that never happened. My navy buddies never knew and the people in the bars didn't care, it was all just business to them. This was the first time that part of me got introduced to the world, into the life I'd made for myself. And the reaction I got was the one I should have known I'd get. It made me feel sick to my stomach, like I had some bug inside me, some virus, some disease, some animal gnawing at me.

When I did go back to work, nothing happened. The first few days I didn't see Tony, he wasn't in the playground, and when he did show up again with a couple of other kids he didn't have a cop with him. He didn't look at me when I walked by and I didn't look at him. We pretended like nothing had happened. Like nothing had ever happened. Like we'd never even met.

It was a huge relief that he hadn't called in his parents or the cops, and I felt this rush of gratitude toward him, like I wanted to hug him and thank him, which was ridiculous. I knew that for the rest of time I had to keep a wall between us—no looking, no talking, no touching, no nothing. He didn't exist. I didn't exist. We lived on different planets. The awful thing about it, though, was the sight of him still made my heart jump. When I heard him call out to another kid, when I heard him laugh or saw him run as I was passing by, it made me ache with longing. I loved him all the more because he hadn't gotten infected with this disease I had. He had kept himself clean.

It was after that I decided I had to do something about all this. I couldn't control it as well as I thought and it wouldn't just go away. I needed to be cured of it. So I went to my doctor, my physician, and told him I was having a little psychological problem, and could he recommend someone. He tried to probe a little bit, to find out what the matter was, and I wanted to tell him so bad I could taste it, but I didn't dare. He was Jeanette's doctor too.

He gave me the name of a psychologist over by the Cascades and I started to see her. She was a nice woman, Dr. King. She was short and kind of cute, the kind of woman I might have wanted to date at another time in my life. She told me she could cure me. She told me this was all about my mother, my father, my brother, my childhood. All about *me* at the age of twelve, an attempt to recapture myself somehow, to recapture my childhood, or maybe to capture the childhood I never had. It made my breath come quick to think all this was understandable, that it was all just simple arithmetic—A plus B equals C. And she was so sure, so businesslike. I felt this hope shooting up in me. This thing I thought I was stuck with for life, I could be rid of it. This twisted part of me wasn't really part of me at all. I knew it! I'd known it all along.

I saw her for two years, every Tuesday afternoon at four, except for holidays and vacations. I sat in her leather chair by the window and watched the cars on Spring Arbor Road and talked about my mom and my dad, my brother Doug and growing up, my involvement in the scouts, all that. And I did come to understand some things. About how my dad used to treat us like we were his property. About how my mom made herself important by being the only one in the house who could talk to everyone else. How my brother used to beat me up.

Dr. King took a lot of interest in the fact that at about age twelve, my dad made us start to fight, Doug and me. He thought it was important that a boy know how to defend himself. In the school yard. Against bullies. Just for his sense of himself. So on Tuesdays he took us down to the basement and cleared a space by the furnace with a single bare bulb hanging over it and sat at the edge of the ring of light on an overturned box. Then he rang a bell and we went at it. Every Tuesday night.

Tuesdays seemed to be my day. Dr. King made a joke about that. For years, she said, Tuesdays meant to me going down into the basement and learning how to fight. That was what growing up meant to me, hurting people, getting hurt. Now we were meeting on Tuesdays, years later, to undo the damage done by that violence. And once that violence was undone, I would no longer feel the urge to try to return to my childhood by possessing little boys. Something like that. I don't know. It wasn't quite that simple, but that was the general idea. It sounded kind of twisted to me, but I didn't have any better solutions. So I talked and I talked and I talked. And I listened to Dr. King.

But on my way home from our appointments I'd pass kids riding on their bikes or fooling around on a street corner and I'd always look in the rearview mirror to catch a longer glimpse of them. Of course I tried *not* to do that. A lot of the time I went around with my eyes fixed straight ahead of me, not letting them wander around at all, for fear of what they might find. I drove with my hands firmly on the wheel—one hand at ten, one hand at two—and my knuckles turning white. But it always came back again, the urge to look, the need to look, and finally the willingness to look. And part of the reason was that when I walked around with blinders on, I blinded myself to everything—missing things that Jeanette was doing, missing things my daughters were doing. I remember one time being so conscious of not looking at this boy at the beach, so determined to keep my nose in the paper, I almost didn't notice June Marie toddling into the water alone.

Sometimes I got mad at Dr. King because it wasn't working. We just kept talking and talking and talking and I kept wanting to look at boys. It pissed me off that my whole life was getting reduced to this. But then she'd always want to know who I was *really* angry at. Wasn't it my father, really? Wasn't it my brother? And by the time she was done I'd be so confused, I didn't know which way was up.

There was one time, though, when I did get mad at *her,* when there was no question. It was when she asked me if I ever had these feelings about my daughters. For one thing, it was a stupid question. I was interested in *boys,* not girls. Here I'd been talking to her for months, and she didn't even understand that much? But the other thing that pissed me off was that it would even occur to her that I might mess with my own little girls. I mean, what the hell did she think I was? That's *incest.* Who did she think I was?

"Well, what if someone did?" she said. "What if some adult did make a sexual advance on your daughter . . . ? With June Marie, let's say. She's how old? Five?"

I slouched down in the chair, covered my face with my hand. "I'd kill him," I whispered.

"Why?"

"Because she's just a little kid!"

She leaned toward me. "And what about Tony?"

I looked at her, stammered a second. "That's different. Tony's eleven, twelve."

"He's still a kid . . ."

"But it's different."

"Is it?"

I looked at her. She leaned closer to me. Then I felt this sliding inside of me, like a whole wall of shelves collapsing, and everything was falling on me, books and boxes falling on me, and I fell apart. "I don't know," I sobbed. "I don't know, I don't know . . ."

By the end, I got to feel like pretty much of a failure with Dr. King. After two full years of treatment, I was still dreaming of Nestor and Tony and other kids I'd seen on my route. Still thinking about them during the day. Still looking at boys on the street. It seemed like I wasn't a very good patient, or maybe she wasn't a very good doctor. So when my insurance benefits ran out, I told her I was sorry, I'd done my best. Although it seemed to me I couldn't really have done my best: If I'd done my best, I would have been cured. But I didn't really understand what more I could have done. I answered all the questions. I opened all the closets, explored every corner of my past, every blind alley of my feelings. I felt like I was a little smarter but I didn't feel like I was changed.

She smiled sadly at me. "Maybe later you'll want to come back and finish what we've started here . . ." Then she stood and showed me to the door. "I wish you the best of luck," she said. She shook my hand and smiled again.

The first week after we terminated—that was her word, "terminated"—I left work and headed out toward her office, just like any other Tuesday. I knew I didn't have an appointment, it wasn't that I'd forgotten. But I just didn't know what else to do. It was Tuesday afternoon, three-thirty. Time to put my house in order. Time to get it right. I couldn't just go home that day—it would have felt like giving up—so I drove out to her office. I didn't know what I thought I'd do. Sit in the parking lot and stare at her door? Watch her with another patient? No, I wouldn't do that. But I still had the feeling she had the answer and I just wasn't smart enough to get it out of her. I had the feeling I ought to go back, and back and back, until I got it, until the cure finally took. So I drove all the way out to her office. But then I just kept going beyond. I knew if I stopped and went in to see her, I'd just sit down in that chair again and we would start to talk again and I'd say all the things I'd said before and she'd say the same things back to me and nothing would ever change. So I drove out to Spring Arbor and had a Coke and then went home to Jeanette.

For all the time I spent with Dr. King in psychotherapy, the only thing that really helped me during that time was Jeanette. Before this thing with Tony happened, I'd never told Jeanette about Nestor. I'd never told her anything about this secret obsession I had. I figured I could control it, that it didn't have to concern her. But after Tony I couldn't not tell her. Even just in practical terms I had to explain to her why I was going to see this psychologist. And she was really amazing about it. She just sat and listened, her gray eyes drinking me in. It was like she was watching a movie, or reading one of her books. She kept her eyes open and watched me, and listened, waiting to hear what came next.

Of course she asked a lot of questions. "Have you always felt this way?" "Did you ever do anything like this before?" "Is it only boys you're interested in?" But she didn't get all troubled about it and start wringing her hands. She just sat there and listened to me, just let me say what I had to say.

Some part of me wanted her to get mad, to punish me for what I'd done. Another part of me wanted her to be scared, so

I could protect her. And so I could feel more guilty, so I could fall on my knees in front of her and beg forgiveness. So she could stroke my head and absolve me, like a queen or a priest. But she didn't do any of that. She hugged me and kissed me on the lips. And then she offered to get a job, to help me pay for the doctor.

That night in bed she snuggled up to me, fit herself up against the line of my body, her head propped on her hand. "Can I ask you one more question?" she said. I looked at her and nodded. "What was it like with Nestor? What did you do together?"

I swallowed. Did she really want to hear this? Did I have any choice? If she asked, I'd answer.

"Anal intercourse," I said.

She looked at me, still expressionless. She looked at me a long moment, then she rolled onto her back. When she spoke again her voice was small. "Was it better than with me?" she said.

My heart fell. It was the first time since we'd started talking she actually showed a concern for herself. And her voice when she spoke was the voice of a little girl, the little girl she still was in some ways, the little girl she sometimes pretended to be in our sexual play. But this time there was no sexual teasing. It was just a small, quiet voice, the tiny voice that resided at the bottom of her stillness, the unprotected Jeanette.

"Nothing's better than you," I lied. It wasn't really a lie, it was true. But it was only part of the truth. I kissed her ear. "I love you," I said. "Nothing could be better than that. Nothing could be better than that." I kissed her neck and her hair. "Nothing could be better than that." She turned to me and grabbed me tight, tighter than she ever had. I held her and rocked her and whispered to her. "Nothing could be better than that." Then I kissed her face, her neck, her shoulders, her breasts, her belly, her thighs, her sex. I rolled her over and kissed the insides of her knees, the soles of her feet. I slithered up the whole length of her and lowered my weight onto her, pulling her hair away from her ear and whispering to her again. "Nothing could be better than that."

"You can try it," she whispered. "If you want."

"What?"

"You know. From behind. If you want . . ."

I thought my heart would break. I rolled her onto her back again and kissed her all over her face, telling her over and over again how much I loved her. And when I burrowed my way between her legs, it seemed to me that we were warmer and closer and more gentle with each other than we'd ever been. That I was penetrating every pore of her and she was penetrating me, that our skins were actually dissolving, that we were becoming one animal, one rolling, breathing, warm, wet thing. And I vowed to myself I would never, ever, ever again give her reason to fear she wasn't good enough for me.

But when I came, I thought of Tony.

3

I drove back out to Francis and headed toward Vandercook Lake, trying to picture in my mind where I'd find a public phone, where Jeanette and I could meet to talk. There was a drugstore there, and a Laundromat. A bar full of hacking old men and smoke. I couldn't see talking to her there. So I stopped at this coffee shop and called.

When I reached in my pocket, I didn't have change—I'd grabbed only my keys and wallet—so I had to go back outside and dig in the glove compartment for a dime. I found a quarter and used it instead. It chimed as it fell through the machine, then I heard a few clicks and then the ring. It was when the clicks switched into ringing that my mind switched over. All at once I was in another room, another stage of my life. It was a holding pattern. *Ring.* What am I going to say? *Ring.* What am I going to say? *Ring.* What can I possibly say?

"Hello?" It was June Marie, back from church.

My voice froze in my throat.

"Hel*lo*?" she said, a little annoyed. I was afraid she'd hang up.

"June Marie," I blurted out.

"Daddy?"

"Hi. Is your mom around?"

"She's in the bathroom. Where are you?"

"Um, I don't know. Vandercook Lake. Look, will you tell her I need to talk to her?"

"OK," she said. She paused a minute. "Daddy? Are you OK?"

"I'm OK, sweetheart," I said. "Just tell your mom I need to talk to her."

She set down the phone and I heard her fading voice call up the stairs. Then I waited. I heard the screen door slam—I'd told those kids not to slam the door—heard the thump of music from Karen's room. I stared at the car lot across the street—the pennants flapping in the breeze, the big soap numerals on the windshields—and listened to the sounds of my home. Then Jeanette picked up the phone. The upstairs extension. The downstairs line was still free, anybody could pick it up and hear what I was saying.

"Jeanette," I said.

"Hi. What's up?"

"I've got to talk to you right away."

"What's the matter?" She wasn't on full alert yet. It was still a Sunday morning to her.

"I can't tell you now. You've got to meet me. Can you come to Vandercook Lake and meet me?"

"Vandercook Lake?"

"At the coffee shop on Francis. Across the street from the used car lot."

"Are you all right?" she said. She was coming into focus now, she knew that something real was wrong.

"I'm OK. But I've got to talk to you. Now. Can you come?"

"Yes," she said. "Sure. What's going on?"

"I'm in a little trouble," I said. "I might be. I'm not sure."

"I'll be there."

I went into the coffee shop and ordered a cup of coffee, then realized I had no money and told the girl to forget it. I went outside and waited, leaning against the wall by the door. It was hot. It was dusty and dry. But I smoked another cigarette anyway, poking the dirt with the toe of my sneaker.

Finally Jeanette's big whale of a car oomphed into the lot. She pulled up next to my car, leaning out the window, looking at me. She was wearing sunglasses and a T-shirt. Before she could speak or get out of the car, I hurried around and got in beside her.

"What *happened*?" she said. She reached out to touch my bruised cheek.

I pushed her hand away. "I'm in trouble."

"What happened?"

I took a deep breath. "Robbie's brother attacked me."

"*What?* Why?"

I stared at the door to the coffee shop. "Robbie told," I said.

She didn't respond for a second. I was just about to look at her when she spoke. Her voice was flat. "Robbie told what."

I glanced at her, then back at the door. "About him and me."

It seemed like a full minute went by before she finally sat back and sighed. I started to breathe again, but then she bounced her hands off the steering wheel, hard. "I thought we were done with all that," she snapped.

"I did too," I said. "I did too." I turned to her to try to explain.

"You *told* me you were just friends. You assured me you were just *friends*!"

"I know."

"Then what were you *doing* with him?" she cried. I didn't expect this anger. Usually her nostrils just flared. But then, this wasn't usually.

"I don't know," I said. "I don't know. I was . . . I don't know. In love with him."

"In *love* with him?" She slapped the seat. "He's only ten years old! You can't be in love with a ten-year-old!"

"He's twelve. I am. I'm sorry."

She pulled off her sunglasses and hurled them onto the seat and sat with her face in her hands. I just watched her. I didn't know what to say.

"What happened?" she said at last, her face still covered.

"I just fell in love with him."

"I mean *today*," she snapped.

I told her what had happened. She sat with her fist in front of her mouth like she was trying not to vomit and stared at the door to the coffee shop. Her eyes were red with tears.

"I don't know what to do," I said when she didn't respond to the story.

"You need to get a lawyer," she muttered, disgusted.

"Do you think they'll prosecute?"

"How do I know what they're going to do?" She fired the words like bullets. She stared at me; she was quivering. Then she sighed again and looked out the window. I looked down at my hands. There was a long moment of silence. Then we both spoke at once.

"I don't know any lawyers," I said.

"What did you do with Robbie?" she said.

There was a lurch when neither responded, neither of us knew whose comment would take the lead. Then she turned to me and went after me like a district attorney.

"Did you touch him?" she said.

I nodded.

"Did you have sexual contact?"

"Yes."

"Did you do with him what you did with that Philippine boy?"

"We've been having an affair," I said. I threw the words up between us like a wall to stop her advance.

"An *affair* you call it? For how long?"

I looked at her, then looked away. "A while," I said. "This summer."

"How sweet," she whispered to herself. "A little summer romance."

I closed my eyes, then looked at her. "Jeanette, I need your help."

She studied me, and studied me. First one eye, then the other. And slowly she started to nod. It seemed like a disdainful nod, to be followed by a sneering comment. *You need help,* I was sure she was going to say, *but you're not going to get it from me. I can't give you the kind of help you need* . . . She had every right to say that to me. I expected her to say that to me. But gradually her nodding grew deeper and slower and she stopped looking at one eye, then the other, and just gazed at me sadly. She took a huge breath and let it out and looked down at her hands. Then her hands curled into fists and she slammed the seat. "God*dam*mit!" she said.

I felt my insides stretching from the weight that was gathering there. I reached over and laid one hand on hers. Both of us looked at it: the bitten nails, the scrape across the knuckles, the wedding ring. Our whole history gathered around us to look. Then she drew her hand from under mine and rapped on my knuckles a couple of times like she was knocking on a door, trying to fight back her anger and tears. "How . . . ?" she gasped. Then she curled her hand around mine and raised it to her lips. I fell across the seat toward her and burst into tears, huge sobs. "I'm so sorry," I blubbered. "My God, I'm so sorry . . ." But she dropped my hand like it was a hot coal and turned to face out the window. I gathered myself. Wiped the tears from my eyes.

"What will we tell the girls?" she said. She sounded far away.

"Do we have to tell them anything yet?"

She whipped around and spat her words at me. "Jerry, you're covered with scrapes and bruises. We've got to tell them something."

I snapped to attention. "Then we've got to tell them the truth," I said. "Before Mrs. VanderVelt does."

"Mrs. VanderVelt?" Jeanette looked at me. Then she rolled her eyes and groaned.

"But how can I tell them the truth?"

"Give me a cigarette," she said. She'd given up smoking a year ago. She lit it with the dashboard lighter, even though I offered a match. She clamped it in her mouth while she waited. Just stared at the lighter while she waited, as if she could will it to pop. When it did, she lurched to grab it and poked it too hard at the cigarette so some of the tobacco came out of the paper and stuck to the coils, smoking. "Shit," she said. She knocked the smoking tobacco into the ashtray, then sat back and exhaled loudly.

"We'll just tell them part of the truth," she said. She was staring at the coffee shop, watching the traffic behind us reflected in the glass. "We'll tell them that Robbie's brother got mad at you for something you said, or did. For something Robbie said you did. Something he said you said, or did. We'll tell them it was a misunderstanding. That he got a little hot under the collar . . ."

"He's always been a hothead," I said.

"Tell them that. He's always been a hothead. Tell them it's a misunderstanding. Tell them it will get ironed out. Be adult about it."

"But what if it doesn't get ironed out?"

She mashed her cigarette out in the ashtray, exhaling all the while. "We'll deal with that when the time comes," she said. "I'll get the name of the lawyer my sister used for her divorce." She grabbed hold of the steering wheel like she was ready to leave, and looked at me. I felt like a child. I stared at the glove compartment. Then finally I looked at her.

"I'm sorry," I said.

She nodded at me rhythmically, like she was considering me, considering what to say. Her lips were tightly pursed. "I am too," she said at last. She looked at the steering wheel. "I am too." Then she just sat there, waiting for me to get out.

"Are the girls home now?"

She nodded.

"Then I guess we'd better go." I got out of the car and closed the door without her looking at me, then walked around to her side. I rested my arms on the door, bent down and looked in. She kept staring straight ahead.

"I'm sorry," I said. She nodded. I squeezed the curls at the base of her neck. "I love you, Jeanette," I said.

She kept staring straight ahead, nodding.

I've never wanted to do anything less than to go home at that moment, to go back onto that sleepy street and confront my daughters. I wanted to do anything else. Drive to Lansing. Drive to Detroit. Drive to Chicago, or San Francisco. Maybe if I drove far enough I could escape the skin I was in, at least until it healed. I could stay on the road for a week or two, until the bruises were gone and the cut was healed, so I wouldn't have to explain. I could say I was kidnapped. Or got amnesia. I could make up any lie, anything. I could say I robbed a bank. Or even that I thought of leaving them all, but found out I loved them too much and came back. Any of those stories would be easier to hear than the one I had to tell them, even though the one I had to tell was a shortened version. The shortened version was too close to the truth. What if they pressed me with questions? What if they figured it out? What were they going to think of me? What would that do to them?

I followed Jeanette back home. Her head looked tiny in that ocean liner of a car, like she was only a child herself, playing at being grown-up. When she held out her hand to signal the turn, she pointed left and down, to the ground, and her bracelets slid down to her wrist. It was odd that she signaled like that. She had her turn signal on, and *I* knew where she was going. But she threw her arm out and down like she was throwing something out the window, or commanding a dog to sit. It pissed me off a little. It seemed a little dramatic, which wasn't like her at all. And if there was anything we didn't need at the moment, it was more drama.

She pulled into the driveway and I parked at the curb. I decided I'd just walk into the house, just go about my business like nothing was too much different, it was just a misunderstanding. Everything would get ironed out. I looked down the street as I rounded the car. Everything was still normal-looking, a peaceful, pleasant Sunday. Maybe it *was* just a misunderstanding. Maybe it *would* get ironed out.

I walked up the driveway to meet Jeanette and we walked in the back door together. No one was in the kitchen. I grabbed a beer from the fridge and went into the dining room. No one was there, or the living room either. There was no music from Karen's room. I looked at Jeanette. She shrugged. She went upstairs, then came back down, shaking her head. We went back into the kitchen and looked out the window. June Marie was in the backyard, sunning herself, listening to her Walkman. There was no sign of Karen or Lynnie.

I didn't know what to do. Did I go out and sit beside June Marie, interrupt her, offer my story? Or did I wait for her to notice, and ask? I would wait for her to notice, and ask. But meanwhile, where were Karen and Lynnie? Gone to the store. Gone to visit friends. Should I ask June Marie? No, that would seem out of the ordinary. All I could do was sit and wait. All I could do was pretend that everything was perfectly normal while I waited for my daughters to come in, one by one, and discover me. It felt like waiting for a race to begin. You're all keyed up and ready to go but all you can do is wait, and wait. Shake out the tension. Pace back and forth. Swing your arms around in windmills.

"Come sit on the porch with me," I said to Jeanette. She

looked at me and screwed up her face. "Everything is fine," I said. "Everything is OK. It was just a misunderstanding." I stared at her like I was willing her to memorize her lines. "Come on," I said. I grabbed the paper. "We'll sit on the porch and read the paper."

Her body went limp and she followed me out. She sat in the wicker chair, I took the glider. I handed her the Metro section of the *Free Press*. She took it and set it in her lap, still folded, smirking at me.

"What?" I said.

"We've never read the paper on our porch. This is real normal."

I smiled, amazed she could find something funny at a time like this. But her smirk did not turn into a smile. It was more like it curled into disgust. She slapped the paper to bend the fold and held it up to read. I held up page one.

I didn't read a thing, of course. I tried, but I couldn't go more than a sentence or two at a time. I kept looking down the street toward Robbie's, waiting for him to come riding my way. Or for his brother to come after me. Or his parents, or a cop. But there was nothing. Just the buzz of lawn mowers, the barking of a dog. The sound of a broadcast ball game somewhere down the street, and the whoosh of the traffic on Francis.

Jeanette crumpled the paper in her lap, then let it slide to the floor. "I can't do this," she said. "I'm going to call my sister."

I watched her get up and go to the door. There were marks on the backs of her thighs from the wicker chair, and splotches of red. I hoped she'd turn and ask if I wanted a lemonade or an iced tea, not because I wanted her to bring me something to drink but because I didn't want her to leave without saying something to let me know she'd be back, that she wasn't leaving for good. But she disappeared without a sound, just a little tap as the door shut behind her.

I dropped the paper in my lap. This was ridiculous. I felt like I was chained to a post. I needed to move, to do something. I couldn't just sit around like this. Maybe I'd go for a drive. Or maybe I'd take the family to the lake. That's it, we'd go to the lake. We'd go visit Frank and Dot.

But maybe I'd call Robbie first. Just to see if he'd pick up the phone. If he didn't, I'd just hang up. Or maybe I'd go out in the car again, to see if I could find him.

I stood, not knowing yet where I was going, and saw my daughters walk around the corner from Francis onto Palmer. They had changed into shorts and T-shirts. I stepped to the top of the stairs a little too soon, a little too eager and nervous. They slowed as they approached the steps and looked up at me, mouths open.

"Hi," I said. "Where you been?"

"Daddy!" said Lynnie. "What happened?" Karen just looked at me.

I shrugged and held up my palms. "I got in a fight."

"A fight?" said Karen. She shrank from the word when she said it, like she was smelling something gone bad.

I nodded.

"With *who*?" She made it sound like no one could care about me enough to fight with me.

"Danny Young," I said.

"Robbie's brother?" shrieked Lynnie.

I nodded.

"Why?" said Karen. Her guard was down now.

"You got in a fight with *Danny Young*?" Lynnie shrieked again. She pressed her palms to her cheeks. She seemed about ready to laugh or cry. She looked at Karen for a cue but Karen didn't give her one; she just waited for my answer.

"It was just a misunderstanding," I said. "He misunderstood something Robbie said. He thought I'd done something . . . you know, that made Robbie mad."

"What?" said Karen. She waited.

"I'm not sure," I said. That was a lie. "I'm not sure exactly what Robbie said." That was better; that was true. "I haven't talked to Robbie yet."

They started climbing the steps. We'd gotten past the first shock, the part where they stood stock-still, frozen in place.

"When did this happen?" said Karen.

"Did you bleed a lot?" said Lynnie.

"This morning. Yeah, I bled a bit."

"Did you hurt him?" Karen asked.

"No, I didn't hit him. I just protected myself until his father pulled him off."

"His father? His *father* was there?"

"Yeah, it happened this morning," I said. There were too many questions coming my way. "It's just a misunderstanding. I'm sure we'll get it all cleared up. Where have you two been?"

"We went to get ice cream," said Lynnie. "We saw this dog? This huge Great Dane? It was almost as tall as I was and it tried to get after my ice cream but . . ."

"What were you doing in Vandercook Lake?" said Karen.

I forced myself to meet her eyes. "I just went for a drive," I said. I held her eyes for two full seconds, then glanced at Lynnie. "You guys want to go out to Gram and Gramp's?"

Lynnie started jumping up and down. "Yes, yes! I'll wear my new suit!"

I put my arm around Karen, not looking at her. "All right," I said. "Let's give them a call." I ushered them both into the house, into the cool, dark shade. It was only then it came to me that if we went out to Frank and Dot's place, I'd have to explain myself to *them*. "I don't know if they'll be home," I said quickly. "Or if maybe they'll have guests? But we could go to some other lake . . ."

"I want to go to Gram and Gramp's!" cried Lynnie.

"You run up and change," I said. "I'll give them a call."

Lynnie bounded up the stairs and Karen followed after her slowly. I hurried into the kitchen so Karen wouldn't have the chance to turn and ask another question. Jeanette was just hanging up the phone.

"Did you reach her?" I said.

She shook her head.

"Listen," I said. "The girls are home. They want to go out to your parents' . . ."

She bugged her eyes and puffed her cheeks. She let out a huge sigh. "Sure," she said. "Why not? Let's just parade this in front of everyone."

I grabbed her elbow and shook her. "Will you stop acting like this? We have a real problem here. I need you to help me solve it."

She ripped her elbow out of my hand. "I didn't get us in this mess," she hissed. "Don't you go accusing me."

I looked up at the ceiling, then closed my eyes and took a deep breath. "OK," I said. "Let's just decide. Your parents'? Or Wampler's Lake?"

"Wampler's," she snapped.

"Fine."

When we finally got everyone into the car, June Marie was up in front with me and Jeanette was in the back on the right, as far from me as she could get, staring out the window. June

Marie took charge. When Karen started asking questions or Lynnie started goofing on the fact that her father got in a fight, June Marie jumped in and stopped them. "Stop badgering Daddy," she said to Karen. "He said it was just a misunderstanding." She reached back and tickled Lynnie. "Hey, you want me to braid your hair tonight?" Then she turned to face front again and squared herself, her hands in her lap. "It's a beautiful day, isn't it?" she said. She must have said it four times.

It was crowded at the beach, or what they call a beach. But we found a corner and spread our blanket and tried to get comfortable. Karen put on her Walkman and checked out immediately. Lynnie dragged June Marie into the water. Ordinarily, Jeanette and I would have talked, I suppose. At least I thought we would have. We didn't go to the beach so often that we really had a routine, I went to the beach more often with Robbie. But she dove into a mystery that had been sitting on her bedstand for months, barely touched. So I just sat and stared at the water, trying to hold myself together.

I didn't understand how Jeanette could lie there and read a book. Every time she turned a page, I looked to see if she'd look up, to see if she wanted to talk to me now, or to see if she'd stopped to think about something. Was she *really* reading that book, or was she thinking about me, about us? She kept her sunglasses on so I couldn't see her eyes.

I watched Karen with her Walkman, eyes shut, frowning at the sun. Watched June Marie teaching Lynnie some kind of synchronized swimming routine. I would have liked to talk to my wife, but I'd already said the worst thing I could possibly say to her; where could I go after that? I closed my eyes and tried to let the sun work its way into my bones, to make me me again.

⋆ ⋆ ⋆

That night while we were getting ready for bed, Jeanette came out of the bathroom, walked to the bed and pulled back the cover to get in, then just stood there, staring at the sheets. Then her eyes glazed over and she was staring at nothing at all, or at some thought inside her head.

"What?" I said. "What is it?"

She broke her trance and looked at me. "Did you . . . ?" she said. "Was he in this bed?" The question was business, matter-of-fact.

I looked at her grimly and nodded. She pulled the sheet back up and dropped it, then turned and went to the linen closet, pulled out a pillow and a cotton blanket.

"Where are you going?" I said, but she didn't answer, just walked away.

The next few days were torture. Jeanette would barely speak to me, Lynnie kept crying for no reason, and every time I caught some motion in my peripheral vision, I thought it was Danny coming after me. Every time I closed my eyes, I saw that woman advancing on me, screaming "Child molester! Molester!" And then I saw Robbie in the street, straddling his bike, saw myself reaching out to him, and saw him ride away.

I was physically sick the whole time. My stomach upset, my vision blurry, I had incredible headaches. But I went through the paces of my day, pretending that everything was normal, pretending that all that had happened was a little misunderstanding, that it had basically passed out of my mind—nothing to get upset about—until I saw Robbie again.

Until I saw Robbie again.

At every free moment, when I wasn't having to talk to somebody, or do something, or fight off vomiting, I tried to figure out how I'd see Robbie next. Obviously, I couldn't call him. Stopping by was out of the question, although I did drive by several times, trying to glance in. But I didn't dare slow down or let it be seen that I was trying to see in, so I just drove by at a slow, steady pace with my eyes self-consciously straight ahead, and tried to catch him in my peripheral vision. After work I drove around the park, hoping I'd come across him on his bike, but I never found him. He'd disappeared from the face of the earth. For all I knew he'd died, just ceased to exist. Which made me think about what if he did, how would I keep living? Which made me think about him still alive, but me unable to see him. And I just ached all the time. In my chest, in my throat, in my stomach, my hands. Everything ached to see him.

I imagined him aching to see me too. I imagined him being kept prisoner. I imagined myself sneaking into his room at night and freeing him, imagined taking off on the highway with all the windows open, the wind blowing wild through his hair and mine, both of us free, laughing, laughing, zooming down the highway into the future. I imagined the radio playing loud, and the lights glowing green on the dash and remembered the glow of those lights when I was a boy coming home from a trip with my parents, my head in my mother's lap, her stroking my hair in a steady rhythm. I imagined stroking Robbie's hair, going over and over his cowlick, trying to smooth it down, imagined it popping up again and again as it always did, as buoyant as his smile, as his spirit. I imagined his head in my lap, looking up at me, smiling. I imagined him rising up to meet me, to kiss me, to wrap himself in my arms. I imagined him straddling my lap as we zoomed down the highway, free, imagined him riding my cock up and down, imagined my nose against his neck, breathing in his sweet smell, imagined his whimpering, his shuddering, imagined my own explosion in him, imagined us rocketing into the sky, still joined, two lovers among the stars. Suspended there for all time, for all the world to witness, and honor. Our love, flaming bright in the sky. I imagined it, and imagined it. And came to crying, my hand full of cum, covered with my own juices.

They came for me on Tuesday. I was home alone, after work, the time when Robbie and I were together most often. I was trying to nap when the doorbell rang. Was it Robbie? Come back to me at last? My throat seized. I hurried down the stairs. I saw the dark blue of their suits through the venetian blinds on the door. I saw the glimmer of silver. The house was still as a tomb. I opened the door. There were two of them. Blue and silver, decorated.

"Jerry Houseman?" said one of them. He was about my height, a bit heftier, with a beautiful, resonant voice, I remember. I remember I liked his voice.

I nodded.

"We have a warrant for your arrest. You have the right to remain silent . . ." I listened to him recite his poem. I watched his lips, the mole near his mouth. "You wanna step out here?" he said. He was gentle. He reminded me of the guy who led us into the haunted house last fall, when Robbie and I went together, the gentle-voiced steering. I stepped out onto the porch. He moved to my side and handcuffed me with my hands behind my back.

He moved to my side.

And handcuffed me.

With my hands behind my back.

I closed my eyes and listened to the sound of the shackles clicking shut. Then he led me down the stairs. I didn't look up to see if any of the neighbors were watching. I kept my eyes on the ground, kept my attention trained to the here and now. The car was silver blue, I'd had one like it as a boy. When you raced the wheels the siren screamed and sparks flew out the exhaust. It was one of my favorite toys.

They put me in the back. There was a grill between me and them, there were no handles on the doors. I slid to the center of the seat, straddling the hump, so I could see through the window between them, to see where we were going. The tall one slid in behind the wheel and we pulled into the street. The radio was crackling, you could hear people talking in codes.

We eased down the street like a parade. As we drove past Robbie's, I looked out the window, then craned my neck to keep my eyes on his house as we continued past. There was no sign of him. But as we reached the stop at the corner, I saw his mother step out on the porch, her arms folded, and look after us.

4

The cops didn't talk to me on the way in. They talked between themselves up front like I wasn't even there—about some little league game, I think. We headed straight down Jackson Street and cut over to the station on Cortland. I was almost surprised to find us at the police station so quickly—I had only a vague idea where it was located. We pulled into a garage and the door clanked down behind us, leaving us in twilight. The one with the voice took me by the elbow and led me to the door. A cop with a crew cut buzzed us into a cinder-block room from his desk. The desk was tall, like the registration desk at a motel.

"Tom," he said to the guy at my side. The guy at my side was named Tom. "This your CSC?"

Tom nodded. The room was white, fluorescent lights. The one with the crew cut dragged a big book across the desk, then turned the page and peered at it like St. Peter at the gates to heaven. "Criminal sexual conduct," he said as he wrote it down. He asked me my name and address, then Tom told me to empty my pockets. I didn't have anything in them; I'd been in bed when he came for me. When *they* came for me. The other cop, I noticed, had disappeared.

The crew cut buzzed another cop into the room from the other side—I thought I could see a jail cell through the door as he came in—and the new guy looked at me a minute like he was looking at an object, like he didn't get that there was somebody looking back at him. The radio was jumping with cops talking back and forth, their microphones clicking on and off, the static garbling their words. Someone had just been arrested at Westwood Mall for shoplifting. The crew cut turned to his computer and watched it print out a form on me. The new guy sat down. "This day gonna end?" he said to no one in particular.

The cop with the voice, my man Tom, led me into a little white room, stood me up and took my picture, then he led me into a bigger room, this one was painted baby blue, and took my fingerprints. He took three different sets, rolling my fingers firmly on the paper like he was rolling out cookie dough or something. He was talking low to me the whole time, asking me where I worked, where I grew up, how long I'd lived in town. "The judge will want to know this stuff," he said.

I found myself feeling soothed by his voice, like he was taking care of me, like he was on my side. But as he was taking my fingerprints, I saw the way his lip curled back and felt the way he pressed on my fingertips harder than he needed to, and I realized it was because he was privately disgusted. His soothing voice and all his manners were just a professional cover-up for what he really thought of me. For a second I could see it in the way he handled my hands—he thought I was repulsive, infectious. I was a child molester.

He led me back to the desk again and had me sit in an orange plastic chair while the crew cut called a judge. Another cop had just arrived with a surly handcuffed teenager, the shoplifter from Westwood Mall. Dressed in a way-too-big sweatsuit so he could wear stolen clothes out underneath. A sweatsuit in August. It was eighty outside. How could this kid be so stupid?

The crew cut turned to me. "You own your house?" I nodded. "Property owner," he nodded into the phone. Then he hung up and turned back to his computer, typing something in. When he was done he looked in my direction. He didn't really look at me. "OK," he said. "Your bond is set at ten thousand dollars, personal recognizance. You're free to go until your arraignment. Which will be Thursday afternoon at one. Up at the courthouse, second floor." Now he looked right at me, saw me. "You're not to have any contact with the boy or his family. You understand?"

I nodded.

"You're free to go," he said.

And that was it, the deal was done. They buzzed open the door and sent me on my way.

"Empty your pockets," I heard the crew cut say to the teenager as I left.

In the cab on the way home, I thought about Robbie, about the fact that I couldn't go near him, never mind touch him or talk to him, and realized with a sinking feeling that at that point I didn't want to. He had become the enemy, the thing I had to protect myself from. I knew in the back of my mind that I still loved him as much as ever, and that in his heart he loved me too, but it was only a thought, a low-level thing. I felt like I was going through myself like you'd go through a summer house, shutting it down for the winter. Covering things. Storing things. Boarding up the windows. But inside with me, there in the darkness, there was still the glow of that pilot light, a small blue knowledge of our love.

When I got home, the house was empty. The girls were at Frank and Dot's for the day; Jeanette and I were to join them for dinner, then bring them back into town. I paid the driver from the stash of cash Jeanette kept in the kitchen, went upstairs to shower and change, then came back down and had a beer.

Jeanette got home about six-thirty, her hair just cut and frosted. She dropped her keys on the front hall table and shrugged. "You like it?" she said. Her voice was flat. She didn't want to sound like she really cared if I liked it or not.

I nodded. "Very nice."

"You sure?" she said, uncertain.

I nodded again.

"Well then, let me change and we'll go," she said.

A few minutes later she skipped down the stairs in her shorts and stopped at the front hall mirror, turning left, then turning right, to examine her hair, picking at it with her fingers to make it curl just so. I stood in the kitchen door and watched her. She seemed like a girl to me, the girl I'd met eighteen years before.

"I have some news," I told her.

"What's that?"

"I was arrested today."

She stopped fiddling with her hair. "For what?"

"Criminal sexual conduct."

She turned toward me, and for the first time in days I didn't see anger there. What I saw was worry and fear. Her cheeks splotched red and her eyes welled up. She gestured helplessly. "I don't know what to say to you . . ."

"Could you tell me you love me?" I said. My voice cracked.

She looked at me with pity, *pity,* then came and gave me a hug. But it was a formal hug and she tore herself away from it, crying, and swiped her keys off the table. "Come on," she said. "I'll drive."

Dinner that night was the hardest thing I think I've ever done. We ate on the porch at the picnic table and watched the light fade over the lake. Dot had made potato salad and Frank grilled burgers and hot dogs. The girls were giddy from being out in the sun all day, and I could tell that Dot and Frank would be glad to see them go, but there was a tired kind of happiness at the table that night for everyone except Jeanette and me. There was a slowness to the evening, the feeling that summer was ending and school would soon start up again. A lazy evening with an undercurrent of coming briskness.

After dinner June Marie got up to help her grandmother. It was clear that Dot was glad to have a companion in her work again, and Jeanette went out and helped them too—the three of them: mother, daughter, granddaughter passing plates from hand to hand: wash, rinse, dry. Murmuring among themselves, now and then burbling up into laughter. "I know! I always do that too!" I heard Dot say at some point, then the three of them laughed. I could see them from where I was sitting on the chaise, out on the porch, with my beer.

Frank and Lynnie walked down to the dock, holding hands. I think they were talking about the stories he used to tell her on the dock when she was a little tyke. Stories about the stars, where the babies came from, and which one she came from. I think they were going to see if they could locate the star she came from.

I sat in the dim light on the porch, sipping my beer, my belly full, and listened to the crickets. This was what I'd always wanted. This was the life I'd envisioned here the summer I met Jeanette. This was it. It was mine, what I'd dreamed of.

Karen appeared in the doorway, quiet as a shadow. "What's the matter, Daddy?" she said so softly she might have been whispering right into my ear.

"Hmm?" I said.

"You seem sad." She sat on the foot of the chaise.

"Oh." I smiled. "End of summer, I guess. Always makes me sad."

She gazed out over the water. "Me too." She tapped my shin. "Make a backrest." I pulled my knees up and she leaned against them, the two of us lined up on the chaise like railroad cars in a train. We looked out at the night, quiet.

"Listen," she murmured. "The crickets."

I met with the lawyer on Thursday morning.

His office was in one of those big old houses on Michigan Avenue, near the Presbyterian church, with the huge old hickories in front of them. Hardly anybody can afford a house like that anymore—most of them have been turned into condominiums, or professional suites. His office was on the second floor at the top of a sweeping staircase that circled around a big chandelier. He met me at the top of the stairs. He was in his thirties, blond and sunburned, like he spent a lot of time playing golf.

"Mr. Houseman," he said. He held the door as I went in, then shut it and stood with his back to it, his hands still on the knob behind him. When I turned back to him, his face snapped into a cheerful grin and his hand shot out to shake mine. "Steve Curtis," he said. "Have a seat."

There was something in that moment when I turned . . . Was it my imagination or had he been assessing me from behind? Had I caught him at it? What did he think, I wondered. What kind of first impression had I made? Was I a person you could defend?

He gestured to a chair by his desk and offered me a cup of coffee. I said I didn't need one, thanks, but he ducked out to get one for himself. I looked around his office. It was small and neat, good light. There was a photo of his family on his desk. I couldn't help but notice his son—blond and cute, a real nice smile—and my interest in him sickened me. What kind of pervert was I, that even in this situation . . . ?

Curtis came back with his coffee mug and sat at his desk. "So," he said, glancing at his calendar. "The arraignment is this afternoon . . . ?"

"Yes," I said. "At one."

"One-thirty," he said. "They tell you one to be sure you'll be there. And you may be there for a while, depending on where you are in the lineup." He sat back and hooked his thumbs in his belt, rocking in his chair. "You ever been through this before?"

I shook my head.

"Well, it's pretty short and sweet. Just to be sure you understand the charge and what your rights are, and to determine whether there will be a preliminary exam. Which there probably will be, since their prime witness is a minor. They'll want to see how he does in court. I trust you've had no contact with the boy?"

I shook my head.

"All right, then," he sighed. He spun his chair and faced the wall, then spun back to face me again. "The charge is criminal sexual conduct," he said.

I nodded.

"In the first degree. Do you understand what that means?"

I shook my head.

"There are four degrees of the crime in this state. Second and fourth involve just touching. You know, in the crotchal or groinal area. First and third involve penetration." He stopped rocking. "There was penetration?"

I nodded.

"Oral?" he said. "Or anal?"

"Both."

"You inserted your penis in his mouth and anus."

I closed my eyes and nodded. That was my first real sense of it, those words. The first real sense of the way the rest of the world was going to see this. Insert tab A into slot B. It was vulgar when you put it that way.

"When?" said Curtis.

I looked at him. He wanted a date? I fished through my mind. "Several times," I said at last. "This summer."

"It's been going on all summer?"

"It's been going on for a year."

"A year." He swallowed and sat up. "And how many times, do you think?" he said. He was taking notes now, sketchily.

I thought. How many times did I hold Robbie in my arms and gaze into his eyes? How many times did I whisper I loved him? How many times did it take to turn my life so inside out? "I don't know," I said. "Two dozen?"

"You engaged in sex two dozen times."

"More or less."

"And you penetrated him each time?"

"I don't know," I snapped. "I didn't keep score."

He looked up at me, then set down his pen. "Mr. Houseman," he said. "I'm trying to help you. These are the questions you're going to be asked."

I nodded, looked down. "I'm sorry."

He picked up his pen again. "You penetrated each time?"

"Probably," I said. "One way or another."

"You mean orally or anally."

"Yes. He didn't like anal intercourse."

"But you . . . initiated him."

I looked up at him, confused.

He shrugged. "They'll paint you as a predator."

"But it wasn't like that!" I said. "He loved me!" I realized as I said the words how ridiculous they must have sounded to him. People don't believe a kid can love a person in that way.

"You had his consent," said Curtis. He raised his chin and looked down at me.

"Yes," I said. "He loved me. He loves me. He was nervous, scared. Of course. He's a kid. But he was willing. Eager!"

"And how did you determine that?"

"That he was eager? He came to my house. He climbed into bed with me."

"But your wife . . . ?"

"In the afternoons. I'd nap after work."

"So he initiated contact."

"He was eager for it! He loved me!"

Curtis set his pen down on the desk and gazed at it a moment. Then he looked up at me, curious. "Mr. Houseman?" he said. He cleared his throat. "Children . . . children are not adults. I think we get in trouble when we think of them as if they were."

"But he loved me!"

He cocked his head and winced like he was hearing a sour note. Then he looked down at his hands, sat back and leveled his gaze at me. "I have no doubt," he said, "that the child felt a special . . . attachment to you. But sexual love . . ." He spread his hands on the top of his desk, then rolled them over, palms up. "Sexual love is not a part of their . . . vocabulary, yet."

I started to protest, but he held up his hand and leaned forward. "At least not in the eyes of the law," he said, dismissing any more discussion. He picked up his pen again.

I looked down at my hands. I knew he was right. What I did with Robbie was illegal, whatever the heart might say. That was the hardest thing of all. I knew I was in the wrong.

Except that Robbie loved me.

"Mr. Curtis," I said. "You said there are four degrees of criminal sexual conduct in Michigan."

"Yes," he said.

"First and third involve penetration."

"Yes."

"What's the distinction between them?"

"The age of the victim." The *victim*! "The age of consent is sixteen. Under thirteen is the most serious. The boy in this case was . . . twelve, wasn't it?"

"He'll be thirteen next month," I said. "I was going to take him to the Chicago zoo."

Curtis nodded.

"What's the penalty?"

"The maximum," he said, "is life."

I felt the floor fall out from under me.

"You won't get that, of course," he said quickly. "But if you're found guilty of first degree, the judge is required to send you to prison. He doesn't have a choice. Of course, he gets to choose for how long."

"You mean like the Jackson prison?" I said.

"Jackson, Ionia. Whatever. But I wouldn't worry about that now." He reached into his desk drawer, pulled out a sheet of paper, a form, and started filling it out. "Will they have any witnesses?" he said. "Other than the boy?"

"You mean did anyone see us?"

"Yes."

"No. Nobody knew."

"No one ever saw you fondle him?"

Fondle him? "No."

"Now, Mr. Houseman," he said. He slid the form across his desk, turned so I could read it. It was called an Attorney Fee Agreement. "In a case like this," he said, "I will need my fee in advance. Judging by what you tell me, by how much time I'd expect to spend on your case, I'd estimate my fee to be at least ten thousand dollars—one hundred hours at one hundred dollars an hour." He pointed with his pen to the parts of the agreement he'd filled in with numbers. The pen was wood and gold. "I'll need a nonrefundable retainer of ten thousand dollars. Cash up front. With any further balance to be payable within fourteen days."

My mouth fell open. I shook my head. "I don't have that kind of money," I said.

He sat back, apparently satisfied. "Then at your arraignment this afternoon, I suggest you stand mute. When they ask you how you plead, say nothing. Then they'll ask you if you want the court to appoint you an attorney. At that point you say yes."

"But are those lawyers any good . . . ?"

"They handle ninety percent of the felony cases in Jackson County. At least ninety percent."

"But are they any good?"

He shrugged. "There are plenty of acquittals . . ."

"Maybe I could mortgage the house . . ."

He held up his hand like a traffic cop. "We don't want you to go through a fire sale. That's why we have these court attorneys."

"Maybe I could borrow the money . . ."

He settled a little and looked at me. "If you want, you bring this back to me signed with a check and we'll get under way." Then he stood and moved to the side of his desk. I looked up at him, stunned for a moment, then slowly got to my feet. He herded me to the door and reached around me to open it.

"Mr. Curtis," I said. I turned to him. "Am I going to prison?"

He let go of the door and took a step back. His face was blank as a wall. "I don't know," he said. "It's a serious charge." He looked at me a minute more, then offered me his hand. "I wish you the best of luck."

When I pulled out of his parking lot, I headed east through town. There were so many flags on the tops of the buildings, snapping in the wind, it looked like the goddamn Fourth of July. I drove out Michigan Avenue, out toward Foote Hospital. I didn't know where I was going. I didn't know what I was doing. I was just driving, blindly. Numb. Like I was shot full of novocaine—numb, immobile all over. It was almost pleasant to feel that way, to feel disconnected, floating, after all the feelings I'd been feeling. But there was an undercurrent to it, the way there is with novocaine when you get it at the dentist's office, that stomach-turning antiseptic smell and the suck of that gurgling thing in your mouth and the light shining in your eyes and somebody sticking their fingers in your mouth, wedging cotton in your mouth, leaning over you, their face so close you could count the pores, and you can't talk; if you try, you'll strangle. It was really a lot like that. A numbed-out stomach-turning feeling. Like being operated on by aliens.

What was I going to do? This guy, this jerk who was ten years younger than me, was sweeping me out his door with a grin and a handshake. Good luck, he says. Good luck. Thanks a lot. And I wish you luck with your golf game. What the fuck was I going to do? A court-appointed attorney. Juggling twenty cases a day, running from courtroom to courtroom, collecting his money for saying a couple of words of legal bullshit code that didn't mean a thing. What the fuck was I going to do?

What if I did borrow money? Who would I borrow it from? My dad? My brother? They didn't have money. Frank and Dot? What difference would it make? That lawyer didn't approve of me. I could see it in every move. It would be the same wherever I went. No one would defend me in this out of any conviction. There was no one in the world, not a single soul, who would take my side. And besides, how could I go to my family and tell them I was going to be put on trial for child molesting?

As if I could keep it a secret from them. As if I had any choice. They were going to know it all soon enough. Everybody was going to know. I'd probably be on the evening news, one of those shots of the guy in handcuffs, hanging his head so the cameras can't see him. Bright white lights, big black shadows. Cops stiff-arming the press. I've always wondered about those pictures. What was the point of hiding your face? Everybody knows who you are. Everybody knows every fucking thing they're saying about you. Why not just let them look at you? Why pretend you can hide?

I hung a left past the hospital and headed out toward the countryside. It took me through blocks and blocks of houses—little houses, modest houses, houses with neat little lawns and shady trees and cars in the driveways. Plaster figures in the gardens. Curtains at the windows. Homes. Families nestled together, nested, keeping each other warm and safe. Taking the days one after the next like nothing was ever going to change, nothing would ever end. It brought me out of the numb, a little. I could feel my heart in my throat, a little.

I got out past the edge of town and headed into the country. It's farmland out there, corn and wheat. Rolling slightly, lots of trees lined up at the edges of fields and along the riverbanks. Pretty country. Pretty and plain. I followed back roads I'd never driven. There was no traffic, few traffic signs. You didn't have to pay much attention. You could just drive and drive and drive, looping around from road to road, looping around inside your mind, around and around inside your mind. Rocking with the sway of the car, looping around in your mind.

I thought about my daughter Karen. My beautiful, dark, suspicious Karen. I thought about how she looked at me, so wary, so accusing. What was going on in her mind? What did she think she saw in me? In the world? I'd tried to convince her that life was good, that life was worth the living. There are things to love, things to enjoy. I wanted her to enjoy. But she was determined to be angry, unhappy. I hoped it would pass. I thought it would pass. But would I get to see it pass?

And Lynnie. My baby. My awkward duckling. What was

she going to grow into? And June Marie. And Jeanette. I couldn't even think of them. I couldn't even hold the thoughts. They were just too precious for me to even think about them now, for me to even bring them into my mind with all the rest of this shit.

What was I going to put them through? What kind of slime would I drag them through? Pictures on the television, stories in the newspaper. Whispering behind their backs, in the markets, in the schools. Father is a child molester. Husband diddles little boys. Wonder if he diddled his girls? Or maybe he likes only peanut-dicks. Hey lady! Your husband likes peanut-dicks! The four of them heading off to church, clean and pressed in their summer dresses, prim and proper in their boat. Your daddy diddles little dicks!

I started driving faster and faster down the center of the road, my eyes so blurred I didn't trust myself to stay off the shoulder unless I was riding the crest of the pavement, straddling the two lanes. So what if a car might come my way? So what if a tractor pulled out in the road? I'd accelerate instead of braking. I'd step on the gas and ram into it. Take the plunge, just take the plunge. Just headlong plow right into it. It would take only a second, an instant. A moment of impact, then *pow,* you're done. It would be the simplest thing to do. Just plow right off the edge of existence, disappear into the stars. It could happen in an instant. I could simply not exist anymore. Their father was killed in an accident. Poor girls, poor girls. Poor good little girls. Her husband died young. Young widow, so sad. But there was insurance and she remarried. Boom, in an instant the problem was gone. The impossible problem lifted away, up and away, as light as air, as the sun, lifted up into the sun, becoming one with the sun. At last.

My little car was racing, racing, whining to shift to a higher gear, but I was already gone, beyond it, raised to some other level. I was floating free, above it, already starting to lift up, to float, to fly, to rise toward the sun. I edged the wheel to the left and headed across the road toward the shoulder, toward the ditch, and a tree. I saw it there like a person standing by the side of the road, motioning to me to come. I aimed toward it, I headed for it. I narrowed my eyes and gripped the wheel and accelerated toward it. All I could see was the tree and me and the two of us coming together. It was so simple. Me and the tree. We were put on this earth for each other.

But as soon as my tires hit the shoulder, my reflexes swerved me back on the road. It brought my tail around and I spun out across the pavement, screeching. I wrestled the wheel back and forth while the landscape skidded around outside the car and finally came to rest on the other side of the road, facing in the right direction, sitting there as simply and neatly as if I'd just pulled off for a second to have a look at a road map.

I rested my head on the steering wheel and felt the shakes come over me. They worked their way in from my edges until my entire body was shaking, heaving, and I was gulping air, gasping, choking, groaning low down in my throat, coughing up sounds I'd never made, sounds like wind blowing out of some cave, sounds that seemed to come from some place and time before the earth even started, helpless sounds, inhuman sounds, human, human sounds. Human sounds.

I looked up, and there was the prison. Just a few hundred feet down the road, shimmering in the heat. The biggest prison in the world. Vague behind layers of chain-link fence glinting with coiled concertina wire. I had driven there without knowing it. I had driven there by instinct. There it was, right in front of me, like some huge sleeping animal that might wake up and swallow me.

I sat up and wiped my eyes. Sat back and looked at it. And I don't know. It made me feel better. It was huge. It was strong. It was secure. There were no questions in that building. Right was right and wrong was wrong and guards were guards and inmates were inmates. It was clear and everybody agreed. Some people belonged in there. For a while, at least. For a while.

I tried to picture the scale of a person inside that huge rectangle. It seemed as big as the Pentagon, as big as the Grand Canyon. It made you feel as small. And that was where I felt something inside me solidify. A floor slipped in underneath me. Four walls closed in, inside me. There was something in the sight of that building that gave me a kind of strength. I don't know if it was the thought of going inside, getting locked away from my own illegal self—that that would somehow purify me, make me right again. Or if it was the fear of that. But I felt that building's solidness in me. I didn't know what my future would be, or what I could do with it. But whatever it was, I would stand up and face it. I would stand, and let them see.

Part III

1

The first time Jerry got in trouble I tried to rise above it, I tried to lift us both above it. That's the way I was raised. I remember one lesson very clearly. It was winter, and Sherry and I, my sister, had been fooling around on the golf course in the park near where we lived. The same park we live near now, but on the other side, over by Sharp Park School. We'd found some old bottles around the pavilion and were throwing them in the road, smashing them against the pavement. We were only eight or nine, I think, and it wasn't exactly the kind of thing that Sherry and I were into, or at least I wasn't into it. But Sherry did always seem like she had something inside of her she wanted to take out on the world. Anyway, we were smashing these bottles and a policeman came along and picked us up, just picked us up in the back of his car, drove us home, marched us up to the door and told our father what we'd been doing.

"Breaking glass in the road?" Father said. He looked at the two of us in turn, peering over his reading glasses. My father is a very big man, a very forceful man, formidable even among adults and thoroughly feared by his high school students. To me, as a child, it seemed like God Himself was looking down on me.

"It was ice," said Sherry, calm as you please. I couldn't believe it. How could she lie?

"I believe it was glass," the policeman said to our dad. I remember he smelled of tobacco.

My father looked at me. "Jeanette?" he said. "Was it glass? Or ice?"

I stood there a moment, unsure. Did I tell the truth and betray my sister? My big sister with whom I shared a room? Or did I risk a lie to my father?

"Ice," I said at last.

My father studied me a moment, turning something in his mind, then he looked up at the policeman. "If my children say it was ice," he said, "then I believe it was ice. I thank you for your concern, Officer. But I've raised my kids to be trustworthy. And I believe if you trust your children, then they will prove to be trustworthy." He met and held our gaze as he said those words. Then he looked at the policeman again, and thanked him, and sent him on his way.

The two of us scurried into the house, giddy with relief and excitement but trying to contain it so our father wouldn't know we'd been lying. He shut the door and leaned against it, watching us take off our coats and boots. "I want you to remember that," he said, watching us carefully. "If you trust people, they'll be trustworthy." He didn't smile. He nodded once. "You're both good kids," he said. Then he went back to grading compositions. And I remember feeling so ashamed of myself at that moment that I had gained his trust with deception.

I remember that moment as vividly as if it had happened yesterday. The sudden heat of the kitchen. The smell of the wet wool. The ponderous weight of my father's gaze and the burden of his faith in me. I'd always known my father loved me, but in that moment I think I felt the price of that love for the first time—the knowledge that his love for me was something I had to live up to. Not a love I had to earn, because he gave it freely. But a love I had to prove worthy of. And I had to prove it to *myself,* not to him. Had to trust that part of myself that believed I was worthy of his love.

It was one of the most important lessons I think I ever learned, from him or anyone else, because in that moment I grasped what love was about. Reaching into somebody and pulling out the best in them. Believing in the best in them, believing their best will prevail. I think that moment with my father taught me more about love and faith than a thousand Sunday mornings in church.

So when Jerry came to me that first time and told me about the run-in he'd had with that boy on his route, that Tony, I let it slide beneath my vision and sought a higher ground. I didn't have to think about it, I just did it instinctively. We were sitting at the kitchen table. It was a rainy afternoon, so dark we needed the lights on. Jerry had put the girls down for a nap, then he came and told me this. And I remember sitting up, actually sitting up and straightening my back to raise myself above it.

Of course I was shocked, I didn't pretend I wasn't. I'd never had the slightest hint that Jerry was . . . *unusual* in that way . . . and at first I just couldn't believe it. I couldn't imagine he'd joke about such a thing, but I also couldn't imagine he was telling the truth. You're sexually interested in *children*? I remember watching him form the words and wondering who the ventriloquist was, who was making him say these things. It seemed as if he were wearing a mask, but a mask that looked just like him. Or as if he'd suddenly stepped in front of one of those department store mirrors, and all at once there were hundreds of him, lined up one after the other, off into infinity: Suddenly there were layers of Jerry that I'd never even guessed at before.

My first thought was for the girls, of course. Had he touched them? Would he touch them? But he said it was only little boys, and something in the way he said it, something in the finality of it, the absolute wall in his words, let me know there was nothing to worry about there. My girls were not in jeopardy. It was my husband who was in jeopardy.

It took me a while to get oriented. I felt dizzy, the way you feel when you first get off the merry-go-round, or the roller coaster, like the ground is tipping beneath your feet. But there we were at our kitchen table, surrounded by all the familiar things of our lives. The cookie jar. The café curtains. The drawings on the refrigerator. This was reality, this was our life. The table had four legs, it was stable. The surface was flat, things didn't roll off.

But I'd never seen Jerry so scared before. Not scared so much that this Tony might tell—by the time he told me he was pretty sure the boy wasn't going to say anything—but scared of himself, his own impulses. Scared of what he'd let himself do and of what that might mean he'd do in the future. It was his idea to see a psychologist and I backed him up on that. I told him I'd get a part-time job if we needed some extra money for it. I told him I wanted to help. I told him I knew he could conquer this, that I knew him too well to believe that he was some kind of sexual pervert. I straightened my back and lifted my head and led him back to his pride by demonstrating my faith in him, by letting him know that whatever happened, whatever demons he had to fight, I knew the higher powers in him would see him through it.

And privately, I prayed. I actually lit candles at church, and went to talk with a priest. I hadn't gone to talk to a priest since we'd gotten married six years before, and even then I was only going through the formalities, giving the church whatever it needed to make it OK for me to marry outside my religion. But I didn't know where else to turn. Ordinarily I'd go to my father, but I couldn't go to him with that news. My father? My lifelong judge? So I talked to Father Doran at St. Mary's, and he told me just what my father would have. Love. Trust. Faith in the good. Find it in you. Seek it in others. Pray to God for help.

And it worked. My faith in Jerry's strength made his strength flow back into him. He became my husband again. And I became, again, the humble recipient of my father's wisdom.

After that, things seemed to return to normal, even better than normal. Jerry started seeing that psychologist once a week, and it seemed to be helping him. He was very attentive to me and the girls, more so than he'd been before: That distracted quality was gone. I felt as if I had him back again, the way he was the summer we met.

And I guess I'd have to say *I* was more attentive afterward too. More tuned to his attention. More conscious of my hair, and my clothes. I lost the twelve pounds I'd kept after Karen. Started getting in the habit of taking baths instead of showers, because they slowed me down, made me feel more receptive. I had a heightened consciousness of Jerry, and of myself, and of the line of tension between us. It was very much like that summer we met, that consciousness at every moment of where the other is, even if you're way across town from each other. That sense, when you're in a room together, there is an invisible tether between you. That every move on one person's part creates a move on the other's part, even if only subliminally, as if all of life were a courtship dance. And that *was* what was happening: We were courting each other again. After that accident in our marriage—I thought of it as an accident—he became my suitor again and I became seductive.

Then Lynette came along, and it seemed that we were starting all over, getting a second chance. The errors of the past had been mended and Lynnie was the proof we were healed. A sign from God. I saw it that way. I feel downright strange admitting it, as semi-lapsed as I am. But I believed God was giving His blessing. And I promised we would be worthy this time.

So when Jerry called me that Sunday last summer—almost a year ago, now—and asked me to meet him in Vandercook Lake . . . Well, it didn't happen instantly. I was so convinced we were over that problem, it didn't even occur at first. When he'd told me that he and Robbie were just good friends, I had closed my eyes and nodded, assuring him I knew that was so. Assuring myself I believed it. But as I was driving to meet him, I felt this cold, hard thing in my stomach, a fear. What if it's That, again? And with that fear, the knowledge that if it were That again, I'd never be able to forgive him this time.

2

In some ways, Lynette is my favorite child. I'd never admit that publicly, I barely admit it to myself. But I guess the youngest is always special, especially when she comes later. She has such a gawkiness about her, she's like a little duckling. And it isn't just that she's eleven. She isn't as pretty as the other two—something happened to her chin: It forgot to grow, or grew too slow. It gives way to her throat at a very steep angle, just kind of disappears. I guess I've always felt a little more protective of her because of that, and because she's the youngest.

June Marie is the prettiest—a natural blond, blue eyes and dimples. She looks like a little doll and has a personality to match: always cheerful, always alert. She was my first, and I'm thankful for that—she was an easy introduction into the trials of motherhood—but her heart belongs to Daddy. As soon as Karen was born, June Marie turned her attention to Jerry. They took care of each other in those first few months while I was busy with Karen and ever after that June Marie continued taking care of her father.

And then there's Karen. Dear, dark Karen. Karen insists on black. I made her a dress for the tenth-grade dance this spring, and she insisted on black. We looked through all the patterns together, all the pastels and puffy sleeves, all the full skirts and lacework—I would have loved to make one of those for her—but she insisted on black. Straight and simple, too severe and much too sophisticated for a tenth-grader, if you ask me. But I don't argue with Karen. She's stubborn as a blueberry stain. Black she wants, then black she gets. I did sneak in an appliqué of bright colors on the inside hem though.

These are my girls, my backup group. My boop-she-boop singers, my own Ronettes. I actually taught them the shoop-shoop song one day a couple of months ago, one of the greatest songs from my day.

Well is it in his face?
Oh, no, that's just his charms . . .
In his warm embrace?
Oh no, that's just his arms . . .
If you wanna know if he loves you so, it's in his kiss.
That's where it is!
It's in his ki-yi-yiss.
That's where it is!

A great song. A truly great song. I got them all lined up behind me, showed them how to twirl their hands and shuffle about just like the Ronettes. Or was it the Shirelles? They didn't know what to make of me. It's never exactly been my style to dance around the house singing, but sometimes in the year since all that messy stuff happened with Jerry I've just felt the need to check out for a while, just become someone else for a while. Anybody. A singer, a stooge. A Flemish acrobat. I feel as if different parts of me are suddenly spinning in different directions, but all the parts are only spinning, I don't gain any traction. I don't always know when this strange sensation is going to come over me and it's a little disconcerting, but I'm trying to learn to live with it, trying to let it go. I figure it's probably good for me to let off a little steam now and then.

It's either that or just lie down and watch TV all day, after all. Just sink into inertia. Eat candy. Smoke cigarettes. Drink. There's a part of me that would love to do that, but I can't, I've got to hold it together. I'm suddenly a team of one, pulling a load that was heavy for two. So if I get a little strange now and then and want to take a vacation . . . well, where is the person who'll judge me for that?

They're everywhere, that's where they are.

Everybody is watching me. Or at least that's how it's felt sometimes.

I ran into Gretchen VanderVelt in the store one day a few months ago, in the produce department. She was fondling a melon, her wattles quivering slightly, her eyes bugging out. I was right next to her before I saw her, and as soon as she saw me she set down the melon and clutched my arm.

"I just want you to know," she said, "I think that it's just marvelous the way you're continuing on with your life." She looked at me with pity. "To be left alone with three young children. And three young children who've been through so much . . ."

I stared at her, too stunned to speak. It had been nine months since Jerry had gone and here she was still talking about it.

"Do you know, at the bank," she said, "the teller was talking about it to me. About how well you seem to be doing."

I looked around to see who might hear and tried to pull

myself free from her, but I would have had to pry her fingers off me with a claw hammer.

"You have a lovely family," she whispered. Why did she whisper that part, I wondered, and trumpet the rest of it? "Those girls are beauties, every one. Well, I'm sure the little one will grow into it. And it just makes my heart break to think of their father—" She broke off and gazed at me, shaking her head. I wanted to throttle her. "Is there any way I can help?" she said.

I patted her hand and kept patting it until I was almost spanking it. "No," I said coldly. "We're doing fine. Thank you so much for your concern."

Finally she let go of me and gave me this condescending smile. I picked up the melon she'd been holding and plunged it into her shopping cart, right on top of her eggs. "Don't forget your melon," I said, and then I marched away.

I was furious for the whole afternoon, to think that she was using my life as a soap opera, something to watch and cluck her tongue about. To think the whole town was doing that, as if there were no people involved, as if we were only actors being paid to say our lines and could go home at night to a different life, probably in a limousine, or go out dancing at a nightclub. Going out to a nightclub, hah. Going out to McDonald's is more than we've been able to muster sometimes, feeling as watched as we have. I felt like I could have murdered that woman, standing there in the market. But I smashed her eggs instead.

I've got to say it felt good.

It amazes me that in the midst of all the public humiliation, June Marie went out for the talent show. I couldn't imagine she'd want to put herself on public display and I asked her if she was sure about it—if she'd really thought it through—but she was adamant. All her friends were doing things, and she wanted to be a part of it. And who was I to say no? She'd always been an extrovert, right from her very first breath, and she was on public view anyway, all the time, as a cheerleader. Why should any of that change? What were we supposed to do, stop living our lives? I just hoped that none of the kids would laugh at the irony of her song. She was singing "Don't Cry for Me, Argentina."

I made her the dress, from the photograph on the album. I got an old wedding gown at Goodwill and rebuilt it to make it look like the strapless white ball gown in the picture. I fudged it a bit, needless to say—I dispensed with the beads and added some sheer fabric to cover her shoulders and arms. Between that dress and Karen's black thing, sometimes I felt like I didn't have time to eat for a couple of months there after Jerry was taken from us. But it was just as well, it was fine. I needed to keep my hands busy. If I'd stopped moving, I would have been done for.

Especially in the middle of the night. There were several months there when I never slept through an entire night. I'd wake up at three or four, regular as clockwork. At first I'd just lie there with my eyes shut, pretending I was still asleep, hoping I could will myself to be "out" for a few hours more. There's such a cruelty in sleep: When you need it most, it eludes you. But then I caught on it was not to be. So when I woke up at three or four, I didn't fight back anymore. I just got up and went about my business, measuring and cutting fabric, pinning, draping, planning.

And life went on. Life still goes on. I go to the bank every morning and do my job. I come home at night and take care of my girls. I listen to their successes and failures, their worries, their plans, their musings. With Jerry gone, I don't have the time to do all the things I used to do. So June Marie does most of the shopping. Karen cleans the house every weekend. And Lynnie sets and clears the table, and puts the dishes in the dishwasher. I used to do all those things myself, but now we have our little systems. I like it, in a way. I like to see the way the girls have accepted responsibility—much, much more than they used to. We manage pretty well, in fact. We run a pretty tight little ship.

But sometimes at night I miss him. Sometimes at night I feel an ache, a longing. Not a yearning for him so much, I think, as for what we used to have together. When something happens during the day, something funny or interesting, I start to tuck it into my mind like you'd tuck a rabbit into your sleeve, to pull out later and amaze someone. Then I remember I have no audience. The girls, they have their own stories to tell, and some of the stories I have to tell I wouldn't tell to them; they wouldn't understand them. I feel like I felt when my brother was killed—this sense of an enormous absence, a void where there's supposed to be something. But when Stevie was killed, I had Jerry to comfort me. Now there is no one to comfort me. Just my pins and needles, my dressmaker's dummy and my books. And my girls. My backup group. My shoop-shoop singers. My reason to live.

3

That first night last August, after I met Jerry in Vandercook Lake and he told me what had been going on with Robbie, I spent the night on the couch. I just couldn't sleep in that bed with him.

I could understand that he had been involved with someone else. I couldn't begin to understand how that other person could be a child, I'd never be able to understand that, but if I tried to imagine him being involved with some other woman, sure, I could imagine that. I guessed I could even imagine him being involved with some other man. What I couldn't understand, what I couldn't ever accept, was that he'd brought that person into our bed. Our *bed.* My *parents* gave us that bed—a four-poster that had belonged to my mother. It was in that bed that we snuggled on Saturday mornings, pretending to be asleep so the kids wouldn't bother us. In that bed that we finally let go of the day and just relaxed with each other, talking, nibbling, tickling. Or sometimes just lying beside one another, me engrossed in one of my books, him in one of his crossword puzzles. Our *children* had been in that bed with us. One at a time, in the middle of the night when one of them had a nightmare. And all together on Christmas morning, when they all came bounding into the room, jumping up and down on us, giggling, laughing, rolling about like a litter of puppies. We'd lived our life in that bed together. We'd *created* life in that bed.

The next morning, Monday, when Lynnie came down and saw the pillow and blanket folded on the living room couch, she was very upset by it. She was at that stage in her life where the slightest thing could take on operatic proportions—if somebody snubbed her at school, she went into a funk for days—and the evidence that Jerry and I were on the outs seemed to really disturb her. This had never happened before. She kept asking me *Why did you sleep on the couch? Why did you sleep on the couch?* I told her I just couldn't sleep so I came downstairs, but it didn't satisfy her, she sensed that something else was up. Karen and June Marie exchanged looks, then Karen started mocking Lynnie—*Why did you sleep on the couch? Why did you sleep on the couch?*—and that put Lynnie into a pout and she went blubbering back up the stairs and shut herself in her room. I couldn't handle the histrionics so I just left them to sort it out among themselves and went into work.

I was distracted all day. I shorted one customer fifty dollars, paid an extra twenty to another, misplaced all my Christmas Club coupons and took almost an hour to balance. It was the thought of Robbie in that bed that just kept nagging at me. I felt as if I were covered with poison ivy, burning with the desire to scratch, and I couldn't do it.

But when I got home that afternoon and found Jerry sprawled on the living room couch in front of the television, watching some goddamn quiz program, all at once I knew what I had to do. The girls were milling about, in and out, so I motioned him upstairs into the bedroom and shut the door behind us. I crossed the room and looked out the window. Mrs. VanderVelt was taking in her laundry.

I turned and looked at him. "I think you ought to leave," I said. He just looked back at me. I started pacing the floor, not sure what I was saying. "I think you should pack your things and go. I want you out of the house." I straightened a picture above the dresser, then turned and looked at him again.

"Where am I supposed to go?" he said.

"I don't care where you go. Just go." I moved to the other window, looked out, then suddenly turned and went to the closet, unbuttoning my blouse. "Go to your parents'. Go to your brother's."

"Jeanette," he said, "you're not making sense."

"Just *go*! I don't care, I don't want you here." I threw my blouse on the floor of the closet and slipped out of my skirt.

Jerry came to me and tried to put his arms around me, but I pushed him away. "I just want you to go," I whispered, backing away.

He stood with his arms hanging limp at his sides. "Jeanette," he said. "Look at me." He waited until I did. "Do you really want me to leave this house?"

He looked pathetic, unprotected. Unwilling to fight me on this, except by peering into my heart. "Do you really want me to leave?" he whispered.

I looked at him a moment more, then lowered my eyes. "Yes." It didn't sound very convincing, so I said it again, more firmly. "Yes. The girls are very upset."

There was a moment of silence, a shameful silence. Then he

turned and crossed the room and looked out the window himself.

"It'll just make things worse," he said at last. "If the girls are upset now, think how upset they'll be if their dad leaves home. Have you thought about that?"

I didn't answer.

He looked at me expectantly, then sat on the edge of the bed. "This is my home," he said calmly. "You're my family. I'm not going to walk away."

"Jerry . . ."

"I'm not going to walk away, Jeanette. You can't just put me out like a dog. Now, you come back to bed tonight. Or I'll sleep on the couch if you want, and you come sleep in the bed."

"I don't want to sleep in this bed!" I cried.

"Shhhhh!" he said, glancing at the door.

I realized I was standing there in my bra and panties. I went to the dresser and rifled a drawer. Jerry lowered his head and sighed—a sigh of regret, a sigh of impatience—waiting for me to come around. I pulled on a pair of shorts and a T-shirt and left him there, still waiting. I didn't even look back at him.

But that night at bedtime I did go back. I washed and bleached the sheets and mattress pad first, but I went back. He lay there in the bed and watched me as I crossed the room, turned back the sheets and slid beneath them. I didn't look at him, I just did it, then tried to bury myself in a book. He kept watching me, hoping I'd say something, but I would not acknowledge him. Finally he reached out and touched my elbow. "Welcome back," he said. But I just pulled my arm away, then got up and left the room and didn't go back until he was asleep.

Even then I didn't sleep well, having him lying there next to me. He had become repulsive to me. The hair on his shoulders. His two gold chains. I was disgusted with it all, and the smell of his breath. It wasn't something I could help, I had no control over it. There was a part of me that wanted to overcome those feelings, that wanted to reach out a hand to him and lift us both to higher ground, but I couldn't do it, I just couldn't do it. I wasn't on a higher ground, and I couldn't find my way to it.

So the next night I slept in Lynnie's room, in the extra twin. It sent more tremors through the house, and it made Lynnie toss and turn in her sleep, restless with me there, but I couldn't help it. I had to sleep, and I couldn't sleep with Jerry.

It took about a week before the word began to get around. The whole neighborhood knew what had happened, of course. They'd all been out on their porches, watching, as if they were invited guests to my husband's humiliation. I couldn't believe that woman had had the gall to scream at him that way. Who were those people, barbarians? Screaming at people on the street, physically attacking people? This is supposed to be a nice neighborhood, people are civilized here.

Of course the word spread like a grass fire. This isn't a very big town. I'd say within a week I was getting looks from the people at the bank, and people stopped talking when I came near. I felt like Hester Prynne with a scarlet A on my breast, but what made it so infuriating was that I wasn't accused of anything, there was nothing I could fight against. I was just being whispered about. Or thought I was being whispered about.

But if I had any doubts, they were cleared up when Lynnie

came home in tears the following Saturday afternoon. I was in the dining room, sewing a skirt for June Marie, when Lynnie barged through the door and charged up the stairs and slammed the door to her room, the room that I was now sharing. I'd been waiting for something like this to happen. I put the fabric aside, took off my glasses and took a deep breath, then made my way up the stairs.

I knocked on the door and went in. Jerry wasn't home yet; he'd taken to going for long drives after work, which suited me just fine. The other girls were off somewhere.

Lynnie was sitting on her bed, tearing pages out of a notebook and crumpling them into little balls, then throwing them on the floor.

"Lynnie," I said. "What is it?"

She tore off another sheet and crumpled it and threw it down. I crossed the room and sat on the bed. My bed, the one I was using, her roommate. "What's the matter?" I said.

Her face was covered with tears already. "They said that Daddy's a molester."

"Who?" I said. "Who said that?"

"Susan Nutter. Tammy Breitmeyer."

My mind went racing in circles. I knelt on the floor between our beds and looked into her eyes. "Tell me exactly what they said."

She tore another sheet from her book. "They said he molested Robbie Young. They said it in front of everyone."

"What did they mean, molested?"

"He made him take his clothes off and then he did things to him."

My stomach convulsed. "What did you do?"

"I said it wasn't true," she cried, and then she broke into

this moan, this awful, horrible wail. I wrapped my arms around her, cradled her head on my shoulder, and she cried like she used to cry as a baby, abandoning herself to her misery.

Then she leaned back and looked at me, sniffling. "Is it true?" she said. She was pleading with me to say no, to make them take it back. I didn't want to lie to her, but how could I tell her the truth?

"No," I murmured. "No, it's not true. Those children were just being mean to you."

"They said that's why Danny attacked him."

"It's not true," I crooned. "Not true, not true." But I'd sung that song to myself before, all the time Jerry was seeing Robbie, and I knew at some point Lynnie would learn that I was lying too.

That night at dinner Lynnie wouldn't eat, even though I made hamburgers. She took one bite, then let it sit there and slouched in her chair just staring at it. Scowling at it, is more the word. Usually she is the one at the table who's most energetic, interrupting, changing the subject, so it was especially obvious. Even Jerry noticed it, and Jerry hadn't been noticing much of anything for the past week.

"Lynnie," he said. "Eat your dinner."

She didn't respond. Didn't look at him.

"Lynnie," he said. "I'm talking to you."

Still no response.

I reached out and stroked Lynnie's head. "She's not feeling so well this evening . . ." I said.

"What's the matter?" said Jerry. He said it to her, but then he looked at me.

"It's nothing," I said. "She'll get over it."

He looked at her again, and chewed, thinking about his options here, what was the best way to handle it. I prayed he wouldn't pursue her further; I hoped I'd put him off the scent.

Finally he swallowed. "Better eat up," he said. "You'll never grow big that way."

I relaxed with relief that the moment had passed. But suddenly Lynnie turned on him. "I don't want to grow up!" she cried. "I don't want to grow up to be like you!" Then she threw her napkin on the floor and ran from the room in tears. There was a moment of stunned silence when all of us looked after her as she ran up the stairs and slammed her door. Then the rest of the family looked at me, all of them, as if I had the answer.

"What's the matter with her?" sneered Karen.

"It's nothing," I said. "It's nothing. Some kids were giving her a hard time . . ." I pushed some beans around on my plate, then set down my fork and glanced up. June Marie and Karen had gone back to eating, but Jerry was still staring at me. His eyes were brilliant, shining, worried. *What is going on?* they said. It was a look he'd shown me a million times before, over the heads of our children. A significant look, a coded look, the look of a partner offering help, or requesting it. A look I imagine trapeze artists must give to each other in the moment before they leap and swing. A lock of the gaze, a solid commitment, a look as tangible as a handshake. It stirred up all my feelings for him, my commitment to him, my reliance on him. He was the foundation on which I'd built my life, and he was still there, as strong as ever. At least in that moment, as strong as ever. But I couldn't hold his gaze. I was sure if I did, I'd burst into tears. Because I knew I couldn't answer the other question in his eyes, *Do you still love me?*

I crumpled my napkin on the table, got up and took Lynnie's plate to the kitchen and dumped it in the garbage. I started to clean the pots and pans, but then I just set them aside and went upstairs to be with my daughter.

4

I wanted to rub Jerry's face in this, to tell him how his daughter had been humiliated in front of her friends. I wanted to make him see it, to see her sitting alone on her bed in her room on a beautiful sunny day, tearing pages out of a notebook and wailing like an infant. I wanted him to be as horrified by that sight as I was, to see what his so-called love affair was doing to his child.

After the dinner dishes were done, I called him into the bedroom to tell him what had happened to Lynnie. I sat cross-legged on the bed and rocked back and forth while I told him, and plucked at a tuft on the bedspread. But once I started talking, it came out of me differently. I couldn't rub his face in it. I needed his help in handling it.

"We have to tell Karen and June Marie," I said.

Jerry was sitting on his side of the bed, leaning against the headboard, his feet straight out ahead of him. "No . . ."

"We have to. They're going to find out anyway, and they're going to find out soon. It's amazing they haven't heard already.

If, in fact, they haven't. Do you want them to hear it like Lynnie did? Isn't that worse? We have to tell them."

He looked at me as if I'd hit him. "I can't," he whispered. "I can't do that."

"You can," I said. "And you will. We're not going to let them hear it on the street."

He covered his face with one hand. I could see his mouth beneath his hand, curled and glistening in a grimace. He cried as if he had the hiccups, or had something caught in his throat, little explosions in his throat.

I plucked at the tufts on the bedspread again. "I'll be there with you," I sighed. "I'll help."

"I'm sorry," he whimpered. "I'm just so sorry . . ."

I closed my eyes and took a deep breath and waited for him to control himself. Then I passed him some Kleenex from my bedstand. "We'll tell them it's a lie," I said.

He looked at me from the corner of his eye, his nose still buried in a tissue. "You want me to *lie* to them?"

"You've been lying to me all along," I snapped. "Don't go all moral on me now." I plucked at the bedspread again. "Besides," I muttered. "That's what I told Lynnie. We've got to tell them the same story." My entire body flushed with shame.

He let his hands fall into his lap and crumpled the Kleenex into a ball. He looked up at the ceiling as if he were beseeching God. He looked to me as if he might break into tears again.

"OK?" I said. My voice was firm. I didn't want more tears.

He looked down at his hands and nodded.

We told them the next day, a Sunday. We called a family conference first thing around the kitchen table. I stood by the sink sipping coffee as the children filtered in. Jerry found something he had to do upstairs at the last minute.

Lynnie came in first, grouchy from sleep, still in her nightgown. She sat down and stared at the table. Karen came right after in shorts and a sweatshirt, her face unwashed. "We got any doughnuts?" she wanted to know. Then June Marie arrived, all dressed and made up, brushing her hair.

"What's up?" she chirped.

"Sit down," I said. Then I went to the door. "Jerry!" I called. "We're waiting!"

I stalked back to the sink and pulled one of Jerry's cigarettes from the crumpled pack on the window sill.

"Mo-om?" said Karen, her lip curling up. "You're *smoking*?"

"Oh, yech," said Lynnie.

June Marie kept brushing her hair. "Boy this must *really* be bad!" she joked.

Jerry finally arrived at the door. He was wearing a blue plaid shirt and gray pants. He looked pale. He looked thin. His watch looked too big on his wrist.

"Your father has something to tell you," I said. I exhaled. "Your father and I."

Jerry came in as if he'd been introduced on a talk show. He sat at the table. "Hi guys," he said. They all just looked at him.

"I have some bad news," he said. He laid his hands on the table, palms flat and fingers splayed. He brought his thumbs together and stared at them a moment. "I've been arrested," he said.

Nice, I thought. Simple, straightforward.

June Marie stopped brushing her hair in mid-stroke. Jerry took a breath to continue, but didn't say any more.

"For what?" said Karen, annoyed.

Jerry closed his eyes and took a deep breath. Lynnie was scowling at the bowl of fruit on the table.

"Robbie Young has accused me of touching him," Jerry said.

"*Touching* him?" That was Karen.

"Sexually," said Jerry.

Lynnie started to cry, or looked like she was about to.

"It's not true," I blurted out. I dropped my cigarette in the sink and it made a hissing sound.

Karen looked at me, then back at her father. "Is it?" she said. "Is it true?"

"I told you it wasn't . . ."

"No," said Jerry. "No. It's not true." He laid down the words like cards on a table, deliberately, emphatically.

Karen kept watching him, studying him.

"Of course it's not true," said June Marie, swatting her sister on the arm. "How could you even ask that?" She turned to her father. "Why is he saying that?"

"It's a misunderstanding," I said.

Jerry nodded. "He's misinterpreted, I don't know."

"Why aren't you in jail?"

"Karen!"

"Well, he's *been arrested*!"

"They let me go on recognizance."

"What's that mean?"

"I just have to stick around and show up at a hearing."

"Are you going to jail?" said Karen.

"I don't know," said Jerry. "We'll see. We'll see. Lynnie?" he said. "I understand some kids were teasing you about it."

Lynnie didn't answer.

"I'm sorry, baby," he said. "I'm sorry to all of you. Karen. June Marie." He looked at each of them in turn. Then he looked at me. "Jeanette."

I held his gaze as long as I could, but I had to lower my eyes at last.

He looked down and pushed his hands out in front of him in a ball, to the middle of the table. June Marie laid one hand on top of his, then covered it with her other hand. "I love you, Daddy," she said.

Lynnie got up and came to me, wrapped her arms around my waist and buried her face in my side. I put my arms around her. "Everything will be OK," I said.

Karen sat back and looked at us all, first at her father and June Marie, then at me and Lynnie, back and forth, again and again, as if she had to choose between us. Her gaze finally settled on her father. She picked up an apple and bit into it.

Within a few days it was clear that we had to do something with Lynnie. Her constant crying was making everything worse than it already was, and when she wet the bed one night, and was so intensely embarrassed by it, I finally made the decision to have her stay with my parents for a while. She jumped at the opportunity. They're just on the other side of the park and their home is like an asylum, all padded and upholstered and quiet, all pastel colors and deep soft cushions. You can hear the ticking of their clock. My mother's presence is very soothing, and Lynnie and her grandfather are "the bestest pals," as she always says. I felt guilty pawning her off on them—my parents had already raised their children, they didn't need mine to raise—but I didn't know what else to do.

I took her there on Wednesday night. It wasn't an easy thing to do. I have always been the one who did things right in our family. My sister Sherry always seemed so angry for no apparent reason—it's just her nature, she's irritable, always ready to take offense. She and my mother never agreed on anything. And of course Stevie was the golden boy, just because he was a boy: My father worshiped him. But when Stevie got himself killed, I felt like it fell to me to see that things went right. Especially after Sherry got divorced and moved away—that left just me to carry on. And as the middle child, the one who always got "neglected," maybe I was extra serious about taking on that role, I don't know. But it always seemed to me that it was up to me to fulfill the legacy of our parents' happy marriage, it was up to me to carry the torch, to pass the message along to future generations. Happiness does exist, you can find it. Keep the faith.

But walking into my parents' on that Wednesday night made me feel dirty. Their house is always so spotless—my mother is a tireless housekeeper—and everything is so carefully placed, so precisely thought out. The porcelain figures on the piano. The plates lined up in the dining room. It made me want to mess things up, upend the furniture, scratch the wood, break every breakable thing. I wanted to destroy this image of peacefulness and complacence. It didn't exist, it didn't. This place was a museum exhibit, it should have had velvet ropes around it, you should have just stood at the door and looked in, *don't touch,* and spoken in muted voices. I hated how tucked in it all felt.

And all the while, of course, I was talking with my mother, talking with my father, being the good daughter I'd always been, or always tried to be. And all the while my ears were burning and I was breaking out in a sweat, my underarms all clammy, and I just couldn't wait to get out into the fresh air again, where I could breathe, where I could move about without fearing I'd knock something over, break something, bring shame on myself.

My mother took Lynnie upstairs to get settled and my father took me onto the porch, the sun porch they had winterized. It was still done up like a porch: wicker furniture, tropical prints, glass-top tables, a parakeet. It seemed too delicate a room for him, too delicate for this discussion.

He sat, and patted the seat beside him. "What's going on?"

I threw up my hands, let them fall in my lap.

"Why's Lynnie so upset?"

"Daddy . . ." I said. I sighed. "Jerry's been arrested."

"Arrested?" he said. All those years I struggled to pry his attention away from Sherry and Stevie, now here he was, all mine. And look what I had to tell him.

"Arrested for what?"

I took a deep breath. "For child molesting."

"What?"

I nodded and closed my eyes.

"With Lynnie?" he whispered.

"No-no-no," I stuttered. "Not the girls, he wouldn't touch the girls . . ."

My father searched me, incredulous. "Who?"

"A neighborhood boy."

He stared at me, showed no reaction. "How old?"

"Eleven, twelve."

"Is it true?"

I nodded.

My father sat back, raised a hand to his brow and rested his head on his fingertips. When he looked at me, his eyes were red. "Did you know about this?"

I shook my head.

"Lynnie knows?"

I nodded. "Kids in the neighborhood. It's all over town, I guess."

"What the hell is the *matter* with that man?" he exploded in a whisper. He jumped to his feet and started to pace.

"Daddy," I said. "I don't know. I'm sure I don't know. But I don't need that from you right now." I was amazed at the firmness in my voice: I actually barked at him. He blinked, to clear his vision of me.

"Now, sit down," I said. He blinked again. "Sit down," I said again, and he did.

"I've told Lynnie it isn't true. I don't think she could handle it right now. I don't think I can handle it right now. Let her talk about it if she wants, don't make her talk if she doesn't. Pretend you know nothing about it. Assume it isn't so. Do you understand me?"

He nodded, paler.

"I'll be in touch every day by phone, I'll stop by after work. I'm just on the other side of the park . . ."

And at that, Lynnie and my mother arrived. The conversation bobbed to the surface like an untethered buoy. Lynnie came and cradled herself between my legs. "Are you going to be OK?" I said.

She nodded somberly.

"I think we'll watch some TV tonight," said my mother.

"That would be fine," I said. "But bed by nine."

"Oh, we'll have her in bed plenty early," she said. "In fact we'll get into our PJs early and watch TV and drink lemonade."

"Oh, that sounds like fun," I said. "Would you like that, Lynnie?"

She nodded. I gathered her to me and rested my lips on the top of her head, inhaling her sweet smell. "I'll see you tomorrow," I whispered. "You be good, you hear?"

She tucked her face into my neck.

"You be good," I said again. Then I gave her an extra squeeze, and stood. Better not make this departure too dramatic. She was there for only a few days, just like she was visiting them at the lake. I'd see her every day, it wasn't anything so unusual. But oh, I wanted to hold her to me, I wanted never to let her go. I felt so chilled when I stood up.

My father came to the door with me while Lynnie and my mother went into the kitchen to make the lemonade. "Do Karen and June Marie know?" he whispered. I nodded. He looked at me, one eye, then the other, his face all furrowed with worry. I'd never seen him speechless before. He let out a little whimper. Then he reached out and drew me into his arms—the way I'd always wanted him to—but I was stiff as a stick.

5

We met with the court-appointed lawyer four times. Once before the preliminary hearing and three times after, before the trial. He wasn't exactly what I'd hoped for. His office was on a traffic island down near Cortland and First. It had once been a shady corner, I guessed, but with all the rerouting they did around there to try to rejuvenate the downtown, most of that neighborhood now is just a tangled snarl of one-way streets through one huge parking lot. I didn't take it as an encouraging sign that he'd been marooned like that; his office reminded me a little bit of Alcatraz. But on the other hand, I figured the man showed some tenacity—he was still there when everyone else had gone. Maybe he was a fighter. Maybe he was the sort of man who would never give up.

When I saw him, though, my heart sank. I was hoping for Perry Mason, or maybe my father: someone big and imposing who had some weight to throw around, someone who could change the tide of events just by standing up. But the man who came out of his office was short and sloppy and out of shape. I don't like to judge people on their looks, but this time I couldn't help it: He reminded me of a hedgehog.

He introduced himself as Attorney Dan Shields, as if Attorney were his first name. When a doctor does that, you think he's ostentatious; when a lawyer does it, it just seems silly. He ushered us into his office and cleared two chairs of papers and magazines, indicating we should sit. He was either entirely disorganized or he knew exactly where everything was; the room was a small city of paper. Books and papers stacked all over—on top of his desk, on the chairs, on the floor, cascading off the side table.

He sat at his desk, leaning forward, and offered us peanuts from a bag. When we both declined—it was ten A.M.—he shrugged and took a handful himself. "Reagan eats jelly beans," he said. "I'm addicted to peanuts." He shelled his peanuts, popped them into his mouth, then tossed his hair out of his eyes and explained to us what our options were.

"One route is just to sit there," he said, dusting his hands over the wastebasket. "You don't say anything and you make them prove their case. Beyond a reasonable doubt." He leaned across his desk and spread his palms up to show how simple it was. "You're presumed to be innocent. You cannot be compelled to testify against yourself. We'll make them prove it. Beyond any doubt. That's not an easy thing to do."

"How can they prove it?" Jerry asked.

"To get you first degree?" he said. "They've got to prove penetration . . ."

"And what's acceptable proof?" I said.

"Oral testimony is fine. Physical evidence is fine."

"What kind of physical evidence?"

"Well," he said, "since this wasn't reported directly afterward, there couldn't have been any semen, right? There could be some damage back there though. Torn tissue, or whatever. But we don't know what their evidence is. We don't even know if he's been examined. It might be just the kid's testimony. In which case it's his word against yours." He gave us a wry look. "I suppose it's too much to hope that he's known as a liar or anything, huh?"

"Well, he's known as a talker," I said.

Shields shot me a glance. "What do you mean?"

"He loves to talk, tell stories."

"Lies?"

"Not lies," said Jerry. "Just stories. He has an imagination."

"He told me once that he and his brother had a juggling act," I said, "and worked at the Westwood Mall on weekends. He had me absolutely convinced."

Shields looked back and forth between us, a hint of a smile dawning on his face. "You say he's known for this?"

Jerry and I both laughed a little. "Yes. All over the neighborhood."

Shields's mouth stretched into a fat, wide grin.

Jerry shifted in his chair. "What's the other line of defense?" he said.

"Plead guilty to a lesser offense and take the consequences. That way you're sure to go to prison, but not for as long as you'll go if you get convicted of first degree. It's all going to depend on the kind of evidence they've got against you, and we don't know at this point. That's what the preliminary exam is for, as far as we're concerned. To see what kind of a case they've got."

"What happens after that?" I said.

"If the judge finds probable cause, then the case is bound over to circuit court, where felonies are tried."

Jerry heaved a great sigh. I paused a moment, then took his hand.

"But at this point," said Shields, "we just go to the hearing. We don't say a thing, we just see what they've got. Then we decide what to do. OK?"

We just stared at him.

"Try to take it easy," he said. "I've been down this road before. I know all the twists and turns. I know where the potholes are. Just try to relax and be cool." He offered us another peanut. I declined but Jerry took one. Shields looked at him and nodded. "The more relaxed, the better," he said.

The hearing the following week was awful. To sit in a public place like that and listen to this little child talk about the ways in which my husband had defiled him . . . To have my whole life reduced to that—an accusation by a child, a child I had befriended, a child now pointing the finger not just at Jerry but at me, because I had chosen Jerry . . . It would be hard to imagine worse torture.

The only thing I could do was to stay focused on Attorney Dan Shields. He was the one person in the room who didn't fill me with confusion. So I kept my eyes on him the whole time. He sat at the table with his hands folded and just studied Robbie. It seemed as if he weren't even breathing, as if he were a bird dog on point, straight and true to his duty. I had the impression that nothing, nothing, was lost on Attorney Dan Shields. And when we went to his office the second time, everything looked different to me. The isolated building, the rumpled suit, the papers, the peanut shells—all of it seemed like evidence of a man so involved with his work, he didn't have time to think of appearances. We had stumbled across the best possible thing—a lawyer who loved his job.

And I was ready for a good lawyer.

At that second meeting, after the hearing, he leaned back in his chair with his hands clasped behind his head, his elbows jutting out like huge ears. There were perspiration stains on his shirt. "I think we're in pretty good shape," he said. He said it like a card player, speculating on a trick.

"Why?" I said. "How?"

He leaned forward, across his desk. "All they've got is the kid's say-so. The kid is good. He's appealing, he's smart. He's pretty articulate. But that's all the evidence they've got. And I think I can work with him."

"What do you mean, you can 'work with him'?" said Jerry. His voice broke when he said it.

Shields smiled and spread his hands. "Well, there's cross-examination and then there's cross-examination," he said. "A good cross-examiner can make anybody look stupid."

Jerry cleared his throat. "What do you mean, you can make him look stupid?"

Shields stretched and sat back, rocking in his chair. "That's what the art of cross-examination is really about," he said. "My job is creating reasonable doubt. That's all I have to do. And all I have to do to accomplish that is to shift his story a bit so it doesn't make sense anymore, so it's not believable. I don't have to disprove it. I just have to show it's not believable."

"And how do you do that?" I asked.

He shrugged. "I make friends with him, draw him out. I get him to tell me more and more. Little by little, more and more. Then I start shifting the details a little, almost imperceptibly, until I've got him saying something different from what he said before. *Oh, maybe it didn't happen that way. Maybe it happened this other way.* I've done this kind of thing before. I'm pretty good at it."

Jerry squirmed uncomfortably.

Shields grabbed the transcript off his desk. He didn't even look, he knew exactly where to find it. "Look," he said. "We have the transcript. We have everything that was said, on paper. And they don't have any evidence. It's just his word against yours. The jury is not going to want to believe there would be no physical evidence. So I put it to them just that way. I lay it right on the line for them. 'The state wants you to find this man guilty of *raping* a little boy. That's a pretty serious offense. Are you going to send this man to prison *without* any evidence? Just because the boy says it happened? This boy who is known for telling stories? This boy whose story keeps changing?' " He looked at us expectantly, then sat back again. " 'Course this kind of approach can be tricky," he said. "The prosecutor has seen me work. He will have warned the boy about me, about what I'll try to do."

"So why do you think you can work with him?" said Jerry.

Shields clasped his hands behind his head. "Because I think the boy likes you," he said. He lifted his chin and looked at Jerry. "I don't think he wants to do this to you."

Jerry's eyes welled up with tears, then he swallowed a sob and looked down at his hands.

Shields gazed at him a moment, nodding, touched that Jerry was touched, it seemed. Then he sat forward again, all business. "Now then," he said. "I must tell you that they've offered us a plea bargain. They've offered second degree, which is only touching, but . . ."

"But that means he admits he's guilty, right?"

Shields stopped short and nodded at me.

"And he's sure to go to prison."

"Yes."

I took Jerry's hand and squeezed it tight. "Then I think we should go for it," I whispered. I glanced up at Jerry. He stared back at me as if he didn't recognize me.

"Are you sure you can get him off?" I said.

Shields raised his hands and shook his head. "I can't promise you anything." He looked back and forth between us. "But I do think we have good reason to challenge."

I gazed back down at my hand, holding Jerry's, then looked again at my husband. He was still staring at me quizzically.

"It's up to you," said Shields.

In the weeks that followed, Jerry sat in his chair and stared at the wall a lot. In the evenings, when the girls were upstairs doing their homework, when I was at my sewing machine, he would just sit in his chair and stare. Sometimes he'd have the TV on, sometimes he wouldn't bother. If it were on, he might as well have been watching a test pattern—he just sat there with his beer and stared. I'd glance up at him now and then over my sewing glasses. He might be sitting with his legs crossed, one finger raised to his puckered lips, as if he were telling someone to shush, obviously lost in some thought. Or sometimes he'd be sitting with his knees drawn up to his chin, gazing at some fixed spot on the television screen, gazing at some thought in his mind, and shaking his head back and forth. And sometimes I'd find him sprawled in his seat, slouched so low he was almost off the cushion, his legs thrown wide in front of him, limp as a rag, undone.

Once he looked at me with what seemed an academic look in his eye. "Do you think God loves us?" he said.

It was a peculiar question for Jerry. He never gave much

thought to God as far as I was aware. I stopped the machine and peered over my glasses. "Of course," I said. "Of course. How can you ask that question?"

He looked at me, one finger over his lips, with this puzzled look in his eyes. Then he dropped his gaze. "Just wondered," he said, and looked back at the television.

I continued sleeping in Lynnie's room, or trying to at least. Most nights I lay awake for hours at a time, staring at the ceiling, tapping my toes against the footboard. I stared at the shapes of the dolls and stuffed animals clustered on her bed, at the size-seven dresses in her closet, the games and puzzles stacked in the corner. I thought of her across the park, asleep in my old bedroom, or maybe lying awake there too, staring at the dolls and games and dresses my mother enshrined there. It seemed impossibly lonely to me, the two of us in exile like that, staring at each other's possessions. I wanted my family together again, I wanted our lives the way they'd been.

On the night before his trial, Jerry came up behind me while I was folding the laundry and put his arms around me. "Do you remember the night we got married?" he whispered. I stopped my work, and nodded. I didn't know quite how to handle this. We hadn't been touching for weeks and I wasn't sure I wanted to start in now. "Remember?" he said. "On the balcony? We saw a shooting star."

"It seemed like a good omen," I said.

He held me tighter. "It was, Jeanette. It was a good omen. It was."

I laid my hand on his arm and stroked it. "It was," I said. "It was." I'd thought that all I'd wanted to do was to make him release his grip, but patting his arm that way and murmuring *It was, it was* stirred something else in me. And when he breathed deep of the smell of my hair and told me he loved me, then left me there to go back to his television, I felt the chill on my back and arms where he'd been pressed against me. It made me realize how unwarmed I'd been feeling for weeks. I wrapped my own arms around me and rubbed to try to generate some heat.

That night I awoke at three as usual and stared at the dark. I went downstairs and poured myself a couple of fingers of bourbon, then did a crossword puzzle, or tried to. I even tried to read the Bible, but nothing seemed to help. I couldn't focus on anything. I listened at the girls' doors; they seemed to be sleeping soundly. I stared out the window at the street lamp. There were no lights in any houses. And then, without really knowing I was going to, I went into our room. I stood in the door and watched Jerry sleep. There was just enough light from the street to see by. The room was so still, so familiar, so foreign. So big, it seemed, after Lynnie's room and Lynnie's narrow bed. My clothes were there. My jewelry was there. My shoes were lined up in the closet. It was an adult's room, not a child's.

I crossed the room and stood over him. He was on his side, facing off the bed, his arms extended in front of him, like a dog sleeping with its legs out. His head was dipped down, like a fetus's head, and his mouth was slack. He was twitching, from some dream, it seemed. His brows were drawn together, forming a crease on his brow, a frown. I leaned over and placed my thumb on the crease to smooth away his worry. He started, almost awoke, but didn't. He rolled onto his back, then back onto his side. I tiptoed around the bed, slipped off my robe and slid in behind him, fitting myself to the curve of his body and putting my arms around him. I buried my nose between his shoulders. Then I stroked his brow to soothe him and finally put myself back to sleep.

6

The trial began at nine. I took Attorney Dan Shields's advice and wore a banker-conservative suit, but I made myself up more than usual—a redder shade of lipstick, darker shadow over my eyes—and wore my higher heels. I wanted to project an image of propriety, but I also wanted the judge to see, I wanted the whole world to see, that I was an attractive woman, a wife from whom a husband would not need to seek an alternative. Jerry wore his dark blue suit and the tie Karen gave him for Christmas—a paisley print but in muted colors. I made him polish his shoes.

Before the preliminary hearing, the only reason I'd ever had to go into the courthouse was to get our marriage license eighteen years before. But having been there for the hearing, this time when we went in it felt uncomfortably familiar. The tattooed guys smoking by the door. The scruffy people in the lobby. A lot of them looked as if they were used to hanging around in public places, waiting for the system to deal with them—at unemployment offices, welfare offices. They brought the entire family: the kids, the in-laws, their brothers and sisters and friends. The lawyers moved among them in their polished shoes and haircuts, murmuring, patting shoulders.

We shared an elevator with a handcuffed man in an orange jump suit and an officer in a brown uniform—he was a sheriff, I guess. He kept his hand on his prisoner's elbow, the way you would touch an old woman you were helping across the street. I stood a little behind them and studied the back of the prisoner's neck and the back of Jerry's. They were not of the same class, anybody could see that. If the judge were used to looking at people who looked like this man in the jump suit, he'd have to see how different Jerry was.

We got off at the fifth floor. The elevator deposited us in a hallway outside the courtroom. The hall was pretty shabby, like all public buildings, I guess. Fluorescent lights, linoleum, everything scuffed and scarred. We took a seat outside the door. Attorney Dan Shields wasn't there yet.

When he did show up, I was struck again by how ill shaped and lumpy he was and how poorly his clothes fit. This was the man who was going to defend my husband? I tried to suppress the thought when it came. I liked Dan Shields, I trusted him, but I wanted him to be tall and strong and handsome and quick-witted. To tower above the rabble here. To lift us to a different level. But he seemed entirely of this place, as if he'd just crawled out of the woodwork. I took a deep breath. Maybe that was just what we needed, someone who knew this place inside out, someone who had this place in his blood. But I did wish he dressed better.

He shook our hands, asked us how we were feeling. Then he looked us up and down. "You look good," he said. "You look great." He stepped into the courtroom and we sat back down.

I glanced at Jerry and smiled. "I wish we could say the same for him . . ." Jerry laughed and looked down at his hands.

I was just about to say something more about Attorney Dan Shields's appearance, something funny to help us relax, but then the elevator opened again and there was Robbie Young and his family. The whole damn family, all four of them, all dressed up as if for church, which they never go to. They stood there, frozen, as if the doors had been a curtain parting to reveal a famous painting: dark suits all and polished hair and Robbie standing in front of them, spotlit, blond as an angel.

The moment seemed to extend forever. Then everything seemed to happen at once. Jerry gasped and tightened beside me. Linda Young grasped Robbie's shoulders and steered him across the hall to the courtroom. Her husband came out behind them, placing his bulk between us like a Secret Service agent. And Danny followed behind them, slower, actually almost sauntering, the only one of them who looked at us as he passed. And he didn't just look, he stared. Cocky. With a sneer on his face.

I lowered my eyes, took Jerry's hand and turned toward him. It was an instinctive gesture, turning to him for comfort and strength—to receive it and to offer it—but Jerry did not turn toward me. He was looking after them, pitched forward in his seat. It was one of the most sickening moments of this whole ordeal for me, that moment he didn't turn to me. There were worse moments to come—there were many worse moments to come—but that was the first time I felt like I might actually throw up.

I reached in my bag, took out a handkerchief and put it over my nose. The smell of its sweet scent calmed me down. It was just the smell of Downy fabric softener, but it calmed me like some exotic aroma, revived me as if it were smelling salts.

Finally Jerry turned back to me. "He looks great," he said.

I nodded. "Like innocence itself."

"A real little trooper."

I closed my eyes and pressed the knotted handkerchief against my mouth. How could this be happening? I was remarking on Robbie's looks as a way of assessing our adversary. And my husband, my dear, lost, stupid husband, my husband who was shortly to stand accused by this little child, my husband whose life hung in the balance, my husband was assessing him as a romantic vision. It was so impossibly wrong, so oblivious of his own self-interest, that it occurred to me, for the first time, I think, that maybe my husband was crazy. Not rambling, dangerously insane. But touched in the head, distorted in some way he had no control over. Didn't he understand why we were there, what they were doing to him? Didn't he understand what this was doing to the rest of us?

Shields stepped out of the courtroom and motioned us to come. I got Jerry to his feet and smoothed my suit, then Shields led us in.

It was a better room than the one we'd had for the hearing. This one was bigger, with better paneling and even a purple carpet. It had a beamed ceiling with indirect lighting. The chairs were green leather with brass studs. And it didn't smell like the rest of the courthouse, that stale, embedded cigarette smell still left over even after years of No Smoking Allowed. Jerry and I sat in a pew. It was not scarred with initials and hearts the way they'd been downstairs. This was a higher floor, a higher court, a higher morality.

We sat in the pew for about five minutes, waiting for things to get started. It was uncomfortably quiet there, quieter even than church, and eerie. Shields sat at the defendant's table, leafing through the transcript of the preliminary hearing; every time he turned a page it crackled loud as a bonfire. When Linda Young whispered something to Robbie, you could hear the hiss of her esses. I glanced at Jerry. His eyes were locked on the back of Shields's head.

Then they led the jury in from the left. I studied them as they took their seats. The fat woman from Napoleon. The grandmother with the champagne hair. The balding pickup-truck salesman from the east side of town. Shields had been pleased with them at the impanelment the day before, but sitting there now they looked to me like a mountain, a mountain with faces carved in it, a miniature Mount Rushmore. I looked at Shields, at the back of his head. Could he really melt them?

They announced the judge and everyone stood as he came in from the right. I took Jerry's hand and stared at it. Rubbed my thumb across his. He leaned toward me and gave me a squeeze.

Then they called his name. He squeezed my hand again, then stood and walked through the gate. I felt like I was sending a child off to the first day of school, or into an operating room. And as soon as he entered through that gate and sat beside Attorney Dan Shields, I felt as if I were watching a film. Everything on the other side seemed two-dimensional, acted out. The real emotions attached to it, the pulse of blood, the welling of tears, all of that was here in the gallery where the spectators sat. It was as if Jerry had passed out of life.

The prosecuting attorney stood up and stepped to the podium between his table and Attorney Dan Shields's. He was tall, good-looking, neatly dressed—exactly the image of who I'd thought I'd wanted Shields to be. He spoke for a full five minutes about how evil my husband was, what a predatory monster he was, how cold and calculating he was, how manipulative. When he gestured to him, he pointed with his arm straight out in front of him like a Nazi salute. When he gestured to Robbie, he spread his hands as if adoring the Christ Child. The jury was glued to every word.

Then Attorney Dan Shields stood up and leaned on the podium. He talked softly about my husband's history—the military, his civil service, his three happy daughters, his wife. He talked about adolescence, imagination and innocent confusion. He talked about rules of evidence. Then he turned and looked at Jerry. "Ladies and gentlemen," he said, facing the jury again. "In this great country, in this great land, we have a fundamental right. Each of us, every one of us. You. And you. You, sir. You. This lawyer here. This judge. This man. Each of us is innocent. Innocent. Until proven guilty. We are here to protect that right today. All of us. Here, for no other reason." He looked at them a long, silent moment, then nodded to the judge and sat. It felt like he had just rung a gong calling us all to prayer. I closed my eyes and said one.

Then they called Robbie Young to the stand. He was wearing a blue blazer; it looked new. So did his gray pants. He looked competent, pulled together. But the collar of his shirt was too big, just a little bit too big, reminding you, in case you forgot, that he was just a child, not yet grown into his clothes. He finished reciting his vow and sat down. I realized that all the "good" people were on one side of the room: Robbie, the jury, the prosecutor. Only Jerry was left to sit alone on the other side of the room. Jerry, and of course Shields.

The prosecutor stood and led Robbie through the preliminaries—his name, his age, his residence. I noticed he had a nervous tic, a way of shaking his head when he asked a question, as if he were shaking off flies, and hiking up his pants. I thought that was good, that he had that tic. I thought it made him seem suddenly nervous, suddenly unsure of his case. It also evened the scales a little, visually, between him and Shields.

Then he asked Robbie if he knew the defendant. How long? How did they meet? How did their relationship develop? It all sounded so innocent so far, sounded like what I always thought it was. A friendship. A special bond. A surrogate father/son kind of thing, Dutch uncle, big brother, a pal. It sounded so perfectly normal. And I realized that some part of me still believed it was. Some part of me wanted to stop the film here, to stand up with a pointer and say, Yes, you see, it's quite innocent. This is just a special friendship. It's just like he says! They were only friends!

But then the lawyer started talking about all the gifts Jerry gave him. The bike. The models. The typewriter. About all the time they spent together alone. It was clear he was starting to tint the picture with the notion of bribery.

I watched as Robbie answered, watched as the picture started to change color, as Robbie turned from pal to prey. He handled himself extremely well—or, rather, the lawyer handled him well: I believed every word he was saying.

"And in all this time," said the lawyer, "did you ever feel there was anything unusual about Mr. Houseman?"

Robbie shook his head. "No."

"Anything strange about his affections?"

"Objection."

"Sustained."

"I'll rephrase," said the lawyer. "Anything . . . 'unexpected' . . . about his affections?"

"No," said Robbie warily. You could tell he knew what was coming next.

The lawyer turned and paced back toward his chair. He raised his voice for all to hear. "But at some point . . ." He turned to Robbie. "At some point, all that changed, didn't it?"

"Yes."

"How did it change?"

Robbie lowered his shoulders. "Mr. Houseman kissed me."

"Mr. Houseman kissed you."

"Yes. On the lips."

"On the lips."

"Yes." His head looked so small and fragile, as if it might topple off his neck any moment.

"Will you tell us about it?"

Robbie took a deep breath. "We were in the park. We'd been riding bikes and it was hot so we sat on some rocks in the brook. We just sat there and talked for a while, then I laid down on one of the rocks and I think I fell asleep in the sun. Then Jerry—Mr. Houseman—lifted me up and kneeled down in front of me . . ."

You could tell the boy was getting scared. He glanced at his father, who nodded at him.

"What happened then?" said the lawyer.

"He told me he loved me."

"I'm sorry, Robbie. Could you speak up?"

"He said he loved me."

"And then?"

"And then he kissed me."

"On the lips."

"Yes."

"Would you characterize this as a 'romantic' kiss?"

"Objection."

"Sustained."

"Robbie," said the lawyer. "What did you do when this adult man, your friend whom you trusted . . . what did you do when he kissed you on the mouth?"

Robbie shifted. "Nothing."

"You didn't encourage him."

"No."

"And you didn't push him away."

"No."

"Why not?"

"I was scared. I didn't know what to do."

"And what were you scared of?"

"I didn't know what he was doing. I didn't know what I was supposed to do."

"So you were afraid. You felt you were in unfamiliar territory?"

"Yes."

"And since you didn't know what to do, you relied on your friend to guide you through?"

"Yes."

"Objection," said Shields, raising his hand. "I believe my colleague is putting words into the witness's mouth."

The judge looked at him, nodded. "Sustained."

The lawyer cleared his throat and ducked his head toward the judge. "Sorry, Your Honor," he said. I looked at the judge to see if he'd liked that little display of humility or if he'd found it too much, but he just sat there, his chin drawn in, waiting to hear more.

The lawyer turned to Robbie again. "Now, Robbie," he said. "Would you tell us what happened next? After Mr. Houseman kissed you."

"I asked if we could go home."

"Your impulse was to leave, to go home."

"It was almost dinnertime."

"And did you tell your parents what had happened?"

"No."

"Why not?"

"I was scared. I was scared they'd be mad."

"At you?"

"Yes."

"And rather than risk their anger, their disapproval, you kept it a secret?"

"Yes. And Jerry—Mr. Houseman—told me not to tell."

"Mr. Houseman *told* you not to tell."

"Yes."

The lawyer stopped pacing, turned on his heel, looked directly at Jerry. He let the moment ring. Then he made a little *hmmm* in his throat, as if he'd just come to understand something, and turned his attention back to Robbie. "And *when* did all this happen?" he said, as if he didn't really know.

"July," said Robbie. "A year ago."

"And you were how old then?"

"Eleven."

"Eleven years old."

"Yes."

As I was watching Robbie unfold the story, I tried to imagine it. I tried to see him as someone you would want to get romantic with. He was certainly a beautiful boy, I'd recognized that all along. Blond and pretty and energetic, a nice personality, bright smile. I'd liked him the moment I met him. And when he started doing odd jobs for me, it was nice to have him around. I liked the sense of having the neighborhood kids come and go in our house, I would have liked it to happen more. I should have known better though. Knowing what I knew about Jerry, I should have known better than to bring this golden boy into our house.

But then, believing what I believed about Jerry . . .

Or did I bring Robbie in to test him? Did I engineer this entire thing? Was this my intention from the start, without my even knowing it, to test my husband out?

"Now, Robbie," said the lawyer. "In addition to the kissing. Did Mr. Houseman ever touch you?"

Robbie nodded. "Yes."

"Where?"

"On the genitals."

"On the genitals."

"Yes."

"And when did that happen?"

"A few weeks later."

"After he kissed you."

"Yes."

"Will you tell us about it?"

Robbie shifted in his chair, cleared his throat. "I went over to Mr. Houseman's house after I got home from school. We were building a model airplane together in his dining room."

"What time of day was that?"

"Three-thirty?"

"And he was home alone?"

"He got out of work at about the same time I got out of school. Mrs. Houseman was still at work. His kids never got home till dinner."

"And what happened?"

"I was working on the model, gluing the body together, and he was leaning over me, reaching around to hold something . . ."

"Good. Go on."

"Then he wrapped his arms around me and hugged me. Then he turned me around and kissed me."

"On the lips."

"Yes."

"And then?"

"Then he put his hand on me."

"Where did he put his hand?"

"On my genitals."

"And what happened then?"

"He put my hand on him."

"Where on him?"

"On his genitals."

I glanced at the court recorder. She was typing madly, her lips pursed tightly, earrings jangling violently.

"And what happened next?" said the lawyer.

"He told me to take it out."

"To take it out of his pants."

"Yes."

"And did you?"

"Yes."

"And how did you feel?"

"I felt . . . I was scared."

"You were scared."

"Yes."

"And then?"

"Then he told me to rub it. Up and down."

"And did you?"

"Yes."

I looked at the judge. He was watching the whole thing with interest, sometimes leaning back in his chair, his chin in his hand, sometimes sitting up, toying with a paper clip. It wasn't possible to read any reaction in his face, but it wasn't possible to imagine that anything he was hearing was doing Jerry any good.

"And what happened next?" said the lawyer.

"We went into the living room and he sat down on the couch. Then he had me sit on his lap."

"His penis was still out of his pants?"

"Yes."

"And then?"

"He masturbated."

"But you were sitting in his lap."

"I was sort of sitting on his stomach."

"So he was masturbating . . . behind you?"

"Yes."

"Did you even know what masturbation was at that time?"

"No. I just felt his arm going up and down real fast and he was starting to breathe harder."

"What did you think was going on?"

"I didn't know. I thought he was having a heart attack or something."

"You thought he was having a heart attack."

"Yes."

"That must have been terrifying."

"Objection."

"Sustained."

The lawyer shook his head. "How did that make you feel?"

"I was scared."

"Did you tell him so?"

"Yes."

"And what did he say?"

"He laughed. He said it was normal. He told me not to worry."

"He laughed when you told him you were scared."

"Yes."

"And told you it was normal."

"Yes."

The lawyer looked at Jerry, then went to his table, poured himself a cup of water and took a sip. Then he leafed through his notes on the podium. It seemed to me that he wasn't really searching for anything, he was just drawing the moment out. Finally he looked up at Robbie again. "Robbie," he said, confused, as if he'd only just then remembered the question he wanted to ask. "Was that the only time Mr. Houseman touched you?"

Robbie shook his head. "No."

"Did these encounters continue after that?"

"Yes."

The lawyer hiked his pants. "How often?"

"Once or twice a week."

"For how long?"

"For about a year."

There! There was a place for Shields to work. A year! He played this game for a year! He had plenty of opportunity to tell his parents about it. Plenty of opportunity to tell Jerry he wanted to stop. If he was such a victim, why did he do it for a whole year?

"Did you try to stop it?"

"No."

"Why not?"

"I was scared. I was scared he'd hurt me."

"You were scared he'd hurt you."

"Yes."

Hurt him? Jerry *hurt* him? I looked at Shields. He was making a note. I closed my eyes and balled my fists.

"Now, Robbie," the lawyer continued. "During that year that Mr. Houseman was engaging you in sexual acts: Was masturbation the extent of it?"

"No."

"There was more? He did other things?"

"Yes."

The lawyer stood in the middle of the courtroom and lowered his voice to a whisper. "Can you tell us?"

Robbie faltered. He looked at the judge, at his parents. He looked everywhere but at Jerry.

"Just take your time," said the lawyer.

Robbie started to cry. I heard his mother whimper aloud. Saw, from the corner of my eye, her husband put his arm around her.

"I know this is difficult," said the lawyer. "But it won't take much longer. Did Mr. Houseman ever touch you in any other way?"

Robbie nodded. "Yes."

"How?"

"He put his penis in my mouth."

"He put his penis in your mouth."

"Yes. And made me suck on it."

"He made you suck on it."

"Yes."

"Robbie," said the lawyer softly. "Is that everything?"

Robbie looked at his parents again, then back at the lawyer. Then he broke into sobs. It was a horrifying moment. He seemed so young, and all at once so vulnerable. I wanted to take him into my arms myself.

The lawyer waited a moment to let us all observe Robbie's anguish. He actually lowered his head as he waited, as if he were uttering a prayer. I looked at the jury; even the men seemed ready to weep. Then the lawyer looked at Robbie. "There was more?" he said gently.

Robbie took a deep breath and straightened up. He lifted his chin and composed himself and nodded quickly, crisply.

"Robbie," said the lawyer. "We need you to answer, for the record."

"Yes," he said, robotic. "Mr. Houseman buggered me."

The lawyer heaved a sigh. "And what do you mean by that, exactly?"

"He put his penis up my butt."

"He put his penis in your anus."

"Yes."

"And how many times did he do that?"

"About a dozen times."

"About a dozen times."

"Yes."

"And you never told anybody."

"No."

"Why didn't you tell anybody?"

Robbie hung his head and started to cry again. "Because I was ashamed," he whispered.

"Robbie," said the lawyer. "I'm sorry. Can you say it louder?"

When Robbie looked up, his face was streaked with tears. "Because I was ashamed."

The lawyer took a long look at Robbie. Then he glanced toward Jerry, then looked at the judge. "I think that's quite enough, Your Honor." He took a seat at his table again.

There was a moment when nothing happened, as if we all were waiting for the cloud to pass from the room. Then Jerry laid his hand on Shields's arm and whispered something to him. Shields turned to him, alert. They exchanged a few words, it was very intense, then Shields squared himself at the table. He stood. "Your Honor," he said. "May I request a recess to consult with my client?"

"How long a recess you need, Counselor?"

"Twenty minutes, sir?"

The judge looked at him, nodded. "The court will recess for twenty minutes."

"All rise," said the bailiff.

Shields stood and hurried Jerry out through the gate, down the aisle past me. I started to go after them, but Jerry motioned me to stay. "We'll be right back," he said. He was very upset—his face was flushed, his voice was choked. I crumpled back into my seat and looked around the room. Robbie was with his family again, sitting in the pew. They were all huddled around him, touching him, talking to him. Their lawyer had left the room and the jury box was empty. For the first time, I wished I'd brought my mother or even my father—someone to help me through this. But there I was, alone in my pew, my husband off somewhere with our lawyer determining my future.

I opened my bag, took out my handkerchief, wiped my nose with it and put it back. I looked around the room again. The bailiff was filling the water pitcher; the sound was as loud as the Cascades. I got up and went into the hall, Jerry and Shields were not to be seen. I followed the hall as it wrapped around behind the elevators but only came upon closed doors. I went back to the elevators and waited.

Finally the prosecutor hurried around the corner of the hall and disappeared into the courtroom. A few moments later Shields appeared with Jerry right behind him. Shields looked at me and nodded curtly as he went back into the courtroom. I arrived at the door at the same time Jerry did.

"What's going on?" I said.

He looked at me, intensely somber. "I love you," he said. "I love you." His voice was trembling. Then he hugged me and followed Shields inside.

I felt a churning in my stomach. Something awful was going to happen. Something awful was going to happen. I teetered back into the courtroom, using the ends of the pews to steady myself. I took my seat—where was the jury?—then stood again when the judge came in. I had an urge to run to him, but then everybody was settling again and the prosecutor was standing up. "Your Honor," he said. "May we approach the bench?"

I felt cold needles pricking me. My throat began to throb.

Shields and the lawyer went up to the bench and talked to the judge a few minutes. I couldn't hear what they were saying, but the judge was nodding the whole time. Then they came back to their tables. Shields sat and poured himself some water. The other lawyer held out his cup to ask for a drink for himself and Shields leaned toward him and filled his cup, then the prosecutor turned and started droning some legal mumbo jumbo.

What the hell was going on?

What the hell was our lawyer doing *catering* to the prosecutor?

The judge nodded and Shields stood up, gesturing to Jerry. Jerry stepped to the podium. The bailiff swore him in.

"Now then," said Shields, stepping away from the podium and facing Jerry. It reminded me of the way a cowboy steps away from a steer he's tied—quickly, a clean break. "What do you now say about indictment 80-143?"

Jerry cleared his throat. He straightened and lifted his head. "I'm guilty," he said. The room went still. "I touched Robbie Young."

There are times, when certain things happen to you, that you lose all sense of time and place. It's as if you slip through some tear in the world and float outside of it for a time, then reenter later and wonder what had been going on while you were gone. When Jerry said "I touched Robbie Young," I slipped through such a tear. I felt this cascading feeling in me, a stuttering kind of collapse, like rows of dominoes knocking each other down. Like lights being turned off in a house, an enormous engine shutting down. He was giving in. He was giving in. He was going to let Robbie's story stand. Worse, he was going to corroborate. I wanted to jump up and scream, to rush through the gate myself and enter the film and tell my side of the story. To tell them about the good father and husband, the veteran, the son-in-law. This was not some common criminal, some predatory sicko. This was my husband. The man in my wedding picture.

But by the time the screaming stopped in my head and I

slipped back into reality, everything was over. Robbie Young was pushing through the gate with his lawyer. His family descended upon him like they wanted to eat him up. His mother knelt down and hugged him, his father patted him on the back, then they moved up the aisle right past me. And I hated them at that moment. I hated their smugness, the simplicity of their feelings. Most of all, I think I hated the simplicity of their feelings.

I waited until they passed, then rose and walked toward Jerry. He was still sitting at the table with Shields, but as I approached they stood and turned and pushed through the gate. I just stared at him. I didn't know what to say. I opened my mouth, but no words would come out.

Jerry looked right into me as if he could pin me in place with his eyes and keep me from flying apart. He came right up to me, right in front of me, and waited for me to hug him, waited just an instant, and when I didn't, he hugged me.

I grabbed his elbows to hold him away. "What . . . ?"

He drew back and looked at me again with that steady gaze. "I couldn't do it," he said.

"Couldn't do *what*?" I was starting to cry.

"I couldn't let Shields cross-examine him."

I wanted to scream at him. *"Why?"* I whispered.

Jerry looked down, ashamed. "I couldn't put him through that," he muttered. "I think I've put him through enough."

I stared at him, mouth open. "You've put him through enough? What about what he's putting you through? And what you're putting your daughters through? What about us? Did you think about *us*?"

He looked at me, disappointed. "I didn't think he'd do it," he said. "I didn't think he'd go through with it."

I stared at my husband, incredulous.

"Right up until the last moment, I thought he wouldn't go through with it." He looked at the door they'd just passed through. Tears were welling in his eyes. "But he did," he said. He looked back at me. "He did it pretty well, didn't he?"

I felt a hole being burned in my brain.

"A regular little trooper."

7

I try to make sense of all this, but I don't know how to think about it. I've always thought of child molesters as dirty old men in stained overcoats they picked up at Goodwill. I've pictured them covered with stubble and grime, missing teeth and stinking of gin. I think I probably always thought they drooled. Just the mention of the word *molester* is revolting, the image it conjures comes so quick. It's something out of Dickens, this image. And I know my husband isn't that.

But I'm not quite sure anymore what he is. The husband, the father, the child molester—it's a puzzle with too many pieces. Is it because my understanding of human nature is too narrow? Too much determined by what I would like to think human beings are about? I never expected my husband to fall in love with a twelve-year-old boy. And I certainly never expected him to sacrifice himself and his family for that love, just to protect the boy from a few uncomfortable minutes in court. It stretches comprehension too far. It can't all fit in the same picture.

But I guess Jerry loved that boy in some way I just can't understand. He didn't see Robbie for who he was, I'm pretty sure about that. Sometimes he referred to him as a "real little man," but Robbie was not a little man. He was a little boy. How could Jerry not understand that?

It's not like he doesn't know children; he has three of his own, and the fact that they're girls has nothing to do with it. He knows what a child is. I think of the way he held our girls and hoisted them onto his shoulders, and I remember marveling at the delicate balance between his gentleness with them and his roughhousing. He always seemed to know where the line was, to know how rough he could get with them before it got too rough. And when he did cross over the line, he was always so quick to gather the child in his arms and gain her trust again. He was marvelous with our children, and not just with ours, with others too. He knows about children. I know this about him. I've raised my children with him.

So how could he do this to Robbie Young?

And what *did* he do to Robbie Young?

Well, we know what he did to Robbie Young. The whole world knows what he did by now, in Technicolor and Cinemascope. They turned that courtroom into a peep show. They turned my husband into a quivering phallus and Robbie into a picture of sweet, unassuming innocence. It's one of their favorite pornographic themes, innocence defiled. Like those baby doll pictures you see in the girlie magazines at the drugstore. Men love that kind of thing. I think it makes them feel big and strong.

I wonder what it made Jerry feel.

I try to imagine what it would be like to find a child sexual. I think of my children when they were younger—the smell of their breath, the touch of their skin, their gurgling helplessness.

I loved them so completely, my girls, it was so all-encompassing that I think I did feel sexual feelings—not sexual arousal, but a stirring of the deepest love. It was very much like how I felt with Jerry when we were making love really well. This sense of fusion, of being touched inside by another person where you never could touch yourself, the awareness of a string inside that could be set in motion only by resonating with another string inside someone else, an adding of dimension and depth, a richening of the soul. I've felt that when I've made love with Jerry. And I've felt that when I've held my girls. Sometimes, even, I've felt almost reduced to tears by it, by my . . . well, my *neediness* seems like the right word. This breathless desire to hold my child close, to keep her dependent, in need of me: my comfort, my solace, my pet.

But as much as I know about how you can desire your children in some way that seems like romantic desire, as much as I might begin to grasp those feelings in myself, those are my feelings for *my* children. I don't feel that passionately about other people's children. How could Jerry feel that strongly about a child who wasn't his? Was it because Robbie was a boy? If Robbie had been our son, would Jerry have fallen in love with him? He says he wouldn't. He says he couldn't. And as much as I don't know what to believe about Jerry anymore, I do believe that.

So is it that, with other people's children, you don't have to be the protector? You don't have to put up that wall against yourself, that wall you put up when you feel your feelings for your own child edging toward sexual arousal? Instinctively, you block those feelings. It's automatic, un-thought-out. But with other people's children, is the reaction, the wall, quite so automatic?

Something allowed Jerry to take that wall down. Brick by

brick, I imagine it. Trembling all the while. Trembling, because I believe my husband violated his own code of ethics. I believe, as he removed each brick, he knew he shouldn't be doing it. I remember that day at our kitchen table when he told me about that boy in the school yard. I remember how scared he was, how horrified at his own impulses. He knew that it was wrong, and he tried to help himself after that. But something allowed him to do it again. Slowly, with intention.

What could bring him to do that? Was the desire, the passion, so strong that he would risk all he risked, and lost, to do it? And was the passion for Robbie? Was he in love with Robbie or was he in love with who he thought Robbie was? A little man? A miniature? But Jerry doesn't *want* a man. He has no interest in men, he says. Just boys of a certain age.

Of a certain age. That is the absurdity of it. Even if he could succeed in loving a boy of a certain age—even if it did no harm to the boy, or to me or our family, even if society had no problems with it—it's a love that's doomed from the start because the boy is not going to stay that age. It's like Sisyphus rolling that stone up that hill. It's an endless impossibility. It's crazy! It's just . . . my husband is touched.

Why is the age the important thing? Is it himself at that age he's yearning for? That's what his shrink was telling him, and you have to wonder. But if it is himself, then why possess it *sexually*?

I don't understand this. I don't understand. I've talked to Jerry about it, to the extent I could, but he doesn't understand it either. All he can say is he loved Robbie. It doesn't change his love for me, he says. He always hastens to say that. But the question in my mind is, how does it change my love for him?

* * *

When I first met Jerry, I wasn't especially interested in him. I wasn't especially *un*interested, but he didn't catch my eye. I was busy working and he was busy reading the paper and talking with the regulars. But over a period of several weeks, I started to get comfortable with him. He arrived every morning like clockwork—he'd just gotten out of the military, and was still operating on schedule—and he stayed every day almost until lunch. He didn't strike me as terribly quick, but he had an easy way with people that I found appealing. He could always think of something to say—no matter where he was, no matter who he found himself talking to, he could think of something to say to keep a conversation going. To me it seemed like a magical gift—me, whose power of speech always ground to a halt right after hello.

And then that summer we spent at the lake—I did enjoy the elaborateness of the pleasure he took in it. The way he would stop in the middle of something and look around and exclaim "This is great!" Then look at me. "Isn't this great?!" It was partly because he'd just gotten out of the service and ordinary life seemed like a miracle to him, but it was also because he just had a great appreciation for life. Me, I liked it at the lake, but I was used to it. I'd spent my childhood there. Jerry's appreciation of it, though, was just so gleeful, so total, it made me appreciate it more. Made me feel that what I had come to think of as ordinary was really a blessed existence. My life, a blessed existence.

And I loved the way he got on with my folks, especially my father. I'd never managed to get along with my father quite that well. I think a lot of it had to do with the fact that Jerry was used to getting up early in the morning, so he was available to go fishing. Sometimes things are just that simple. He and

Stevie and my father would set out onto the lake at dawn. . . .

I wonder about Stevie. Stevie was about ten that summer. I wonder now, looking back on it, how much of Jerry's enthusiasm for my family was about Stevie. It's not a thought I can hold for long.

Seven years later, when Stevie was killed, Jerry sort of took his place with my father. He became my father's only son. They still went fishing every Sunday morning, the two of them, all through that summer. I'd get up and look across the lake and see them sitting there—just two of them where there used to be three—sitting with their backs to each other, fishing lines in opposite directions, symmetrical as an inkblot. Who knows what they talked about out there, or even if they talked at all? But Jerry nursed my father through that loss—he nursed *me* through it as well—and as much as I'd come to love him already, that summer my love for him grew wings.

My brother was a pistol. Reckless, willful, a risk-taker. He was saving for a motorcycle, that was his big dream, and that's still how I think of him. I never even saw him on a motorcycle, but the image of him zooming down the road at five hundred miles an hour with the wind blowing through his hair and a great big grin on his face—that's my image of Stevie. He would have been at his peak, doing that. He would have been thoroughly Stevie, his inside and outside perfectly matched. I like to think he was experiencing something like that when he was killed. He was driving fast, that much we know, and he'd had a bit to drink. Did he have all the windows open? Was the wind blowing through his hair? Were his nerve-endings singing, was he in perfect form at the moment his life ended? I like to think of him that way. I like to think of him traveling fast, so fast he just escaped the bonds of the earth and sailed to heaven.

My sister came home for the funeral, stayed a week, then went back to New York. I was the only one here to tend to them both, my mother and father. They weren't able to help each other much. My mother wanted to talk about it, and talk about it and talk about it, but my father just clammed up. Zipped lip, not a thing to say. Then he'd explode at her for not being able to let it alone. He was really awful to her, really nasty, many times. I saw it. It was obvious he was in terrible pain.

My father thought the planets rose and set on his boy Stevie. That was why he always got so angry at his recklessness. He loved Stevie's Wild West spirit and hated it at the same time. It was a very *involving* relationship for him, so involving it sometimes seemed he had nothing left for Sherry and me. And it was clear, when Stevie was killed, what was happening. It was as predictable as porridge: He just tried to stuff everything. When I tried to talk to him about it, or to get him to lay off my mother, it only made things worse: Then he got mad at me as well. And I got to feel as I'd always felt—that nothing I did was enough for him, nothing I could even imagine doing would ever be enough for him. Because nothing I could do would make me Stevie, would make me his son.

If Jerry hadn't been there that summer, I don't think my parents would have survived. I think they would have destroyed each other. But with me taking care of my mother and Jerry taking care of my father, we got them through it. And got through it ourselves.

I love this man. I'm indebted to him.

I believe in that, in indebtedness. I believe in loyalty.

The question is, I guess, does he?

It's not even that I feel betrayed. If he'd been with another woman, or even with a man, I think I'd feel more betrayed. If he had been with another adult it might have been a relationship, two people sharing their lives in a way that would have been a threat to our marriage, and it might have eventually won. But a twelve-year-old boy? It's so preposterous it makes me shiver. How can I feel betrayed by that?

How can I not feel betrayed by that? Especially since he put Robbie's interests ahead of his own family's.

But how do I put that together with all the other memories I have? Like those early Christmases, when the girls were really tiny, before Lynnie was even born. I think of how much pleasure Jerry took in playing Santa Claus. One year we played this trick on them . . . While I was getting them dressed and making them brush their teeth before they went down, Jerry snuck down and got himself up in this Santa suit he'd borrowed. One of the guys at work had been Santa at some hospital and Jerry had borrowed his suit. It didn't fit him at all —the legs and the sleeves were way too long. It was ludicrous. But he got himself up with the beard, the whole works, and let the girls find him there at the tree when they came downstairs. I came down ahead of them so I could get in their way, to give him a chance to get away. And he took off running out the front door and down the street yelling HO-HO-HO, ON DONNER, ON BLITZEN, ON RUDOLPH, GOODBYE! and disappeared into a neighbor's house. We had it all arranged; he had a change of clothes waiting there. And while the girls were still looking out the window, he snuck around the back of the house and climbed up on the roof of the porch and in through the bathroom window, then came strolling down the stairs, wondering what all the noise was about. June Marie and Karen were absolutely beside themselves and Jerry listened all wide-eyed. It was rich, it was really rich. We've got pictures of it somewhere, but the pictures don't compare to the memory. . . . The sight of him hightailing it down the street in these boots three sizes too big for him, trying to hold up his pants so he doesn't trip over the fake fur cuffs. Whenever I need to cheer myself up, that always will do the trick.

I have to say I never really expected a man as good as Jerry. Not that he was perfect, he wasn't. He never had a shred of ambition. He seemed pretty much content to let one day just melt into the next. He never seemed to think it mattered that he should make more money, should be a better and better provider. For all his strengths as a husband and father, providing was not one of them.

But the boys I'd met before Jerry always seemed more interested in themselves. They were funny or clever or handsome or smart, or different combinations of that, but in the end I always felt as if I were a sidecar with them. We always went out with *his* friends. Spent time doing things *he* liked to do. The focus was always on him.

But with Jerry, well, he didn't have that many friends, even though he was so easygoing, because he'd just come back from the service. So we spent time with *my* family and friends. And he was happy to just hang out with me while I was making clothes or working in the garden. He did a little gardening with me, did a little cooking. He seemed interested in *me,* in what I could do. And when I got the promotion at the bank and was scared I couldn't handle it, he just shrugged and said, "Well, of course you can. You're smart."

He never had any doubts about me. Whenever I got down on myself, he simply would not buy into it. He believed I could do just about anything I set my mind to. I never knew where he got the idea. It's not as if there was a lot of evidence around. But he reached into me like you might reach into a game of cat's cradle, and he pulled on just the right string to make the result come out "you can."

The bank is the biggest example, convincing me I could really manage an entire branch by myself. But the real magic was in the smaller moments. The offhand assurance after a party that I hadn't come off as witless as I'd feared. (He was always surprised, in fact, to learn I'd thought I hadn't done well.) The unsolicited compliment on a dress I'd made, how I seemed to have a gift for envisioning things. ("How can you start with this," he said, holding up a dress pattern, "and turn it into that?" "You just follow the steps," I told him, laughing at his befuddlement. "No," he said. "It's more than that. You do it in the kitchen too.") Or the times he came to me for advice. On his clothes. On how to handle the girls. Even just crossword puzzles.

Even just crossword puzzles. It was new to me to be around someone who thought I might have the answer to something, especially after growing up with a man who had all the answers. Never mind that I didn't always have the answers Jerry wanted, he was always convinced I might. And more and more, it seemed, I did. It was a change he worked in me just by being around me, just by assuming competence and sociability. It's hard for me to remember now how insecure I used to feel, how ashamed to have the world see me. They seem like feelings that must have belonged to somebody else, back then. But I'm not fooled by that illusion. I remember who I used to be, and I know who I am now. And I know that Jerry is the reason. Jerry is the magician, the genie who transformed me.

Jerry was sentenced on the Friday of Columbus Day weekend, just before June Marie's seventeenth birthday. We didn't take the girls to court. I didn't want them to see their father led out of the courtroom in handcuffs, especially since officially they still believed he was innocent. I hadn't been able to tell them yet; I didn't know how to tell them. But I also didn't take them to court because I wanted that final moment to be just between us, the adults. It seems ironic to me now, to think that was the reason. To think that we shared some privilege or responsibility as adults, separate from those of children, when what had brought us to this point was Jerry's denial of that notion. In some way Jerry didn't really belong to the world of adults anymore. And of course he didn't belong to the world of the child. He existed now, in my mind, in some limbo, trying to straddle the two, trying to have it both ways and ending up having it no way at all, ending up outside of the loop, neither here nor there.

We spent the morning with the girls. Lynnie was still staying with my folks, but they brought her over for breakfast. She was quiet, almost eerily so. Too composed, too in control. She seemed like a little British girl, built all of manners and form. She kissed her father on the cheek, a peck, then took her seat and sat up straight, as if waiting to be dismissed.

June Marie tried to cheer her up. "Hey, Squeegie," she said. "Welcome back!"

Lynnie turned to me. "Can I see my room?"

I nodded and she went upstairs and stayed up there for quite a while. It seemed OK to me that she should spend that time alone in her room, finding her grounding again in this house, having some time to herself to do it. But it did leave an obvious gap at the table and after twenty minutes or so I went upstairs and brought her down.

June Marie sat next to Jerry and kept up a steady line of chatter: She really inherited that from her father. She promised to write him, she promised to visit. She promised to bring him books and keep him posted on the high school football season that she was cheering for. She told him she knew he'd be paroled. Karen just sat and observed their talk, as if she were planning on painting a picture; she took it all in with no reaction on her face at all.

At the end of the breakfast I brought out a cake I'd bought at the supermarket—I just didn't have it in me to bake one—Karen drew the curtains to darken the room—and we sang "Happy Birthday" to June Marie. For a moment, when she made her wish, her face let go of its professional excitement and I saw it without the smiles and chatter. The muscles were all taut, contorted. It almost made me gasp to see it, she looked to be in such pain, and lit by the flickering candlelight she looked like some scary African mask. But then she was full of animation again, blowing out the candles and laughing, opening her presents. Karen gave her a couple of tapes, Lynnie gave her some hair bows and lipstick, my parents gave her a sweater, and Jerry and I gave her a typewriter. It was a pretty fancy one with a memory and it was more than we could afford, but we were so in debt at this point, a little more didn't make much difference.

When she saw it, her hands flew up to her face. "This is great!" she kept saying. "This is great!" It wasn't lost on me, and I don't believe it was lost on June Marie, that Jerry had given a typewriter to Robbie the Christmas before. A used typewriter, yes, and not as fancy as this one. But the fact remained, he had tended to Robbie before he'd tended to June Marie. There wasn't a hint of that from my daughter though. She was all excitement and gratitude. Although it did spill over, finally, into tears and blubbering, and she went to her father and put her arms around him and sobbed into his shirt and he held her and patted her hair and cried. I rose and stood behind Lynnie's chair, stroking her brow with my palm, and laid my other hand on Karen's shoulder. Karen put her hand on mine. It was not a characteristic gesture for Karen to show gratitude. But then I realized she wasn't thanking me for the comfort. She was comforting me.

Before we left, Jerry gathered the girls in the kitchen. "I want you all to know," he said, "I love you. I'm sorry for what's happened. I'm sorry for the heartache it's causing you. Don't ever doubt for a second I love you." He hugged each one of them in turn, and then we left the house.

It was the same courtroom, the same judge. Danny Young was in one pew; no one else from his family was there. Attorney Dan Shields made a gallant plea, but the judge gave Jerry five to eight years in the Jackson prison anyway. Then they locked his hands behind him in handcuffs and led him out of the room.

8

Sundays, now, I sit on the porch and watch the world go by, what part of the world goes by on Palmer Street. It's something I've never done much before. I was always busy gardening, or working at my sewing machine. And truth to tell, I have much more work now that Jerry's gone, even though it's true that the girls pitch in more than they used to. But I'm just too tired to do it, most Sundays. After a full week at the bank, after evenings of cooking and sewing and cleaning, after all the errands on Saturday . . . I figure I'm entitled just to sit for a little while. Even if the porch does need painting. Even if the lawn does need mowing. Even if that broken window in the bathroom still needs fixing.

Once it occurred to me to hire a neighbor boy to come in and help, and I swear I actually felt my heart turn a flip-flop, like a fish on a line. Remembering, of course, that that was how Robbie Young came into our lives. I see Robbie every now and then, riding by on his bike. He seems to be happy and healthy enough, as much as you can tell from watching him ride by in your peripheral vision: My eyes always dart the other way as soon as I catch a glimpse of him. I don't know what I'd do if our gazes ever met, even though some part of me wants to talk to him. Some part of me wants to apologize, and ask him how he's doing. It even occurred to me at one point that maybe I *should* ask him to come help out around the house. I don't believe I ever really entertained the idea as an actual possibility, but the thought of it stuck in my head for a while. The thought that he would visit us, that he'd become a friend of the family's, a sort of honorary son. It's the weirdest thought I've ever had. But it seemed that it might heal things, in some way. If I could extend myself to him, if we could build a bridge of some sort, it might ease a lot of pain.

He did only what he did, after all. And Jerry did what he did. Now we're all doing what we're doing. You can't do much about it except keep putting one foot in front of the other until you come out the other side. I wonder sometimes what the other side is going to look like once we're finally through all this, but I really don't have energy to think about the future much now. When I sit on the porch on Sundays, I don't really think about much of anything. I'm just trying to catch my breath before another week gets started.

It's kind of funny, actually. When Jerry was here, we seldom used the porch. That one Sunday, when all of this got started, the day Danny attacked him, we sat out here to try to make things look normal, but that wasn't normal at all. So it's odd for me to be out here now, out in public view, offering up my solo presence as a constant reminder to everyone that Jerry is gone. If I had a brain I'd stay inside, away from public scrutiny. But I have the porch. I have this day. I have this one moment to sit and rest. Why shouldn't I take advantage of it? I guess I'm just too tired to worry about what people think of me. They're going to think what they think anyway, regardless of what I do, so I may as well make myself comfortable. That's the way I see it.

I wasn't entirely sure that spring was going to come this year. I guess I'm never quite sure, after these endless Michigan winters. But it came, just like it always does. First the trickle, then the gurgle and rush of melting snow, and the smell of Xerox machines in the air. Hasn't anyone ever noticed that melting snow smells like Xerox machines? Or vice versa. I think I'm the only one. Has something to do with ozone, maybe. I haven't the slightest idea. And I don't know how to find out since no one else knows what I'm talking about. Melting snow? Xerox machines? They nod and move away.

But spring did come. The sun started shining, the earth thawed out, the trees started getting hazy with green. Flowers, slowly. Fragrances. A gentle touch to the air. And the world was returned to us.

June Marie finally sang her song at the talent show. I wasn't sure she was going to make it. The night we did the final fitting, I expected her to look radiant, like a blushing bride in her wedding dress. But she looked haggard, worn. It wasn't the first time I'd seen it, of course. I'd been seeing the crease in her brow, the burning quality in her eyes, the hard *set* look to her mouth. But it wasn't until she put on that dress and tried on the jewels and all the rest that I saw it for as bad as it was. I actually started to cry right there, at the sight of it. I blinked back the tears and made myself busy pinning up a tuck at the waist, and I'm sure she thought I was crying because she was wearing a wedding dress.

I said it, just in case, to be sure: "My baby! In a wedding dress!"

But it wasn't until later on that night, when I found her brushing her hair, that I knew how bad it really was. She was sitting in her room at her vanity, brushing her hair as she always did, a hundred strokes every night, when I walked by and saw her there. She wasn't just brushing her hair, she was attacking it, dive-bombing her brow with the brush and yanking it through her hair. I hurried to her, took the brush from her hand. "June Marie!" I said. "Take it easy!" She turned to me and her face turned scarlet. Then she burst into tears. I knelt down next to her.

"I . . . I . . ." she blubbered.

I stroked her head. "I know," I said. "I know."

"I'm just so sorry . . ."

"It's not your fault."

"I'm just so *sorry* . . ."

"It's not your fault."

I led her over to her bed and lay down on it with her, moving her stuffed monkey aside. I cradled her head on my shoulder and stroked her hair and murmured to her. "It'll be OK, it'll be OK." What else was I going to do? There was nothing to say to make it better. So I just lay there and stroked her hair until we both felt calmer.

"Mom?" she said finally. "Why did he do it?" Her voice was muffled against my shoulder.

I stopped stroking her hair. She knew? Or was she making the assumption as a way of finding out? Why was I making the assumption she couldn't handle it? I started stroking her hair again. "I don't know," I said at last. "People are complicated, I guess."

She lay still for a moment. "Is he sick?" she said finally.

"I guess so. Or maybe disturbed in his soul. Honey, I'm sorry we didn't . . ."

"It's OK," she said. "I understand."

I stared at the circle of light her bedside lamp cast on the ceiling. "Do Karen and Lynnie know?"

"No." She shifted her weight. "Karen might."

"I don't know how to tell them."

She pulled back from me, looked up at me. Her face was open, simple. "I'll help you," she said. "When the time comes . . ."

I felt every cell in my body sigh. "Thank you, honey. Thanks."

She started to settle back into my arms, then pulled away again. "Mom?" she said. "Is Dad going to be OK?"

I gazed into her face, the beautiful face of my almost-grown-up daughter. "I hope so, honey," I said. "I hope so." We lay there a moment just looking at each other. Then I wiped the tears from her cheek with my thumb. "And what about you?" I whispered. "Are you going to be OK?"

She nodded, snuggled up closer to me, curling her face back into my neck.

"I think you're going to be fine," I said, stroking her hair again.

The next week, she sang her song. She followed a tap-dance chorus line. As they shuffled off into the wings, she appeared from the shadows at the back of the stage. At first, all you could see was the dress, this glowing ghost in the dark. Then she emerged, all aglitter in rhinestones, her hair pulled back into a bun, revealing the fine bones of her face. Her eyes were shining in the light. And she sang. She sang it beautifully. At least I thought it was beautiful, and the crowd seemed to think so too. It was such a ridiculous song for her to be singing under the circumstances: "Don't Cry for Me . . ." Everybody knew that her father had just been sent to prison, and why. In a way, the song was laughable, because it was just too applicable. But she sang it, she made it work. And I think when the people applauded her—her friends, at least; when her friends applauded—I think they were applauding *her,* her survival as well as her singing. I think they were encouraging her to sing, keep singing, keep living on. That's what I was doing, anyway. That's why I was applauding.

Lynnie came back to live with us as soon as Jerry left, and moved back into her old room. She was changed after her stay at my parents'. It amounted to only a few weeks, but of course it wasn't the visit that changed her. She was much more subdued than she'd been before, not as gawky, gee-whiz about everything. She had corners now, hidden places, shadows. She loosened up over the winter, became more of a little girl again, more ready to laugh and have fun. But whatever changes have happened in her as a result of this thing with her father are confused by the changes that are starting to happen now in her body. She'll be getting her period any day now, I think. And I wonder how those changes are going to mix with the emotional changes that surrounded the trial.

She won't talk about it much. I've asked her what she thinks of it all. I've tried to ask her at casual moments, when we're folding laundry or something, to make it easier for her, and for me. It's easier to talk, sometimes, when your hands are busy. But she shrugs it off.

Her teacher tells me the kids were pretty cruel about it at first, some of them. There were some comments made on the playground, some whispering behind her back. That hasn't made it easier for her, and her response has been to withdraw. She's always been on the shy side, but she was starting to get more confident with the other kids. Now this has pushed her back into her shell at just the moment she's going to need all the friends she can get—this awful period of puberty, when the only thing that keeps you from feeling like a total alien is knowing that the other kids are going through the same thing, and having them as friends.

She does have friends, of course. Sissy Sanders and Dawn Lamar have stood by her. They are the Three Musketeers. Or the Three Stooges, I don't know which. She still fools around with them after school. I think the sound that makes me happiest now is the sound of them in her room, shrieking, giggling over boys, or whatever it is they're talking about. Just the sound of Lynnie engaged with the world—with her world, the people around her.

Maybe she's not going to talk about this. Maybe she's not going to talk to me. The counselor is there at school, she knows, if she ever wants to go, and she did go once or twice. But she decided it was stupid. Maybe she won't want to talk about this until she's older. Or maybe she just won't ever talk at all. People do things differently. All I can do is be around and keep a watchful eye and try to encourage her to be more outgoing. Other than that, it's in God's hands.

And she seems to have put herself in God's hands, that's the one thing she hasn't withdrawn from. In fact her interest has grown more intense. She goes to church *every* Sunday now, whether the rest of us go or not, as well as Sunday school. She seems to be developing a real relationship with God. Maybe He's a new father for her, I speculate about that. But she doesn't talk about that either. She just keeps her door shut a lot. And when I knock and go in and ask her what she's doing, as often as not she says she's praying. "What about?" I say. She shrugs. So I kiss her on the top of her head and tell her I love her and leave her alone. I don't know what she's doing, but she seems to be doing all right with it, so I'm respecting her wishes and just leaving her alone. And in the meantime, I'm praying too. That this is the right thing for me to do. That she will get through this OK.

And then there's Karen. Karen, who drapes an arm across Lynnie's shoulders casually, without drawing any attention to it, just to let her know she's included. Karen, who brought home little gifts for everybody on Valentine's Day. Karen, who now participates. This is not like Karen at all. It's almost like her suspiciousness, her judgmental attitude toward the world, was exorcised by all of this, or passed along to Lynnie. But it's not that the darkness in her is gone. It's that she's grown beyond it. When she sits back and stares at people now, the way she always used to, you don't get the sense she's judging them. There seems to be a softness, a kindness in her eyes. She still sits back and studies people, still sees what it seems she always saw, but it seems to me in the last nine months my daughter has developed compassion. Compassion and maybe courage.

It was Karen who took me to see him. I hadn't been able to go myself. It had been six weeks and I still hadn't gone. Twice I had driven out to the prison and twice I had turned around and come home. I just couldn't face him yet, couldn't face him there, couldn't see him in jail. I know it was small of me, I know it was wrong, but I just couldn't bring myself to it. When I got to that prison and saw the huge, appalling bulk of it—I was just willing to put it off. And as time went on, it seemed I was willing to put it off indefinitely.

It was Karen who helped me get over that. We were having a sandwich at a coffee shop near the Westwood Mall. We'd been shopping for some fabric. She ordered her tuna fish and Coke then put the menu aside. When the waitress left, she settled back. "I talked to Daddy," she said.

I froze, then leaned in toward her. "What do you mean?" I whispered.

"He called the other day," she said simply. "You were out. He called from the prison yard. He said he had to stand in line for half an hour to make the call."

I peered at her. "What did he say?"

"He misses you. He wants to see you."

"Is he all right?"

She nodded. "But he really wants to see you."

I cupped my coffee in both hands.

"Why don't we go this weekend?" she said. She leaned across the table toward me. It was like we were huddled over a campfire.

When I set down my coffee, it rattled in the saucer. "I don't know if I can. I've tried . . ."

"I know."

I looked at her.

"I know," she shrugged.

I sat back and stared at the napkin I was balling in my hands. "I just don't want to see him there."

She leaned forward and placed her hand on mine. "I do," she said. "I want to see him. And they won't let me go alone." She held my hand tight and looked straight into me. "Will you go with me?"

So we went, on a Sunday morning. June Marie took Lynnie to church; Lynnie didn't want to come and neither did June

Marie, I suspect. It was an unseasonably warm and sunny early November day, all black shadows of limbs on tree trunks, and Karen did the driving. She'd just gotten her learner's permit and she wanted to try it out. She was completely competent, not nervous in the least, I thought. At least she didn't show any nervousness.

We parked at the north end of the lot near a little graveyard set up outside the walls of the prison. There were maybe two dozen headstones there, all different, all tilted at different angles. I wondered who could be buried there. Was it prisoners who died in prison? Guards who died in prison riots? It looked like something out of a Wild West movie, a ghost-town graveyard.

As we crossed the lot, I could hear what I thought was roaring coming from the prison. It sounded like the roar of animals in a distant zoo, but it was so muffled I couldn't even be sure I was really hearing it.

At the desk where we checked in and got a locker for our coats and bags, they made Karen put on a smock because she was wearing a V-neck sweater they thought was too provocative. It made me feel like we really were going into some kind of zoo. "I feel like a dental hygienist," Karen joked, yanking the smock around to try to make it fit better. While we waited, she bought a photo ticket from a vending machine so we could have our picture taken with Jerry, and thumbed through a magazine someone had left. I was conscious of not meeting anybody's gaze until I realized no one else was going to meet mine anyway.

We saw Jerry arrive at the other side of the gate as we were being frisked. He rose up on his toes as if he were trying to see a parade and smiled, tight-lipped, to hold back his tears. They allowed us to embrace and kiss once at the start and once at the end, but other than that we couldn't touch. We had to sit in adjacent chairs which faced in the same direction. The room looked like a bus station, except that no one was going anywhere. There were guards keeping watch all through it.

He was wearing blue pants and a blue work shirt. He seemed to be OK. He said the food was all right. He was subdued, a little vacant, I thought, as if he were in shock. We bragged about Karen's driving there and he was all congratulations. Karen told him funny stories about the Halloween party she'd gone to dressed as a jack-o-lantern and that got me telling stories about the trick-or-treaters who'd come to the house and how I scared one with the old-hag's mask Lynnie had worn the year before. We told him about June Marie and Lynnie and promised they'd come to visit soon. He said his brother had promised he'd come.

Then we went back home. Karen drove again. She stalled the car once on Cooper Street, but other than that she was fine.

"I'm impressed," I said as she pulled in the drive.

"Thanks," she said with a satisfied sigh. She dangled the keys in front of me and dropped them into my palm. Then she lifted her chin and looked at me. "I'm impressed too."

The hardest part since Jerry left has been dealing with my father. From the start, his attitude has been that I should get out of this marriage, that it was a blunder from the get-go. I don't know where he came up with that, after all the time he'd spent with Jerry. He'd taken him on just like his own son and he turned on him on a dime.

"I just don't see the point in being married to a child molester," he said.

"Will you stop calling him that?"

"Why stop? He's admitted to it. Publicly. Is this a man you want to be married to?"

"He's my *husband,*" I said. "Doesn't that count for something?"

He snorted and looked away. We were sitting on the sun porch again, looking out on the snow-covered backyard, the cardinals perched in the trees as if they were waiting to take a vote. "If I were you, I'd take my children and get away from him, right now. You're just lucky nothing's happened yet. And are you sure it hasn't?"

"Dad!"

"Well, he *says* he hasn't touched the girls. And maybe they say he hasn't. But you know how these things go. The kids don't always admit it. Hell, the kids don't always remember it. You think he was touching the girls?"

"No! He told me he didn't, and I believe him."

"You believed him before."

"Yeah," I mumbled. "Well, he's not interested in girls."

My father considered me for a moment, then snorted and looked away, as if he were looking for somewhere to spit. "I knew a guy like that once, when I was a boy," he said. "Gym teacher at school, interested in all the boys. Hanging around in the locker room. You could practically hear his heart start to race whenever one of us came near. He was a laughingstock, Jeanette. Everybody knew, everybody made fun of him. And it would have been funny too, if he hadn't been so dangerous."

"Jerry isn't dangerous."

"Then why did they put him in jail? What do you think he did with that boy? Rock him to sleep a couple of times? That kid'll have nightmares the rest of his life. He may never get unscrewed from this. If you'll pardon my pun."

"I don't have to listen to this," I said.

"You *do* have to listen to this! You can't just pretend this didn't happen." He hunched toward me and lowered his voice. "You have to get rid of him, Jeanette. You have to make a public statement, to your children and to the world, that you do not ally yourself with that man. That you will not welcome him back in your life. Cut your losses, Jeanette. You listen. If you won't do it for yourself, then do it for your children."

He silenced me. I couldn't speak. Then, or ever again with him when this subject came up. And it came up a number of times, this winter. Christmas night, when he'd had too much brandy. One day in March, when he was down with the flu and I brought him some soup I'd made. Then again around tax time, when he was helping me with my return. Every time I was with him, I was afraid he'd bring it up again. And the thing that frightened me about it was not only that I couldn't respond, not only that the only thing I could do was sit there and stare at my lap like some kind of errant child. It was also that some part of me believed him. Some part of me wanted to make that break, to make that public declaration that I had nothing to do with Jerry, or with his dirty deeds. I wanted to feel clean again, or maybe clean for the first time. I think I almost began to feel that if I did that, if I divorced Jerry, if I stepped away from his side to the other side of the playing field, if I joined the other team, whatever the opposing team was . . . if I did that, then maybe I would have finally done what my father wanted. Maybe that would be enough. Maybe this at last was the thing I could do to convince him that I was good enough. And if I were good enough for him, well, wouldn't I be good enough for the rest of the world? Wouldn't I finally have my place? Securely among the good people, the

God-fearing people, the righteous? Renouncing Jerry was renouncing sin. How could I not do that? How could I not make that choice for myself, or set that example for my children? When I listened to my father, I found it harder and harder to remember why I shouldn't do that.

Except that Jerry was my husband. Until death do us part.

I still don't know what will happen. When I see Jerry at the prison now, I'm worried for his safety. He says that people hate him in there. There's one guy in particular, one of the inmates, who finds a way to bump into him every time he can, just accidentally bump into him and push him up against a wall. Then he's full of false apologies, but he pops Jerry one before he walks off, knuckles him one in the thigh or the rib. Jerry says he's never seen such a cold hate in someone's eyes. He says it's like this guy is made of stone, he's that unreachable. Just stone, imposing his bulk on Jerry, stone looking down at him. One time the guy came over to him while he was eating dinner. He stood right over him, so close his hips almost touched Jerry's shoulder. Jerry just kept his eyes down. He didn't dare look up. "What's the matter?" said the guy. "You won't look up at me? What's the matter, you scared of me? You're scared of me, aren't you, you little butt-fucker. You little baby-fucker. Why don't you look up at me, huh?" Finally Jerry looked up at him. The guy's lips curled into this horrible sneer, then he spit in Jerry's face. The guards came over and moved him away, but when Jerry looked around the room, he saw everybody looking at him, like cats on their haunches, just watching, grinning. Even the guards were grinning. We've mentioned it to the warden and he's said he will look into it, but I really don't know what good it will do. The damage is being done.

I'm concerned about how depressed Jerry is. He tells me this when I go alone, he never tells the girls, but one time he actually broke down crying right there in the visiting room. "Jesus!" he said. "Our Father really fucked up when He made me, didn't He?" He looked at me, then laughed and cried. "He really fucked up the wiring in me." It scared me to hear him talking like that. I'd never known him to talk about God in such a personal way, as if he thought God really played a role in his life. I'd always wished that Jerry would take more interest in religion, but being as ambivalent about the church as I was, I never really pressed it. Now he's going to chapel, though, and talking with the chaplain. He's been reading the Bible. And now that he's taking an interest, something about it doesn't feel right to me. Maybe it's just my ambivalence showing itself again. But there's something about the way he quotes Scriptures that makes me feel uneasy. And the question I always bring home from the prison is, How can I walk out on Jerry in the middle of all this?

And the answer is, I just don't know. I don't know if I can stay married to him, and I don't know if I can divorce him. But for the time being, for five years at least, I guess the point is moot. I have time to decide. I have time to decide. So I sit on my porch in the Sunday breeze and wait for the answer to come to me. To see what the warmth of the sun might bring me. To hear what I might hear from the birds. I've always loved the birds, especially the mourning dove, that coo-coo-coo. Such a sad and yearning sound, like a lover calling its lost mate. *Coo. Coo. Coo.* Sometimes I call back to it to see if it will answer. It never does, you can't fool those birds, but I keep trying anyway.

PART IV

1

At first I wasn't sure I wanted to go to my high school reunion. I mean, here it had been ten years and I still wasn't out of college yet, still working as a bartender while everyone else was probably off becoming millionaires by now. I'd heard that Eddie MacEldowney had some fancy job in the State Department and Milo Smith was working at some brokerage outfit on Wall Street. Not that I'd want either of those jobs. Law? Finance? Not my style. But still, in that kind of context, it wasn't going to sound so hot for me to say "Oh, me? I'm tending bar. Still picking up classes for my bachelor's . . ." I imagined people smiling politely, then seeing somebody else across the room and moving along.

High school reunions are always like that. At least that's what everybody was saying—Nick and Phyllis and Reuben, all of them—and I figured they were right. People were going to be very busy checking out each other's credentials, and I wasn't sure I wanted to subject myself to that, to *their* expectations, *their* sets of values, *their* ideas of what makes a life.

But I finally decided, Fuck it. I was just too curious not to go. I wanted to know what happened to those guys. Donny Lee Harrington. Buzzy Kaser. The Wall twins. Sharon Carraher. Those were some pretty great kids, in high school. Some of the things we did together, I still get a kick from thinking about. The time we stole the Christ Child from the crèche in front of the Catholic church and left it on the steps of the Florence Crittendon Home for Unwed Mothers. The time we put detergent in the Cascades, and the whole damned waterfall turned into one big foaming bathtub. And some of the parties we had, especially when somebody's parents were out of town. We had a lot of fun in high school. We were like a pack of animals—everybody moving one way, then another way, then another—we were one big family, one big herd. I loved feeling *part* of something like that, instead of just me by myself, alone.

Of course there were parts that weren't so much fun—getting caught breaking and entering, once even shoplifting. But none of us were ever serious criminals in the making, we were just kids with too much energy taking dares from each other. At least I guessed that's who we were. That's why I decided to go back: Line everyone up against the wall—*OK, you guys. How many of you are here tonight on parole?* Who knows? Get us all together again, maybe the Cascades would mysteriously start to foam in our honor.

And besides, I wanted to see Patty. Wanted to know what had happened to her. I hadn't seen her since the Christmas of our sophomore year at Western, just before I split. Hadn't even talked to her since I left her there on her doorstep and took off into the night. That felt like unfinished business with Patty. Which is what it always was with her, in a way, right from the start: unfinished. But I wondered if she still thought about me, like I sometimes thought about her. Not that I sat around mooning about her, but sometimes when I thought about her it did make me smile in a sad kind of way. I figured she was probably married by now, had a couple of kids. She probably had some great job. That was good. I hoped the best for her. I didn't have any big ideas about us getting back together, I just wanted to see how she was doing. Maybe pay my respects to what we'd had. And maybe, in paying respects, to feel a little of that feeling again. Just a little. For maybe a moment.

So a couple of days before the reunion, I decided to go after all. I still felt kind of weird about it, still felt like there was a pretty good chance I'd come away feeling like a doofus, but there was nothing new in that. Feeling like a doofus was always an option for me, anyway. And Nick assured me I'd be OK so long as I wore his magic tie—a fat old forties thing, really nice, that he said would protect me from the power of the past, especially against the truly awesome forces of old girlfriends. So I packed the tie, called my parents, got Phyllis to cover me at Charlie's and drove up on Friday night.

I don't like the drive from Chicago to Jackson. Besides the fact that I always feel like I'm on a collision course with my past, I don't like the aesthetics: All those cornfields look alike. I always think of how they look in November at twilight—row after row of broken-down stalks stretching as far as you can see, covered with a light dusting of snow. Off in the distance there's a farmhouse with a yellow light in the window. Inside there are people and the smells of food cooking. Maybe there's a fire, and a dog. But I am always out in the field, a long ways away, looking at it. Even in July, that's the way that landscape feels to me. The sky is always gunmetal gray.

That's why I decided to drive it at night, so I wouldn't have to look at it. Just put on some tunes and crank up the sound and coast along through the dark. I could be anywhere, who knew? It reminded me of the days when I wandered around the country by bus pretending I was Jack Kerouac or something, half stoned all the time. A part of me still loves that feeling, floating in limbo in the dark, unconnected to anything except my bag, my books and my music. But I have a tendency to get bored with that kind of stuff faster these days. More and more I'm starting to feel like I ought to be getting someplace in my life, like floating in limbo in the dark isn't quite the thing anymore.

I like my life in Chicago. I like the people I know. They're more complicated than the people I grew up around. Like Phyllis. Ran away from home at sixteen to get away from her father who kept chasing her around the house with an enema bag. Actually working as a model by the time she was seventeen. Hooked on coke by eighteen, clean by twenty, a mother by twenty-two with no sign of the father in sight. Now managing Charlie's Saloon. This woman has been around the block and there's nothing going to get her down, she just keeps moving on. She makes you feel like anything's possible, just by continuing to put one foot in front of the other.

And then there's Nick. Old Nick. Old better-get-hold-of-yourself-pretty-quick-or-you're-gonna-die-in-a-gutter Nick. It's the booze that's going to get him, if he doesn't die of AIDS first, the way he fucks around. But you can't help loving him, he needs to be loved so much. Besides the fact he's hilarious. We keep telling him he ought to go audition for Second City or one of these other comedy troupes, he could be a star in no time. But he just can't get himself to it. He'd rather pop another beer, tell another story. Seduce another woman.

And then, of course, there's Reuben. Reuben, the diva of Douglas Street. The biggest, blackest, most outrageous queen in all of Chicago. How this man *will* wear the makeup and nails and wigs and strut his ass at the Lucky Horseshoe. At first I have to admit I didn't know what to make of him, I thought he was sort of ridiculous. But then, as I got to know him, I realized his dress-up was just a reflection of how he felt inside, and I could relate to that. I can relate to feeling like there's more than one of you inside. And I think it's sort of brave of him to dare to give both those people a life. Besides, he keeps us all from taking ourselves too goddamn seriously. Not that we're inclined, as a group, to take ourselves too seriously. But we can always count on Reuben, if things start getting too much the same, to come up with a new outfit at least.

It's good to have a life at last that's out in the real world instead of the middle of some cornfield. And I love being in the city, always having people around. No matter what time it is, no matter where you are, there's almost always someone else there—driving by, walking by, sitting at the next table. I really get off on watching them all. I have this whole collection of them across the alley from me—it's like an Advent calendar, a different scene in each window. I know these people's comings and goings, their habits, even their private habits that maybe no one else knows about. Like for instance I know this one guy is seeing two women at the same time, and I can tell from the way they cook for him they don't know about each other. And I couldn't count how many times I've watched this other pair making love. Of course, sometimes it can get to you—you can start to feel like everyone else in the city is a couple and you're the only one by yourself. But whenever I get to feeling like that, I just go down to the Loop and walk around among all the buildings. I love those monster buildings, and the canyons they create between them. If I'm feeling sorry for myself, I just go walk in those canyons awhile and my problems start to feel kind of small.

So I'm happy enough with my life. But every now and then I do have to wonder, is this as good as it gets? I mean, what's going to happen to us? In ten years, let's say, or fifteen. Nick will probably be dead. Phyllis's daughter will be leaving home, and Phyllis will be alone. Reuben will be an aging queen, not a ripe young thing anymore. And as Reuben reminds us every day, nobody, *nobody* is interested in an aging queen.

And where am I going to be? Still watching other people's love lives out of my back window? Still tending bar at Charlie's? Maybe I will have finished my bachelor's and moved along to a master's, taking one course a semester to keep myself convinced I'm actually headed in some direction. Or maybe I will have just given up, just accepted the fact that mixing drinks is what I'm made for. And maybe that would be OK.

But I did always think I'd like to try teaching.

Kids, I think. Little kids.

I always start thinking this way when I know I'm going to see my father. And what always fucks me up is, I don't know whether it's him or me talking. Sometimes I get myself all worked up over where I'm going in life and then I realize that every thought I've had has been *his* voice, *him* talking in my head.

And then I think, I don't have to do what *he* says.

But then I think, What if I *want* to?

But no, that was my *father's* idea.

Or at least I thought it was his idea; maybe it was my idea.

And on and on and on it goes, and where it stops, nobody knows.

When I got as far as Kalamazoo I pulled off the highway and went into town to drive around the campus and stop at the grill I used to hang out at. I knew there wouldn't be anyone there that I'd recognize, but I wanted to see if my initials were still carved into the booth there. There'd been this one booth I used to hang out at during my last days at Western, after I'd stopped going to classes, and I'd branded it with my initials—using the diagonal stem on the R as the start of the Y, then carving a circle around it. It took me a couple of days, while I was just hanging around feeling bummed. And I figured that since this trip was about my past, I'd stop and see if my artwork was still there. But the place had been turned into a pizza parlor, all lit up with fluorescent lights, and the booths were all molded plastic. Orange and gray. They were orange and gray. It's funny what people think are improvements. But it did sort of depress me, too, to think there was nothing left of me there. Not even my crummy initials.

I hopped back in my Honda and drove as fast as I could to Battle Creek, then slowed down and opened the windows to see if I could smell the baking grain even from the highway. I wondered if people from Battle Creek smelled like baking grain themselves. If you met one in Alabama, would you know they were from Battle Creek? And what would Alabama smell like to them? Anything at all? I bet their noses were so screwed up by smelling cereal all the time, they couldn't even smell anymore. Did florists do badly in Battle Creek?

Then I was back on the road again, tunneling through the darkness on I-94 and singin' along with the Boss: ". . . take a look around, this is your hometown . . ." And finally there it was: Jackson. Garden spot of southern Michigan, home of the Cascades, and site of the largest prison in the world, beneath one roof. My hometown. I hadn't been there since Christmas. I pulled off the highway at 127 and took West Avenue up to Morrell, then headed out Francis Street toward home.

I pulled up in front of the house about nine. The light was on in the living room, another one under the kitchen stairs. My mom would be watching TV, my dad would be down in the basement, probably fixing a broken toaster. There was a comfort in it, the sameness, that made me kind of squirm. I could almost smell the basement from here—oil and must and paint thinner. It smelled like my father to me, in a way. It put me right back down there with him, watching him fiddle around with a screwdriver, whistling, sweat running off his temple. *Now, if we twist this a little bit further* . . . He'd talk like that all the time he was working, pretending to be talking to me, but he was really just talking to himself and I happened to be there. Lately I'd come to think that he really *had* liked my company, even if he hadn't quite known what to do with it. But still, I couldn't forget that feeling of being there but not being there, of feeling like I was playing second fiddle to a toaster.

I grabbed my duffel bag and stepped up onto the porch. Sure enough, my mom was on the couch, watching *Larry King Live*. I could tell she was more or less just waiting for me to arrive; she had the remote control in her hand ready to shut the thing off. It reminded me of the way she used to wait up for me at night, when I was out on a date: She'd sit there in the dark and just wait, like she didn't have anything else to do. I opened the door and she looked up and smiled, then dropped the remote on the couch and came to meet me at the door.

She looked shorter, or maybe wider. Her hair was a slightly brassier version of what it used to be naturally and the curly do she'd taken up with made her look fatter, I thought. Her bifocals hung from her neck on a chain. She came toward me with her arms extended like she was going to hug me. I almost started to back away, but then she grasped me by the elbows and gave me her usual hearty shake.

"You're so tall!" she said. As if she hadn't seen me since I was a kid. "Ken!" she called. "Rob's here! Come up!" She turned back to me. "How was your trip?"

How are you supposed to answer that question? *My trip was boring. My trip was spectacular. Succulent. Sinful. Erotic. Cosmic.* What did she want to hear anyway? I told her it was OK.

My dad appeared from under the stairs, ducking to get through the door even though he didn't have to, wiping his hands on his pants. He had a big grin on his face. "How you doin', son?" he said. He shook my hand, clapped me on the shoulder. Now, how was I supposed to answer that question? *Doing great!* Or, *Doing shit!* Or, *Doing nothing at all! What do you think of that!* I told him I was OK.

We went into the living room. My mom and dad sat on the beige couch, I sat in the tweed recliner. My mom killed the TV with the remote, and there we were, in silence, just sitting there, staring at each other. I felt like I was on *Meet the Press*. I expected them to ask me about land reform or taxes. But it was really good to see them too.

"So how are things in Chicago?" My dad.

"OK," I said. Then I realized "OK" was the only word I'd spoken since I arrived. "Fine," I said. "It's great. They're great."

"Your Sox are doing good," he said.

"Yeah," I said. "Not bad . . ."

"Are you hungry?" said my mom. "Want me to fix you a sandwich? I've got some ham salad all made, your favorite . . ."

"Nah," I said. Then I thought, what else? "Yeah," I corrected myself. "OK."

"Oh!" she said, sort of surprised. "Oh, great!" She clapped her hands and dropped them in her lap, then pushed herself to her feet. "You want some chips?"

"Sure," I said. "Chips are fine."

"Pickle?"

"Pickle," I nodded. "Pickle is good."

She hurried out of the room. "You want milk?" she said, popping back in. "Or beer! My goodness—milk! You're a full-grown man. You want a beer?" she said.

I nodded.

"Hey, Linda!" My dad. "What about me?" Then they had to negotiate his sandwich, his potato chips and pickles. It was quite a brouhaha. But finally it was just me and my dad, sitting across the room from each other.

"So how you doin'?" he said. "Everything OK? No problems?"

I shook my head, smiled. "Everything's fine."

He nodded rhythmically. "Good, good. You sure?"

"I'm sure."

"Good."

"I'm taking *Learning Theory* this summer."

"*Learning Theory,* eh?" he said. "Learning anything?"

I shrugged. "Theoretically."

He laughed and nodded, didn't pursue it.

"I'll have my degree by the turn of the century," I said. Joking, sort of apologizing. "If everything goes all right."

He kept on nodding, didn't respond.

I cleared my throat, resettled my weight. "So how are things at the store?"

He spread his hands, shook his head, smiled like an umpire pleased to say "Safe."

"Hezekiah still helping out?" I went to high school with Hezekiah. Dumb as dirt, sweet as sugar. I sat next to him in study hall, the times I showed up in study hall.

"Still there," said my dad.

"Do you know if he's going to the reunion?"

"I think so," he said. "Said he'd like to see you. Everybody'd like to see you. You'll come into the store tomorrow?"

"Sure," I said, feeling wary. I looked forward to going into the store to see the folks I worked with there when I was in junior high and high school, but I dreaded the conversation that I always had with my dad there. I felt myself tense up for fear he was going to start in now, already, before I even got my pickle. *When are you going to come back to Jackson and take this store off my hands, eh, Rob? Why do you think I built this store? From the very first day? For you. Hey, your brother's not interested. Come back home.* I took a deep breath. If he started, I was going to recite the words with him. But my mom came back with the sandwiches.

"So!" she said, setting a plate on the table/lamp combo at my elbow. "Meet any nice girls since we saw you last?" She gave me a mischievous grin.

"Nobody special," I said. "Not yet."

"Better get cracking," she said. "Or all the good ones will be gone!" She put a paper napkin on the arm of my chair and patted it.

"For Christ's sake, Linda," said my dad. "He's only twenty-seven. Give him a chance to have some fun."

My mom looked sort of hurt by that, or maybe it was my

imagination. I never understood my parents' relationship. In some ways it seemed like no relationship—he spent his evenings in the basement being Mr. Fix-It, she spent her evenings in front of TV, then they went to bed together. In a way, I guess it wasn't so bad. I mean, they always had that comfort of knowing where the other one was, of knowing they weren't alone. There's something really nice about that, about having somebody else in the house even if you're not in the same room. But still. The same thing every night? Him in the basement, her in the living room? They hardly even spoke to each other. I wondered if they ever made love when they finally went to bed. I *used* to wonder if they ever fooled around with anyone *else*. I guess everybody wonders if their parents ever fool around. I was pretty sure, though, my parents never did—with anyone else, I mean. They were too much into routine.

We talked about my brother and his girlfriend in San Diego. They were thinking about getting married after living together for five years. Then we talked about my cousins awhile, and how well Stan was doing at MIT. Then we talked about who had come into the store. And by eleven o'clock I was fluent in the ebb and flow of Jackson life. Then we watched the news and they went to bed.

I figured it was probably too late to call anybody, and I didn't know who I'd call anyway. Didn't know who was still in town, didn't know who was coming back, or where I'd be able to reach them. But if anybody was up and about, the Hunt Club would probably be where they'd be. I knew it was a long shot, but I was too restless just to hang out at the house and watch some boring old movie, so I hopped in my car and headed out.

There was no one I knew at the Hunt Club, just as I'd

figured, but I had a beer anyway and a couple of cigarettes and watched a little TV. Then I climbed back in my car and went touring around the town. Drove down Michigan Avenue, the main drag; it was really spooky. All lit up by streetlights, as if they expected traffic, but nobody in sight. Most of the stores were boarded up. It looked sort of like a downtown version of those broken-down cornfields—bleakness everywhere—but there was no farmhouse on the horizon.

I drove up Wildwood past the old high school, took a turn around the parking lot, then drove past Patty's house. It felt like being in high school again, driving past her house late at night. I used to do that all the time just to feel her presence, to know she was sleeping, peaceful. Patty was the closest I'd ever come to being in love, so far: We'd gone together all through high school. Well, at least the last two years. If you could call it "going together." It was more like a series of breakups with just enough "going together" between to give us something to break up again. I didn't know what it was about us. I was always so jealous of her, always so afraid she was going to be fooling around with somebody else. If she so much as talked to another guy, I got fucked up about it. So she talked to other guys all the time. Maybe she'd always been that way, and that's why I hooked up with her. Or maybe, when she saw what it did to me, she did it again and again, to see me dance at the end of her string. I don't know. It was all fucked up.

But it was also incredibly sweet. There was something so delicate between us, sometimes it really scared me. I'd never had anyone treat me like that—so gentle, so soft, so warm. Sometimes she made me feel so weak, I got scared I was going to come apart in her hands like a soggy Kleenex. Then I'd feel this roiling inside of me, like a storm building up in my stomach, and it would build and build and before you knew it we'd be having another fight about some guy she'd been flirting with. It was all incredibly dramatic. It kept us occupied and interested for a couple of years, and more. And, I sometimes think, distracted. But distracted from what, I'm not quite sure.

All I knew was, I missed her now. Not her so much, not Patty herself. But I missed what we'd had together. The quiet parts, between the fights, before the roiling started again. I wanted to have that in my life. Just that. Just simple companionship, love. It seemed to me if you had that, you didn't need money or position or whatever else people thought they needed. Just someone to live with, watch TV with, eat with, sleep with, have a life with. Easy, comfortable, side-by-side.

There's this one couple in the city I watch. The girl used to work at a clothing store around the corner from me. The guy has some kind of office job, wears a suit every day. I see them all the time on the street, and just the way they move together—they are so entirely at ease with each other. There is no hurry to get things said. Maybe they're really dull people who just don't have anything to say. Even so. Whenever I see them I drink them in, almost like I'm thirsty. Recently I noticed the girl is pregnant, just beginning to show. I saw them one morning at brunch, saw him lay his hand on her belly while he was reading the menu, just absently stroking its roundness, and it almost made me cry.

Sometimes I get that easy feeling when I've just had sex with a girl, a woman, and we're lying in bed, smoking and talking, entwined with the sheets and each other. Sometimes I feel as loose and relaxed as the smoke uncurling toward the ceiling. Lazy, unhurried. There. It isn't the real thing, exactly, but it seems to be the best I can do, so I do it a lot. And it does give me what I need, for a moment. But it's always gone the next morning, or the next day, or the next week. One girl I saw for a while said every time we got together, it felt like we went back to square one and started all over again. I didn't tell her the reason was I simply didn't love her, that I wasn't even sure I *liked* her. Maybe I should have told her that, but I didn't want to hurt her feelings so I didn't say anything, just didn't respond, and eventually she moved back in with her previous boyfriend, the sculptor.

That's the way it happened, a lot, even with women I really liked. One woman I did get sort of close with, this woman who had two kids, said sometimes I felt to her like one of her kids, constantly tugging at her sleeve, needing something from her, but I couldn't make it clear what I needed. I knew the feeling she described, knew how it felt from my end. It was that feeling of straining against something, a leash, and the tightness it made in my throat, almost like a piece of food was stuck in there, or a piece of my heart. It felt like I was ready to cry if I only knew what to cry about. But I guess I made her feel like I was asking her for something—no, *nagging* her for something—and eventually she moved on. To Houston, I think, or maybe Dallas, and married a businessman.

Sooner or later, they always moved on. To the casual observer I was just doing what every other bartender in town was doing—meeting and laying as many beautiful women as I could. And sometimes I sort of liked to pretend that I was just a guy on the prowl, intentionally avoiding getting hooked, like a clever old fish. It was good for my image to pretend that. And good for my self-image too. But that woman, Susan, was right. I did always snap back to square one. Or I didn't snap back, exactly—it was more like I was reeled back in. So I knew there was something else going on. I knew there was something that wasn't working, I just didn't know what it was.

I got back home about one A.M., had another beer, checked out the movies and went up to bed. I stopped at Danny's old room and looked in. Most of the traces of him were gone—the posters, the rocks he'd collected. The whole room had been done over like something out of a magazine—pastel carpet, sheer drapes, flowered wallpaper. I guess this was what my mom puttered at while Dad was puttering downstairs. It looked pretty good, I was impressed—the colors, the balance of everything—she'd always been good at making things pleasant. I'd always especially liked that about her, that she was always taking care to see that people were comfortable. Like the first thing she did when I got home was make me a ham salad sandwich, my favorite. She was always tending to people that way. She was never so happy as when she knew she'd made somebody happy.

But when I went into my room, it felt weird to see it was the same as it had always been. My bats were still in the corner, exactly where I'd left them. The turtle tank was by the window—no turtle now, but ready for one if I decided to move back in. It was like a museum exhibit. Kind of a neat exhibit, actually. The Pink Floyd poster. The swim team clippings. The acid wash clothes in the closet with all those useless zippers and buttons and flaps. Seeing all that stuff again was sort of like seeing old friends. But I couldn't get over the feeling that my parents had somehow given Danny permission to leave home and make a life for himself in California and they were trying to keep me there by keeping my room intact. Trying to make me feel at home so I'd come back and take over the store and live out their lives for them. Or at least live out the life they imagined for me.

Once or twice I'd actually thought maybe I *ought* to take over the store. A part of me would have loved to have a life that unruffled, unstirred-up. Just putt-putt-putter my way through the years. Maybe take up golf, maybe join the Rotary Club. It wasn't like I was getting anywhere doing what I was doing, really. And at least there would have been some kind of security in the store. Maybe running the store would have made me feel like I had a place in the world, even if it wasn't *my* place, exactly. I don't know. I don't think I ever really considered it seriously. But sometimes it seemed to me like I should. Just because if I'd done it, I guess, it would have made my parents so happy. And maybe after all these years, it would have been nice to make my parents happy for a change.

2

I hadn't spent much time with my parents since I'd been in high school, mostly because my father was always getting on my case, always so worried about me being a juvenile delinquent. Sometimes I think I got in trouble back then just to yank his chain a little, just to see him get upset. Then I'd tell him to go back down to the basement, life was better upstairs without him, which would always get my mother going, and before you knew it the house was like a chicken coop with a fox in it, and I got to be the fox. It wasn't much fun at home in those days, especially with Danny off in the navy. So when I graduated from high school, I got out and I didn't come back.

I started out at Hillsdale College. I wasn't sure about college at first. I guess I knew I was smart enough, but I wasn't convinced I could hack it somehow, or wasn't convinced I wanted to, maybe because that was what my father wanted me to do. But when I considered the options—working in a gas station, working in my dad's store—I decided to give it a shot.

I wound up at Hillsdale because I didn't get my shit together soon enough to apply to a better school, and it was like exile in a labor camp. There wasn't even a town there, just this little college in a cornfield. But I did it, like I said I'd do, and I did OK. In fact I did real well. And somehow, getting away from home and all the screaming and shouting there—I don't know, I started to think I wanted to go to college after all, that maybe I could even, maybe, make something of myself.

I talked to Patty at Christmastime and she said Western Michigan was the greatest, and maybe I ought to transfer, so I moved on it. I guess I wanted to go where she was, to see if things might spark again—they did at Christmas, a little—and if that didn't happen, then just to have a look around and see who else was there. I'd gone out with a couple of girls at Hillsdale but nothing really clicked, and I thought that Western at least would increase the possibilities. And besides, I wanted to be in a place that had more than one movie theater. So I talked to my dad and he said OK, I could transfer in the fall.

I spent that summer in Chicago. Patty was working as a counselor in a camp in northern Michigan and I went home with my roommate, Tom. My dad would have liked me to come back to Jackson and work in the hardware store again, but I convinced him I'd make more money working for Tom's father. His dad owned a construction company and we worked on one of his houses that summer. Nice house, big one. With balconies. I really liked being out there in the sun, in the heat, in the smell of the sawdust. I liked the banging of hammers and tossing comments back and forth with the guys. Or sometimes not talking at all, just going about our work, just quiet. There's something nice about that, just working quietly with other people, not feeling like you have to talk, or think of something to say every minute. It gives you time to think. And I liked making use of nails instead of just sitting there staring at them sitting in a box on a shelf, the way my father did all day. Every nail became a kind of a point I was driving home. It was sort of like meditating. You set the nail, then you start to pound, and for a moment your whole existence gets focused just on that nail, on driving it straight into the wood. I really got so I loved that. They started calling me Jackhammer. Then they shortened it to Jack.

I told them to shorten it to Hammer.

By the time I got to Western I was feeling pretty good, like maybe I wasn't destined to be a delinquent all my life after all. But then, that fall, all hell broke loose. I don't know what it was exactly. The place was bigger, that was for sure, and it was harder to figure out where the hell you fit in. And I didn't like my roommate much—Arthur Anderson, the Fart King. But if everything else had stayed the same I could have handled all that. Mostly it was Patty, I guess. Here I'd thought we'd get back together, or at least we'd hang around together, but when I got there I found out she already had a whole life going on. A couple of guys she'd been dating the year before were still hanging around, sort of interested, and she belonged to this sorority, Kappa Crappa Globulin, or something. . . . She was just so busy, so popular, so happy all the time, so breezy. I found myself feeling jealous not just of the other guys who were interested in her, but of *all* her other friends. She didn't seem to have time for me anymore, and even when she did make time, it wasn't the same with her. There wasn't that same sense of having a little world that was all our own.

Then I flunked a midterm. I actually flunked the midterm

in organic chemistry. I'd never flunked *anything* before. And when I went to see the professor about it, he wouldn't even look at me. Just said *Your work is not good enough. You're going to have to work harder.* Which really got me depressed. I mean, here I was in this new school and I didn't have any real friends and I couldn't even get my chemistry professor to talk to me. What the hell did I think I was doing?

That was when I started to slide, and it was all downhill after that. I mean *way* downhill. By Thanksgiving I had pretty much stopped going to any classes at all and was spending most of my days in the dorm watching game shows on TV. Either that, or hanging out in the video arcade. That seemed to be the one place in the world I could make some headway, the one place I could win. Just keep punching those buttons. Then of course I flunked organic chemistry at the end of the term, along with two other subjects. And by the time I went home for Christmas I was already on the road, in my head at least. I didn't tell anyone I was going, except Patty, the night before I left. Everyone else—my parents—thought I was going back to Kalamazoo. But instead I went down to the bus station, plopped my money on the counter and bought a ticket to Las Vegas, the biggest, loudest, highest-rolling game show of them all. The Pay-Your-Money-And-Take-Your-Chances Great Arcade in the Sky. The Wheel of Fortune. The Price Is Right. The Future Is Now. Good-bye.

It took about fifty-seven years to get to Vegas by bus, but that was OK with me. I loved being on the bus. I'd take a seat about three-quarters back by a window on the door side—too far back to be a part of any conversation with the driver, but not all the way to the back of the bus where the peculiar people sit—then slouch down in my seat with my knees against the seat in front and my backpack on the seat beside me. I liked having everything I owned in that backpack. I liked knowing just where everything was, and that it was all within reach. And that, if it wasn't there within reach, it didn't matter, it didn't exist. I'd go with what I had, and I had everything I needed. There wasn't any feeling I liked quite as much as that one. Then watching the fields fly by outside, watching the towns creep up. Or sleeping and waking up not knowing where the hell I was. Or reading a book, just putting myself someplace else altogether. There was nothing quite so good as that, that feeling of moving along. The hum of the wheels on the pavement. The people coming and going, always changing.

I even liked the bus stations. The garish light, the low-life. I wouldn't have wanted to live in one, the way some people seemed to, but I did like passing through them. I liked being part of that scene for a while, just long enough to wait for my bus. I liked to feel the torpor of it, the shuffling endlessness of it, the buzzing sense of being beaten. I liked the horror of bus stations. Because just as it reached up and threatened to drag you down inside it, to trap you forever in its muck, you stepped onto a bus and it pulled out and you were on your way. Escaped again. Another close call. Freed at the last second.

I spent about two weeks in Vegas. Gambling a little, eating a lot, mostly just looking around. Talk about the bus station, that whole *town* is a bus station. All the lights, the game show sets, all the crazy people. I used to just wander around the casinos, watching people gamble. I remember this one old woman—all dressed up in high heels and a dress, her hair all tucked and curled, working three slot machines at once. She'd drop in a coin and pull a handle, then move along to the next machine, drop in a coin and pull the handle, then move along to the next machine, drop in a coin and pull the handle, then move back to the first machine. She was turning *into* a slot machine—drop, pull, drop, pull—and in between she was waving a hundred-dollar bill at the changer like she was waving a white handkerchief, like it was a matter of life and death that she get more coins before she ran out.

It finally got kind of depressing. I mean, I did win some money. In the end, I guess I broke even. But all those people taking their shot, all of them sure they were going to hit it. It made me feel sorry for them, sad. Like this was what life was like for them—hoping for that one big hit, then hitting it and turning around and hoping for the next one. Just one thing after another. Just one thing to grasp for after another. Was that what life was really like, just one thing after another? Just dropping coins into a machine and pulling on a lever? I finally got so depressed about it, I had to get out of there. So I sent my parents a postcard with a picture of a couple getting married in a parking lot, just to let them know I was alive, and split for California.

On the bus I met this woman named Linda. Linda. Ha, my mother's name. She had a black enamel cigarette holder clamped between her teeth but no cigarette because they wouldn't let her smoke on the bus. She sat slouched down in her seat like me and cocked her head when she looked at me, letting it wobble back and forth like the heads on those little dogs that people put in the back windows of their cars. We started talking, sort of flirting, sort of feeling each other out.

She was comfortable as an old shoe, to talk with. She seemed kind of wise and worn in. And when I told her that Linda was my mother's name, she threw back her head and laughed this terrific, raucous laugh, because she figured she was old enough to be my mother herself. Which I think she was. But we got pretty friendly on that bus, and she finally asked me if I wanted to get off at Barstow with her, where she lived, and hang out for a while. She was just divorced, she told me, from some guy she called the Trucker, and she was feeling a little lonely. So I did. I got off at Barstow with her and ended up staying a month.

I liked hanging out with Linda. I liked having breakfast with her in the morning before she went off to work. She worked as a secretary at some sort of packing outfit and I hung around her house and made myself handy, tending to stuff the Trucker had never bothered with—fixing steps and leaky faucets, painting the garage. I wired her house for music. And then when she came home, it was great. We watched TV. We ate. We drank. And we fucked all night. I never met a woman before or since who was so into being fucked. Inside out, upside down. At one, then two, then three. It was exhausting. It was great. And I liked being her gigolo, her kept boy, for a while. It made me feel kind of gritty and real in a way I'd never felt before.

But I knew it couldn't last very long, and she knew it too, I think. After a while I ran out of things to do, so she got me a job loading trucks at her packing outfit. It really sucked. I couldn't even talk to most of those guys because they didn't speak English, so I found myself just hanging myself on a hook eight hours a day until it was time to go home with Linda. And as time went on, she came to feel like such a sad person to me.

Alone. No kids. The Trucker was gone. All she had was this college kid she picked up on the bus, who she knew was going to leave her. That she had, and her bottle. Once the novelty of it wore off, I got overwhelmed by the sadness of her, and that's why I finally left. I mean, she was old and drunk and worked as a secretary in a packing plant. She was the bus station, in a way. So when she went off to the store one Saturday morning, I wrote her a note and left.

My next stop was San Diego. Figured I'd spend some time with my brother, I'd been planning it for weeks. I called him when I got into town and he came to get me at the bus station. I was watching *L.A. Law* on one of those little coin-op TV sets when he came through the door. He looked good. He looked tan and kind of tough. He was grinning at me.

"Hey, little brother," he said. He punched me. "You look like a dude on the road."

I shrugged. "I am," I said.

He took me to a bar downtown and bought me a burger and beer while I told him what I'd been up to. His eyes were shining all the time I was talking, like what I was doing was just the right thing, like that's what he wished he was doing. He liked the part about Linda a lot, whistled through his teeth.

"Little brother's out getting a taste of the world," he said. He laughed and shook his head at his beer.

I settled back and propped my boots up on his side of the booth. It was so great to see him and talk. It felt like I hadn't talked to anybody who really knew me for years. Everybody who really knew me was back in Michigan, and I didn't want to go back there. Partly because they really knew me, I guess. Or because they didn't know me at all. But sitting here in this little bar, talking with my brother . . . I felt like this was great, like I could put up at my brother's place, hang out with him in California. Maybe we could travel together, go up to the Oregon coast. I felt like I used to feel at Lake Michigan, when we'd go over there in the summer and stay late on the beach and build a fire. You had a sense of the huge blank lake just beyond, in the darkness, but here by the fire it was warm and cozy. You were out in the elements, out in the world, but you had your little fire. It was like that, sitting with Danny.

But then he took me to his apartment and I met his girlfriend Janice. I liked Janice well enough. She wasn't a woman I'd choose for myself, too skinny, but she seemed to be nice and friendly, and if that was who Danny wanted to be with, that was OK with me. But it was obvious from the start she wasn't excited about me being there. They had a pretty small apartment, one bedroom, and they put me up on the couch in the living room. It was obvious I couldn't stay there for long. Which really, *really* depressed me. Where the hell was I going to go next?

That night Danny convinced me that I had to call the folks. He said they'd been calling him all the time to see if he'd heard from me. They were worried sick, he said. He made it seem kind of funny—he'd gone through this kind of stuff with them himself—but he also understood their worry, he could see it from both sides. So we talked about it for a while and had a couple more beers, and after a time it got to seem like maybe it wasn't necessarily such a bad idea to call. I mean, I didn't want to give them a heart attack or anything. I didn't want *that* on my conscience.

So I called. Janice went into the other room, staying out of the way. And while the phone was ringing, I was feeling a little uncertain, wary. And a little drunk. Then as soon as I heard my mother's voice . . . I could picture her there in the kitchen, the way she leaned her head to the side when she answered the phone so her hair would fall away from her ear to make room for the receiver. I could smell the smell of that house, the Lemon Pledge she always used for dusting. And it made my throat start to ache, just ache. Of course, as soon as my mother heard my voice she started to cry, then she started to laugh and cry at once, and that got me choked up and tears started to fill my eyes. "I'm OK," I said, "I'm OK." And then that really opened the floodgates. First I was crying because she was crying, but then I was crying because of what I was saying—*I'm OK, I'm OK*—for some reason, that really got me going. Danny was sitting there on the couch, and he just lowered his gaze. He didn't leave and he didn't watch. He stayed there, but he lowered his head, like some kind of gesture of respect, offering me my privacy and his companionship at the same time. I leaned on the end table and put my hand over my eyes and sobbed.

Then my father got on the line. He wanted to know if I was OK. He wanted to know if I was in trouble. And once those things were out of the way, he took a deep breath and lit into me. He wanted to know where the hell I'd been. He wanted to know what I thought I was doing, why was I screwing up like this. I told him I needed to get away.

"Get away from what?"

"I don't know. Everything."

"But you were doing so well."

"I flunked three courses!"

"Before that, I mean. You've proven you can handle college, you were doing really well at Hillsdale. So why do you want to screw things up?"

"I don't *want* to screw things up."

"If you didn't *want* to screw things up, you wouldn't have taken off on the lam. This is just willful, Rob. The same old shit you pulled in high school. What are you hoping to accomplish?"

"Does everything have to be an *accomplishment*?"

"Now, Rob," said my mother, "he just means . . ."

"I can talk for myself here, Linda."

"Ken . . ."

"You don't need to get mad at *her,*" I cried. "*I'm* the one who's fucking up!"

"You're not . . ."

"Oh, yes, I am! You heard what he said! I'm the fuckup of the century! And I'm doing it all on purpose! Yeah! I can't wait to fuck up my life bigtime!"

It went on like that, escalating, and before I knew it we were screaming again and I hung up on him. Which really made me feel like a shit. But I also felt like I had a right. My mother called back half an hour later to try to explain him, as usual. *He's hurt that you didn't come home this summer. He's hurt that you didn't come to him if you were having troubles at school. He's bent over backward for you,* blah, blah. She tried to get me to call him back but I said we'd just start fighting again. We always started fighting again, and I was tired of the same old fight. But I finally told her I'd think about it.

The rest of that night I talked with Danny about joining the navy. He said the navy was the best thing that ever happened to him. Got him away from home, got him out to see the world, taught him a few skills, so that now he had this pretty good job at a radio station as an engineer. He got pretty excited about it, telling me about it, and I had to admit it sounded neat, sailing all around. He said he'd take me down to the navy yard and show me the boats and stuff. He seemed pretty much convinced this was the answer to my problem, just join the navy and that'll solve everything.

I wasn't exactly sure I was looking for a *solution* to anything, but I considered it. It did give you a paycheck and teach you some skills and give you a place to be. And if I wanted to travel, well, you sure get to travel in the navy. And Danny was there, nodding along, approving of all the advantages I was parroting back to him, and Janice was there making jokes about how I'd become an admiral, and it all sounded pretty good. But when we went down to look at the boats, I just couldn't bring myself to it. The thought of living on that boat and not being able to get off, of being trapped on that boat with a thousand other guys—it made my neck start to burn. Even though the thing was moving, it seemed like being in jail.

So a few days later I borrowed some money from Danny and hit the road instead. I headed north, toward Seattle. Maybe I'd get a job in a coffee bar. Maybe I'd wash dishes, who knew? All I knew was, I couldn't go home. Not yet. I knew at some point I would, I knew at some point I wanted to, but first I wanted to find out if there wasn't *someplace* in the world I could be where I didn't feel like a shit. And I knew for sure that place wasn't home.

I met this guy on the bus who told me that Portland was the place to be and that he had a friend who owned some apartments that he might be willing to rent on a weekly basis. So I got myself a place to hang, basically just a furnished room, and found a job through the paper selling encyclopedias. I wasn't very good at it, but there was a chance to win a trip to Hawaii, so I stuck with it awhile. What we used to do was, the trainer, Ted, would pick us up every day around three at the publisher's offices. There were four of us in his team, and he'd drive us out to some little town and set us loose. Drop one here, drop one there, drop one on the other side of town—like he was setting traps for mice, except we were attack dogs. We'd prowl through the neighborhoods, knocking on doors, trying to get people to sign up for these books.

The deal was that they got the books free—although Ted reminded us all the time never to use the word "free"—as long as they agreed to buy the yearbook every year for the rest of their lives, or something. The whole deal ended up costing them hundreds of dollars, but it was parceled out in a way it didn't really look like that. It made me feel a little slimy, especially when some of the people I was talking to could barely read, but I had to be someplace doing something and Ted kept telling me how much money I was going to make, which was just what I needed to hear. And it was kind of neat to have someone believe in me like that, especially when I wasn't giving him much reason to yet.

Even if it *was* Ted. I mean, Ted was a little weird. He was a whole different kind of person than what I was used to, and not the kind of person I was particularly attracted to. Too much ego, too much bragging. In a way kind of overbearing. But he really took an interest in me. Every time he dropped me off, he always said "Go get 'em, Tiger." And even though I wasn't exactly overly good at this, he acted like he could see the potential, like he knew all I needed was a little experience and confidence. It made me think that maybe I'd finally found where I belonged, in sales. I mean, as a kid I did always like going around to people's houses, going in and talking to them. Wasn't that what a salesman did? Maybe it was right for me. Maybe all I had to do was find that part of myself again, and learn some of the ropes of the trade, and I would have found my place in the world. Not that I'd always work for Ted, and not that I'd necessarily always be a salesman either. But this could be the start of a whole new way of seeing myself. As somebody who could do something. Somebody who could do something well. It made me weak in the knees to think that maybe I was OK after all.

Then one day after Ted had dropped the other guys off, he headed out toward the highway. "Let's have a beer," he said. I said I wanted to work, didn't he want me to work? But he said there was time for that, he was thirsty. Maybe we'd talk about my possibilities in the firm, he said. So we go into the cocktail lounge of this Motel 6 or something and he orders us a couple of beers. The place smells of cigarettes and chlorine from the swimming pool, and it's dark in the middle of the day. We sit in a booth and then he starts talking about how he's really bored these days, he's so bored these days he's even bored with sex. Really, he says, he's just getting tired of doing the same things over and over. He's in the mood for something kinky, something different, you know? "You ever feel that way?" he says.

I kind of shrugged and shook my head. "I don't know."

Then he rubs his ankle next to mine. "Hey, Rob? You ever feel that way?"

I could feel this stuff creeping up inside me. It felt like a vine crawling up my insides, this kind of coiling revulsion. Or excitement, I couldn't tell which.

He moved his leg closer to me, then put his foot between my feet, rubbing his calf against mine. "Hey, Rob?" he said. "You ever get bored? Want to try something different?"

I took a slug of my beer. I felt like I was going to explode. I was out in the middle of the country somewhere, I didn't know where I was. He was my boss. I needed the job. "I'd better get to work," I said.

"Don't worry about the work."

"I need the money."

He put his foot up on my side of the booth, right between my legs. "I'll see that you don't go hungry," he said.

I looked down at his foot and felt this little hard knot in my throat, like I was going to choke, or throw up.

"Come on," he said. "Let's get a room."

I stared at my beer. I was quivering. He stood up, threw some bills on the table. He was huge: six foot three, 280 maybe. He put his hands in his pockets and rattled his change. "Come on," he said.

I followed him into the lobby and went to the men's room while he got the room. Then I followed him outside and down the sidewalk to the room, watching the trucks zoom by on the highway. We passed a maid with a bundle of sheets—"*Hola!*" she said—but I looked away.

He opened the door, I followed him through, then he shut it behind him and locked it. A double bed with an off-yellow spread. A chair, a table, a mirror. Pictures of a matador. Ted turned around and grinned at me, this kind of knowing owner's grin. Then he took off his jacket and his tie and lay down on the bed with a big sigh. Shortsleeve shirt. Ham-shaped forearms. Creases at his wrists. "Hot out there today," he said. He looked at me. "Take your shirt off." I reached for my tie, but just loosened it. I could feel the seething in me find its place, choose its direction.

"Come here," he said. "Don't be nervous." I went over and stood next to him. He laid a hand on the back of my leg. Then he sat up on the edge of the bed and started to unzip my fly. I thought I was going to slug him. I thought I was going to take off running and hitchhike back to town. But I didn't. I let him do it. I let him do it because I wanted him to. And that night I left for home.

3

That Saturday morning in Jackson. Waking up in that room, the smell of cut grass curling up through my window. Hearing the lawn mowers going outside, dogs barking, the sounds of kids playing. Not exactly the same as hearing the El rush by my window. I lay there and stared at the ceiling awhile, watching the light move toward the corner, and listened to the sounds. They were pretty much the same sounds I heard in the mornings when I was a kid, as if they had this neighborhood sound track on an endless loop. I remembered lying here just like this listening to the day as a kid, then getting up to feed my turtle and going downstairs to breakfast. Maybe Mom would have made creamed eggs. I could smell it cooking downstairs, even now. And then I'd hop on my bike and be gone for the day. Visiting friends. Making new friends. Exploring the world outside.

My parents gave me a lot of freedom. I've got to say, that was nice. Of course my dad was always at the hardware store or down in the basement—it wasn't freedom so much as negligence—but I liked being free to go off on my own. It was when he tried to be my friend that it drove me nuts, taking me down in the basement with him like that was some kind of privilege. I didn't want to spend my time underground, especially when I knew my mom had put him up to it. I was happier going off on my own. I would have liked to feel closer to him, but if he wasn't interested, hell, I could entertain myself.

And I did, I had a great time. I was a real little adventurer. It kind of amazes me now, the sense of fearlessness I had. I didn't know where it came from, and I didn't know where it had gone, but lying there in my childhood bed in that drowsy state between sleeping and waking, listening to the sounds of my childhood summers, I felt it again, that sense of being unafraid. It was like a dream, so sharp, so real, but just out of my reach: If I tried to touch it, it disappeared. It made me aware of how far I'd come from those boyhood summers.

But everything looks better in hindsight. And I've studied enough psychology to know I was probably just as full of fears and doubts about myself then as I was now. But it didn't *feel* that way then, at least I didn't remember it feeling that way. I don't know. All I knew for sure was that I thought I remembered a time when I felt better than I did now. When I didn't feel afraid of what I might do, or what I might become, or what I had become. And there was a part of me that wanted to go back to that time, to be a little kid again, to have things taken care of for me. To have breakfast waiting for me when I woke up in the morning. To have nothing to do all day except hop on my bike and go touring around. It was an incredibly strong pull, stronger than I'd thought. Lying there in bed that morning made me realize how much I wanted to go back.

Just like my parents wanted me to.

I threw off the covers, pulled on some shorts, and padded down to the bathroom. I was feeling kind of strange and disjointed, almost like I had motion sickness. Getting out of that bed was exactly what I needed to do, to shake myself free of that nostalgia, but putting myself in motion made me feel a little sick. I found myself weaving down the hall like I didn't have any rudder.

I stepped in the shower and lathered up. It felt good to be naked, adult, with hot water rushing over me. It took that vaguely sick feeling and shot it through with adrenaline, made the nausea start to tingle and uncurl into something else. I lathered up my dick and my balls and felt the tingling focus there, felt the uncurling reach down into my groin and make it grow. It felt like there was a serpent inside me uncoiling its muscular self, reaching down and extending itself through my dick, reaching up and out my throat. I lathered up my ass and slipped a finger into my butt. I felt the serpent extend to its fullest length, formed in a perfect circle now, chasing its tail inside of me. I ground my hips into my fist.

Then my mother knocked on the door. "How soon do you want breakfast?"

I stopped. "I don't know," I called. "Five minutes."

"Shall I bring you some juice?"

"I'll be down in a minute!"

"Orange or pineapple?"

"I'll be *down*!"

I listened a minute. She seemed to have gone. My dick had started to soften. I yanked on it and shook it up to get it back in line, then finished what I'd started. But when I came, it wasn't release so much as a kind of painful bleeding.

★ ★ ★

I spent the morning with my dad at the hardware store. It was good to see the gang there—Hezekiah, Arnold, Cynthia—and I've got to say my dad behaved well. He didn't give me the litany of all the reasons I should come back, didn't give me any lectures about finishing school, or getting my life on track. But I did feel him watching me move through the store, talking with the others, and I knew he was trying to picture me there as the manager. I knew he was watching for signs that I was warming to the idea.

It felt pretty much familiar. I'd felt like my dad had been *watching* me ever since that business with Jerry Houseman fifteen years before. All of a sudden, after that, he took this enormous interest in me, always poking at me with questions. *How are things at school? You making friends? Anybody giving you trouble?* But if I started telling him about school, or about my friends, pretty soon his eyes would glaze over and he'd go back down to the basement, which really made me feel like a shit.

It became clear to me after a while that he didn't really want the answers, he just wanted reassurance. Wanted me to tell him he was OK, he was a good father. I wasn't fucked up, I wasn't a mess, Jerry Houseman hadn't made me a raving maniac after all. That was about the time I started doing everything I could to convince my father otherwise, just to piss him off. Got in my little scrapes with the law, started screaming at him to leave me alone when he started pestering me. Which made him get even more concerned and start asking me even more questions.

I think it was when I took off across country that he finally started to settle down. I think it made him see I meant business. Or maybe it was the fact that I came back from that outing a little less arrogant, a little less sure I knew what was best for me, or for anyone else. But in either case, we both seemed to get more civilized after that. I agreed to go to junior college until I got my grades back up, and eventually he agreed to let me transfer to Chicago. He still hovered around me sometimes, but only rarely did he actually voice his questions anymore. Now he just hung around, watching me, the questions thickening the air.

The reunion that night was at the Holiday Inn out at the intersection of I-94 and 127, across from where my mom used to work. The parking lot was practically full. I had to park way out at the edge near the Chinese restaurant and hike back to the entrance. It was a balmy twilit evening, a three-quarter moon rising over the highway, the trucks zooming by beneath it with their running lights already on.

When I walked into the lobby, I could hear "Thriller" throbbing down the hall: The party was in full swing. Debra Donovan and Paula Wysocki were at the reception table, passing out name tags and directories. The Viking statue from the school's trophy case was on the table beside them. Paula shrieked and ran around the table to give me a hug; Debra didn't recognize me. Everybody looked pretty good, although an awful lot of them seemed respectable before their time. One guy was even wearing a suit.

I hadn't been there ten minutes when Nancy Lamley grabbed my elbow and told me Patty was looking for me. Nancy was our runner in high school, the one who always carried messages back and forth between us when we were having our fights. It made me laugh to think that ten years later here she was again playing the same role, as if everything were fixed out of time and no matter how much time went by nothing would ever change. Nancy Lamley would always be running messages between Patty and me. And Patty and I would always be looking for each other.

I didn't find her right away. Every time I took a step I ran into someone else covering up their name tag to see if I could remember who they were. It was a pretty frantic party, everyone talking a mile a minute, every conversation getting interrupted by another. It was a relief to discover that nobody had their shit *that* well together that I had to feel so bad. Everybody was just getting started. So I was a year or two behind, so what? It wasn't a race. It didn't feel like a race.

They played records from our high school days. Huey Lewis. Elvis Costello. Depeche Mode. Police. When I heard REO Speedwagon start up with "I Can't Fight This Feeling," I immediately looked around for Patty, automatically. It was just like the dances in high school—whenever that song played, we'd find each other, even if we hadn't been speaking the whole night, sometimes. I saw her by the pool, sort of waiting, sort of expecting me. I was near the dance floor, she saw me, so I just sort of cocked my head toward the floor to ask her if she wanted to dance. She smiled this kind of wistful smile, and slowly walked toward me. More womanly now, more confident. Blonder now than she'd been before. Smoky eyes. White dress. Bare shoulders.

She brushed past me—"Nice tie," she said—and walked out on the floor, just barely touching me as she passed, her fragrance just a suggestion. I followed her onto the floor and we slipped into each other's arms as if we'd been dancing all night long. We knew exactly how to hold each other, knew exactly how our bodies fit, even though our bodies were different now. We tried to talk a little at first, but after a while we just danced. And I felt that feeling with her again, that quiet, gentle unfolding. Just the slightest hint of it, almost just a sensory memory triggered by the scent of her hair, the warmth of her neck, the touch of her hand. I closed my eyes and we just moved, although as the song went on we moved less and less, until by the end of the song we were pretty much just standing together there, holding each other on the dance floor. Another song started up and people started brushing past us, jabbering at each other. We pulled apart and looked at each other. She had that same look in her eyes, that wistful this-can-never-be look she used to get sometimes in high school after we'd had another fight, a look she always wore in the moment before we fell in love again. Then she smiled, a weary smile. "Old times," she said, and she blinked real slow. I nodded and took a deep breath, let it out.

"Buy you a drink?"

She nodded.

I got us a couple of beers and we took a seat on the far edge of the pool, away from all the crowd. She took off her shoes and dangled her feet in the water and told me about this computer outfit in Colorado she worked with. When I told her I was working as a bartender, still going to school, she didn't even make me feel like a shit. She sounded kind of appreciative, even. "I figured you'd do some exploring," she said, "before you settled on something."

She showed me her engagement ring and told me about her fiancé, an architect in Denver. I watched her as she talked about him, watched the shy kind of smile it gave her, and it made me grin. Then we talked about some of the people we'd seen. How slick and rich Brian Carter looked, how fat Ellen Corbin had gotten, how brave it was of Sam Esposito to come even though he had AIDS. We shared a laugh over Nancy Lamley still running messages.

Then she tossed back her hair and turned to me. "So how about you?" she said. "Are you seeing anybody?"

"Nobody special," I said.

She nodded, then looked down at her feet. They looked kind of green and ghostlike in the underwater light.

"I haven't seen anyone special since you," I said. I couldn't believe I'd said it.

She swung her feet back and forth in the water, smiled a little smile. "Why not?"

"Oh," I said, making a joke of it, "no one could compare."

She shifted her weight and squinted at me. "Then why did you run off?" There was something in her tone that wasn't altogether a joke anymore.

"I don't know," I said. I looked at her feet. "I couldn't do it anymore."

"What's that?"

I looked at her again, then at the party, then back at her feet. "You remember what we were like," I said. "The on-again, off-again, on-again stuff."

She grinned and bumped a shoulder against me. "I think it was just the on-again stuff. I don't think you ever really liked love."

I bumped her back. "I like love," I protested. I didn't know what else to say. I turned to her, shrugged, shook my head. "I used to have this dream that you and I were getting married . . ."

"You did?"

"Yeah," I laughed. "All the time." I crossed my legs beneath me, campfire-style, and lit a cigarette. "I was in the room in back, in the church, where the groom and the best man and the preacher hang out until it's time? My best man was there, but it wasn't Danny. I never knew who it was. Never saw his face. I was always busy straightening my tie, smoking a cigarette. And then I'd hear the music start the wedding march. And we'd go to the door—me, the best man and the preacher—and I wouldn't be able to move. I wouldn't be able to go through the door. It felt like there was some force field there or something that repelled me. I couldn't pass through it." I looked at her but not at her, I was looking at the dream. "I haven't thought about this in years, I'd forgotten all about this. I never figured it out. All I knew was, there were all these people out there waiting for me, but I couldn't go through the door. I don't know what I thought was going to happen . . ." I gazed at the dream a moment more, then looked back at Patty.

Her face turned into a puzzle. "So that's why you broke off with me?"

I drew back and looked at her. "*I* broke off with *you*?"

She leaned toward me, peered up at me. "Well, you're the one who left town," she whispered. She was smiling at me.

I stared at her, then laughed. "Oh, yeah," I mumbled. "Forgot about that."

Her shoulders lurched a little with amusement, then she tossed back her head and ran her fingers through her hair a couple of times. She planted her hands on the edge of the pool and settled into herself. We sat there staring at the water, watching her feet swing back and forth in that eerie underwater light. They were playing "Private Dancer," another song we used to dance to a lot. She bumped a bare shoulder against me again.

"Old times," she whispered.

"Good times," I said.

The next day there was a picnic at the pavilion in the park for everybody who didn't get reunited enough at the party. I didn't have anything else to do, so after breakfast with my folks and a look at the *Free Press,* I headed over to check it out.

I stopped at the Rix on Prospect first to get some cigarettes. There were a lot of people there—an unusual number for Sunday morning, I thought—and only one cashier on duty. I watched her while I waited in line. A high school girl with fingernails, pimples and a wad of gum, a ring on every finger. She must have been more hung over than me. She picked up every object delicately, as if it gave her pain, and sort of *fondled* it as she searched for the price tag. The woman she was waiting on was buying five years' worth of diapers.

I turned around just to shift my weight and change the view a little and caught eyes with the woman behind me. She looked up at the instant I turned around and looked directly at me. There was no pretending I hadn't seen her, no pretending for her she hadn't seen me. I tried to look away, but my gaze snapped back to hers as if it were on a short, yanked leash. It was Mrs. Houseman, Jerry's wife. Her face went slack and paled three shades. She looked tiny standing there clutching her toothpaste, gazing up at me through her glasses. I wanted to brush her off me, the way you'd brush an ant off you at a picnic, but it felt like she was stuck to me. It was that hollow-eyed, horrified stare, the kind of stare that could burn you up. I tried to look away again but couldn't. And it suddenly dawned on me that she couldn't look away from me either. It made me feel softer toward her, like we were survivors in the same lifeboat. I nodded, to release her. "Mrs. Houseman," I said.

"You're so handsome!" she blurted out. Then her horror doubled for saying something so stupid. I smiled and glanced away, sure that the spell had been broken. But when I glanced back at her again, she was still staring at me. It made me want to smack her.

"How's *Jerry*?" I said. The words just burst out of my mouth. It's not like I really wanted to know, I just said it to scare her off, to make her stop staring at me. Or maybe I did want to know. But as soon as I said it, I was sorry I had.

She opened her mouth in a little O. Her whole head seemed to empty out somehow, like there was a wind blowing through it. She seemed lost, a little child, a confused old woman who realizes she's in unfamiliar territory and doesn't know how to get home. "He died," she whispered. "In prison."

My stomach jumped. I opened my mouth but no words would come out. My gaze seemed fastened on her now just like hers had been fastened on me, and she was left to figure out how to get me off her.

"They said it was suicide," she said. Her voice was a little stronger now, but shaky, quavering. "Some people say it was murder."

Was she accusing me of this? Was that the weirdness in her voice? Or was it just the weirdness of having to say this while standing in line to buy toothpaste at Rix on Sunday morning from a girl with rings on every finger?

"I . . . I'm sorry," I stammered. "I didn't know."

She nodded and looked down.

"Next," said the girl, cracking her gum. I glanced around. "Marlboros," I said. I started fishing in my pockets for change. "When?" I said to Mrs. Houseman.

"Several years ago."

"Two twenty-five," said the girl.

I paid her, then backed away from the line. "I'm sorry," I said to Mrs. Houseman as she stepped up to the cashier. She nodded again, set her toothpaste on the counter, asked for some Tylenol.

It felt like I ought to stay around and talk to her or something. I mean, she just told me her husband was dead. You don't just walk out after that, do you? Or do you? But she was busy with the cashier and I didn't have anything to say. And I never wanted to get out of someplace so bad in my life.

"I'm sorry," I said again, more to myself than to her, then I turned and walked into the electric-eye post that opens the door. It got me right in the crotch and I doubled up then hurried out the door, bent over. I beelined for my car and got in, then fumbled to open the cigarettes. I ripped one open in my struggle, spilling tobacco in my lap, then punched the dashboard lighter and waited, tapping my foot, just staring at it. I started rocking back and forth to try to urge it along. Just kept my eyes on the lighter and rocked. When it popped, I stopped for a moment, not sure what to do. Then all at once I grabbed it and jabbed it at my cigarette, bending the paper and pulling some tobacco out in the process.

I exhaled and looked out the window. Mrs. Houseman was crossing the parking lot and getting into her car. I wanted to gun my motor and run her over, then keep on going. I clutched the wheel with both hands. She opened her door and tilted as she got into her car. Her head looked small in the driver's seat. She pulled out of her space and crossed the parking lot on the diagonal, very slow, the sun gleaming off her chrome, then took a left on Prospect, heading up toward town. I started my car and pulled onto Francis, just to get off that fucking hot asphalt, and headed in the other direction.

Murdered. Dead. Suicide. That stupid fucking fool. That stupid fucking imbecile. What the fuck did he think he was doing, fucking around with a little kid? What the fuck did he think he was doing? Didn't he know he was going to get fucked? Didn't he know they'd string him up and carve their initials in him? What a fucking *fucking* asshole.

Dead. He killed himself for *that*? For a couple of rumbles in the sack, he went and offed himself? How did he do it? Did he shoot himself, stick a gun in his mouth and shoot? That would have been appropriate. But he couldn't have gotten a gun. So he slit his wrists. Or hung himself. Or jumped off a railing or something. How do you kill yourself in prison?

Or did he get killed? Cut up? Beat to death? How did those things happen in all those cellblock movies? Who was it that killed him? One guy, or a bunch? Where were the guards? What the fuck did it matter?

Why didn't anyone tell me about it?

I drove out through Vandercook Lake then got on 127 and zoomed north. When I hit I-94, I went west. I ran the car up to seventy and tried to hold it there, just concentrated on the speed to see if I could keep it exactly at seventy, not slowing or speeding. I aligned myself with those dashboard numerals, the seven on one side, the zero on the other, and drove straight down the middle. I listened to the wind in the windows. Watched the flatness of the sun on the road.

Jerry Houseman, dead. In a way, I'd been wishing for that

all my life. Wishing that I could just wipe him out of my past, reverse his force field or something so that he never even existed. In some way, I'd willed this to happen to him, I'd willed him out of existence. It scared the fucking shit out of me to think I had that power. I knew it didn't make any sense, I knew I hadn't made it happen, but it felt that way and it scared me.

And in a way I did make it happen. I was the one who sent him there. I was the one who told the police. And even before that, I was the one who made him do what he did.

I didn't make him do it.

He was the one who made me do it.

And do it, and do it, and do it.

Then why did it feel like I was the one who was at fault for this?

Jerry Houseman, dead. Why did this have to come back to me now? I'd done my best not to think of him for the last fifteen years. After all that courtroom shit, I made the decision I'd never think about him again for the rest of my life. I knew I'd never really forget it, but I didn't have to think about it and I wasn't going to. Besides, everybody else was thinking about it plenty enough for me. My dad with all his fucking questions. My mother with her, her I-don't-know-what-it-was. The counselors at school, the kids. It was like I'd disappeared, like all that was left of me was what had happened with Jerry Houseman. All anybody saw when they looked at me was sexual acts. And they either snickered or got all flustered and bothered and didn't know what to say or they handled me as delicately as if I'd just had surgery. They got over it, in time, most of them. And there were always a few good friends who treated me just the same, all through it. But some of the people really loved it. The snickers, the horror, whatever. They dug it.

I was a walking tabloid. And after all that, I never wanted to hear Jerry Houseman's name again.

I never talked about it, except with Patty once or twice. And with Linda, in California. But with Linda I kind of used it, strung it out to her as a sexual tease to let her know I'd had affairs before with older people. I thought she'd get off on it, and she did. She got off on the strangeness of it. It made me exotic to her because I didn't seem upset by it. I told it to her like it was a goof, like I'd had this affair when I was just twelve, like I was such a stud I was already doing it before my pubic hair had even filled in. I didn't tell her about the prison or the courtroom stuff. I just let her know I'd had this affair, let her know she wasn't the first in my pants, and wouldn't be the last. It made me feel sly, to do that. It made me feel like what had happened had been of some use to me, or at least that I could put it to use. It wasn't your run-of-the-mill experience. I wasn't just another kid off the bus. I had a history.

With Patty it was different. With Patty it was harder. One night she just asked me, straight out, "What was it like?" It came out of nowhere. We were parked in my car in the Dibble School lot, where we always went to be alone. It was a nippy night in October during one of our quiet times, in between our fights.

I didn't have an answer ready. "It wasn't like anything," I said. "It was like itself, I don't know. It was sort of . . . I don't know. It hurt." She just cuddled up next to me and sat there waiting for more, so I started talking about it and ended up telling her all about it. The things he made me do, the way people treated me after. I cried about it a little. When I finished, she didn't say anything, she just reached up and touched my cheek, and we made love after that. I felt closer to her that night than I'd ever felt to anybody. I felt healed, like her love had come inside me and set things right at last. She changed the chemical balance in me. Realigned my molecules, set everything to humming. That was the first time I'd ever talked about it to anybody and they hadn't gotten all upset about it. It was the first time anybody just left it alone, just let it lie.

But the next day, or a day or two later, she said she'd been thinking about what I'd told her and it just made her so mad she wanted to kill that guy.

"Stop it," I said.

"But it makes me so mad . . ."

"Just let it be," I said.

And we never talked about it again.

Now Jerry Houseman was dead. After all those years of not talking about it, after all those years of not thinking about it, I didn't know what reaction to have. I sort of hoped if I kept driving, if I kept the car at seventy and never let it slow down, I could outrun any reaction at all. But what exactly was I outrunning? What was I supposed to be feeling?

Well, it was clear what I was *supposed* to be feeling. That was clear from the start, from the moment I told my mom about it. My mom's reaction. My dad's reaction. Danny's reaction. The kids at school. The lawyers, the teachers, the counselors. Even one fucking reporter who waited for me after school. It was clear what they all thought, and felt. And I guess I thought it and felt it with them. It was like whatever *I* thought about it, whatever *I* felt about it, just got folded up like a tent and slipped in a trunk someplace. There wasn't any room for it, I was so busy fielding everybody else's reaction. Now, where was the trunk I'd put myself in? Was there anything in there still?

When I finally came around enough to actually notice where I was, I was almost to Battle Creek. I thought about driving right on to Chicago, just escaping back into my life, lift off in Spaceship Shy-Town. Maybe I'd talk to Phyllis about it, or get drunk with Nick. Maybe we could all get together, have a little party. Reuben could turn it into an outfit. I didn't know, we'd find a way. But when I got to Battle Creek, I did a U-turn on the overpass and headed back toward Jackson. I had to get my clothes, anyway. I had to say good-bye to my folks. And besides, I did have a place to go.

By the time I got to the picnic, the softball game was already under way. Patty was hanging out on the sidelines, waiting for her turn at bat. Sleeveless blouse and tennis shorts, hair pulled back in a ponytail. She waved. I went and stood next to her.

"How you doin'?" I said.

"*Creamin'* them," she crowed. She looked at me closer. "You OK? You look a little peaked."

"Oh," I said. I glanced away, then looked back at her. "I just found out Jerry Houseman died."

She got this sort of hurt-puppy look of automatic sympathy, then her eyes flicked recognition. "Was he that guy in our algebra class . . . ?"

I started to tell her no, but all of a sudden there was all this shouting and she turned to look at the game. Someone had just been thrown out at home and the teams were changing places. Jim Donnelly trotted past and threw her his glove, but it bounced off her head and she lurched after it. She took a step toward the field, then hesitated and looked at me.

"Uh . . . how did it happen?" she said.

"Oh," I said. "Car accident. Or something. I'm not sure of the details. It's no big deal. We weren't close. I just thought you might remember him."

She shrugged and shook her head. "Sorry."

I gestured toward the field. "Knock 'em dead."

I watched her run out to center field. Some of the guys on her team called to me to get a glove and join in—they had something like seventeen people on the field—but I waved them off and grabbed a beer from the cooler instead. I watched the game for a little while; it was really pretty funny. Everybody was just the same as they'd been in high school. All the personalities, just the same. Either people never changed, or high school reunions made them revert. It was fun, it was like the night before but funnier, more relaxed.

I found myself watching Patty in center field, bent over, her hands on her knees, calling out insults to the batter, and I had this strange feeling come over me that she was irrelevant to me. She had been important to me once, and was still important because of that, but now she was sort of off the point. She wasn't any less interesting, or any less good, or beautiful. It wasn't that she didn't matter. It was just that she wasn't part of my life. She was basically an acquaintance now, essentially just a stranger. It wasn't an unpleasant feeling, exactly. But it did make me wonder if she'd been a stranger all along. Or if everybody was always strangers. And it did make me feel a little alone, under the circumstances. So I finally grabbed another beer and wandered off by myself.

It was a beautiful, buzzing day, a few fat clouds cruising by, real high. I walked over to the rose garden and through the abandoned zoo where I used to practice popping wheelies, then wandered down the service lane that led to the back of the park. An ugly little mutt came barreling down the tobogganing hill and danced around me a couple of times, wagging his tail like he'd been looking for me all his life. I knelt down and rubbed his ears and his belly and he shellacked my face with his tongue, then he took off running again as fast and furious as before, looking for the next adventure.

I wandered on down the lane, still sort of smiling from the puppy, and finally found myself at the dirt bike hill where I used to ride in the summers. And the brook, where Jerry kissed me. It made a tightening come up in my throat, and a stirring below my throat, near my chest. The brook where Jerry kissed me. I stood on the hill and looked down at it. Felt the heat of the sun on my shoulders, felt the breeze in my hair. I sidestepped down the hill, then reached the bottom and looked back up. It was hotter down there, less breeze. The world felt more concentrated. I was absolutely alone, the only sound was the brook and the buzz of the beetles.

I sat on a stone in the sun and stared back up the hill. The sound of the beetles, the smell of the grass, the bubbling of the brook, it all took me back. Back further still than my high school days, back now to my childhood. I could almost see myself riding my bike up and down that hill, and feel myself do it, at once. Could feel the heat and sweat, the strain, the effort to get to the top. The falling back, the trying again, the triumph when I made it. Then skidding back down the hill again to start the whole thing over. The freedom in that repetition, the total concentration, and the exhilaration of it. Those were the days. Those were great days. Those were the days I was all of one piece, just one person, whole. And it seemed to me, sitting there on that rock, I hadn't been just one person since.

I sat there for quite a while, watching myself, watching who I had been, before I realized that I was sitting on the rock that Jerry had sat on to watch me when we came here together. It almost made me get up, move away, as if it were an electric chair, but then for some reason I took a deep breath and let myself settle into it, let myself get comfortable. I pulled my feet up under me and lit a cigarette, then watched the smoke drift up into the air and dissipate. I took another puff and let it out and watched it dissipate too. Then watched a bird fly by real high.

I'd loved having him for an audience. No adult had ever taken such an interest in what I was doing. He seemed to get as much of a thrill from it as I did. He followed my progress up the hill, winced when I fell, cheered when I reached the top. I loved that sense of being watched, of knowing someone was there. I became a circus act on that hill, leaping, spinning, doing my tricks, with my audience of one. Sometimes Jerry tried it too, and it always gave me a kick to see him struggle and fail at what I could do. We were on my turf at the dirt bike hill. The rules were all upside down.

It seemed like I'd never felt that before, better than an adult. I must have, though. A kid always has more energy than his parents do, he can always run and jump better. But somehow this was different. Grown-ups always laughed when you beat them, always waved their hands in the air in surrender and gasped for air, complaining about how old they were getting. Jerry never did that. Jerry just kept trying. It was like he really *wanted* to ride his bike as well as I did, or something. It was neat to have a grown-up friend who didn't pull grown-up stuff on you, like pretending they didn't care anymore when you won the race. I don't know. I liked having him there.

But when he kissed me. Jesus Christ. It was so weird to think of it now. I remembered how big his face was. I remembered how bristly his mustache was. And I remembered how scared he looked. That's what I remembered, the fear in his eyes. It felt like he was scared of me, and that made me scared.

But I also felt . . . God, could I remember this? I felt excited by it. Was it just the fear that excited me? I don't know. It was all mixed up. Fear and excitement and pleasure at being touched that way. No one had ever kissed me like that. I wasn't even sure what it was, except I'd seen it in movies. But I'd never seen a man kiss a boy. I knew it wasn't right and I could tell Jerry knew that too. But he did it anyway. I could see how scared he was and he did it anyway.

And all those feelings in me—the fear, the confusion, the pleasure, the stirring—they all got mushed together somehow, forged into some new compound, some new feeling I'd never had before. One feeling, but full of components, the components all too confusing if you tried to separate them out, but when they were combined they became this incredibly powerful pull, like the pull of the current on your feet. Strong, insistent, steady. But this was in my chest, inside. Somewhere just below my throat. Somewhere just above my heart. This powerful sense of being needed.

But all of that came later. That first time, all the confusion didn't really come together yet. It was only later, in remembering it. Only later, when Jerry tried it again. Then another time, when he did it again, and my fear began to subside. I wasn't being hurt by this, I was surviving this OK. Then the other feelings started to grow. The being needed. Being wanted. Being stimulated. But especially the fact that he liked me so much he'd do what scared him most. It made me feel lit up.

After a while I got used to being caressed, and even kissed. I didn't like the kissing so much, his face was so scratchy, his mouth was so big. But I didn't mind the caressing, the caressing felt kind of good, exciting. I knew this was something secret, something no one should know we were doing. He was very explicit about it, although he didn't have to be, I knew. Maybe that was part of the excitement. But I'd never felt my body come alive like that.

Then he took it further, had me touch him. I remembered the first time, how disgusting it was. His loose-fitting skin, the hair everywhere, the worminess of it. The smell of his crotch was like peanut butter. But then, thinking about it later, I was fascinated by it and the next time we were alone I touched him through his pants, unasked. I wanted to know more about it. What was that thing? What would it do? Would my thing do that too? I was scared at every step of the way, but Jerry led me through it, always urging me on a little but never pushing too hard. He never made me do anything I didn't agree to do.

Shit. I couldn't believe I was sitting there thinking those stupid thoughts. I was just a little kid, I didn't have the power to agree or disagree. I couldn't believe I was sitting there actually thinking that what Jerry Houseman did to me was not so bad. It *was* so bad. It was disgusting. I was disgusted with it myself, at the time. One day I came home after being with him and drank a glass of water—to purify myself, I thought—then broke the glass in the sink on purpose as part of the ritual because I was so ashamed of myself.

But then a few days later I went back to him, went over to his house and crawled into bed with him, naked. I remembered I looked forward to it. I thought about it all afternoon. It felt like exploring a cave, some underground cavern. It was dark and scary and full of echoes, but it was intriguing, exciting. And I was very curious.

Was that the secret I'd folded away and put in a trunk fifteen years ago? No one would let me say that. No one would let me say that I had enjoyed my time with Jerry Houseman. Not that it was the greatest thing that ever happened to me. Ultimately it was probably the worst, with all the stuff that came after. But it was a part of my experience. It was a part of my history. And it wasn't just something that happened to me, the way everybody said. Nobody wanted to hear that, and I sure didn't want to say it. In the middle of all that outrage, I wasn't going to stand up and say I was as bad as Jerry Houseman, even though I felt it.

I never intended for it to turn into the circus it did. I was just pissed off at him that night. I was just getting tired of it. As time went on, I'd started to feel like there was going to be more and more, that his need for me just kept growing and growing, that he was going to gobble me up. He wasn't just exploring a cave. He was leading me down into it and wanted me to live there with him, wanted me to stay underground. Just like my father. Underground. All the men were underground. They never gave you much up top, you had to go down in the dark with them and do what they wanted to do.

But I wanted my life to be mine again. I wanted to hang out with my friends and get to know girls and go to parties. I wanted to be a kid awhile longer. Or, I don't know, *not* a kid anymore, hanging out with an adult. I wanted to be a teenager, hanging out with teenagers. I wanted to do something else. But every time I told Jerry I wanted to go off with my friends, he came up with more things for us to do, gave me bigger and bigger gifts. I liked the gifts. I liked my bike, my typewriter, I liked my models and tapes and books. So I kept seeing him. But I kept resenting it more and more and demanding more and more presents from him until finally that night at the mall, I'd had it.

I didn't mean him to go to prison. I didn't mean him to get killed. I just wanted him to stop. But once I told, it went out of control and all I could do was fold it all in, pull myself inside my shell like my turtle and wait for it to pass. Which I did. And it finally passed. But somehow I never came out again. Fifteen years, it was fifteen years, and I was still in hiding.

4

By the time I got home, it was almost three. My mom was in the kitchen, cutting strawberries for the shortcake she'd promised. I angled off the refrigerator and wedged in the corner of the counter.

"How was the picnic?"

"OK, I guess." I took a cookie out of the jar, nibbled on it, stared at the floor. My body felt like a double exposure, out of alignment with itself. "I saw Mrs. Houseman at the drugstore," I said. I didn't know I was going to say it. "She told me Jerry's dead."

My mom stopped cutting, then started again. "I know," she said, not looking up.

"How did you know?"

"I heard."

I stared at the kitchen floor, the flecked yellow squares I used to crawl around on when I was a little kid. I could hear my dad mowing the lawn out back, could smell the fresh-cut grass. "They say he killed himself," I said.

"I know."

"Some people say it was murder."

"I hadn't heard that part."

I looked at my mother, still cutting. Her mouth was set, the lips pursed tight. She looked down at her work through her bifocals so she seemed to be looking down her nose at something she found distasteful. "How come you didn't tell me?" I said.

"I didn't think you'd want to know." She placed a berry on the counter beside her without looking up. Was it meant for me? I couldn't tell.

"Why didn't you think I'd want to know?"

"It's over. It's in the past." She rinsed her knife beneath the tap and set it beside the berry. The water beaded up on it, dropped onto the countertop.

"But he's *dead,*" I said, staring at the knife. I looked up at her again. "Didn't you think I'd want to know?"

She hosed the sink with the spray nozzle, sweeping the strawberry greens into the disposal. "Why should you want to know?"

"Because I *knew* him."

She curled her lip. "You'd be better off if you hadn't." She flicked on the disposal and the whole counter shook with the suck and growl of the greens getting pulverized. I waited until she turned it off, until the residual whirring stopped and the room was silent again except for the sound of my dad out back.

"But I did," I said. "I did know him."

My mother dumped the bowl of strawberries into a colander and shook them under the tap. "I thought it would be better if you just left it behind you," she said, glancing over at me. "There was nothing you could have done with that information except get upset by it. And there's nothing you could have done to prevent it." She turned off the tap, shook the colander and dumped the berries back into the bowl—crisp, brisk, efficient. Then she wiped her hands on the dish towel, satisfied that her task was done, preparing for the next one.

I felt something move inside of me. I looked at the kitchen floor again. Settled lower, shifted gears. "I didn't have to send him to prison."

She froze, her hands still balled in the towel, and looked at me sideways, wary, annoyed. "What else were we supposed to do? Slap his hand and tell him 'bad boy! Don't you ever do that again!'?"

I held her gaze as long as I could, which wasn't very long at all, then lowered my eyes to the floor again. Why was my neck on fire, all at once? Why was my stomach tightening up? I swallowed to open my throat. "You didn't have to call the police."

My mother turned to face me full on, the dish towel balled in one fist on her hip, the other hand propped on the counter. "Now, wait just a minute here," she said. "Am I getting this right? Are you standing here telling me I was wrong because I tried to protect you?"

I felt a roiling in my stomach sort of like the feeling I'd always get in the moment before I'd start another fight with Patty. "You didn't protect me," I heard myself say. "What did you protect me from?"

My mother's face went slack with shock. "From that pervert!" she cried, indignant.

"You didn't *protect* me from him," I said. "He'd already *done* what he did."

She stiffened as if against a strong wind. When she spoke her lips barely moved. "And he would have gone right out and done it again to someone else, you can bet."

"So you *weren't* protecting me," I said. The words came out like a cry, a whine. "You were protecting everyone *else.*"

She looked at me, exasperated, then let out a long sigh. "I wanted him punished," she said flatly. "I wanted him prevented from ever doing that again." She shook the dish towel over the sink. "I didn't know what else to do."

I watched her tuck the towel into the ring below the counter, and for a moment she looked different to me, like she was a different person, someone I'd never seen before. "What exactly do you think he did?" I said.

She slid me a slow, cold stare. "I don't have to tell you," she said. "You were there."

I held her gaze until she looked down, and felt something slip into place in my mind. Now I recognized her. She'd been a stranger in the moment before, but now I recognized her. "You're right," I said. "I was there." The words were strangely hard to say. I leaned toward her, incredulous. "And you've never forgiven me for it, have you?"

There was a moment when nothing happened. Then she muttered a muffled "What?"

I edged out of my corner toward her. "You've never forgiven me for it," I said. "You've never forgiven me for what I did with Jerry Houseman."

"That's ridiculous," she rasped. She started searching the cupboards for something, opening doors and closing them.

I took another step toward her. "You stopped touching me after that . . ."

"I did not." She turned away from me and angled out into the room, then glanced around, disoriented.

I felt a cloud roll up in my chest. "Whenever I went to kiss you good night, you turned your face away—"

"I did not."

I rocked back on my heels, off balance. "I don't think you've kissed me since that happened . . ."

"Robert," she snapped. "Now stop this." She beelined back to the window as if to call my father in for help. I realized the mower had stopped.

I took another step toward her. "Every time you touched me," I said, "I was aware of how hard it was for you. How your hand didn't change, didn't move, didn't grab hold of me. It was frozen, like the hand of a statue."

She turned and looked at me, curious. "That's not true," she said, uncertain.

I took another step toward her. "I remember watching TV with you. Watching you from the corner of my eye to get a fix on you, trying to figure out just what you really thought of me. Some part of me wanted to sit with you, to put my arm around you or something. But I could feel how tense you were. Your whole body went rigid when I came near."

"Robert, that's just not true," she said. She dodged around me back to the sink, grabbed the towel and wiped the counter.

I spun around and faced her. "I have a *photograph* of it!" I cried. "It's a picture Dad took of us that Christmas, right after Jerry went to prison!"

She threw the towel into the sink. "Robert!" she said. "Now stop it!"

"We're sitting on the couch. Remember? You look so cold in that photo! So *mad*! But you're holding it all in like you're afraid you're going to explode! And there I am, sitting next to you, looking like *I'm* afraid you'll explode!"

She shook her hands beside her head to keep my words out of her ears and started edging away from me, fluttering about the room like a bird trying to get out of its cage, banging against the counter, the oven, the table, the refrigerator.

"Don't you remember that photo?" I said. "There we are, the two of us. Just as rigid as we can be. Both of us trying not to move. Not to look at each other, or touch, for fear of what might happen."

"Stop it!" she snapped. "Just stop!"

"I thought you *hated* me," I cried. "I thought you couldn't stand to be near me!" She froze in the corner by the oven, quivering, her back to me. I stopped, afraid to go further. But then I heard my voice go on, quieter, more curious. "You were nice to me," I said. "You were always nice to me. But you were almost *too* nice to me, like you had to cover something up." I reached toward her. "You know? And I knew if I hadn't started all this you wouldn't be acting this way. I knew if I hadn't started all this, I wouldn't have made you feel so bad that you had to hide it from me."

She turned to me, pleading. "Rob, you didn't . . ."

"It wasn't just bad what I did. It was bad because of what it did to you. And what it did to Dad. And Danny. I made you all ashamed of me."

"We've *never* been ashamed . . ."

"And *mad*! I mean, Danny was so *vindictive*. And Dad was so *happy* that day in court—it was like his football team had won." I turned and moved into the room. I wasn't talking to her anymore; I was talking to myself. "I kept thinking, *prison*. Jerry's going to *prison*. I had this picture of him in my mind, sitting there in this cell, staring out through the bars, reaching out to me to free him. And there was Dad, savoring it. And

Danny, actually cheering." I sank into the chair at the table and looked back at my mother. "He was actually *cheering,*" I said.

She stared at me, stunned, exhausted. Then her shoulders slumped. "Rob, I was never ashamed of you," she said. "I was ashamed of my*self.* I was . . ."

The screen door creaked and my dad came in, wiping his hands on a rag. "Well," he sighed. "I'm glad that's done. How—" He stopped short and looked at us, wary. "What's the matter? What's going on?"

"Jerry Houseman's dead," I said.

He looked at my mother. She yearned toward him as if to apologize, but for what I wasn't sure. Then she collapsed back into her corner and let out a long sigh. "He thinks it's all my fault," she said.

"That's not what I'm saying at *all,*" I cried. "It's just the way you treated me after—" I looked at my dad. He peered back at me. He really didn't have a clue. I leaned across the table toward him, palms flat, my chin almost touching the surface. "I was scared to be with you in those days. I was scared to be in a car with you, because I couldn't get away. I was always scared you'd start asking me questions. *Are you OK? Are you OK? Are you sure you're OK?* All these questions all the time, like you were afraid I wasn't going to be able to tie my shoes anymore, after what Jerry did to me. Like I was going to just sit in a corner and drool."

"He was *concerned* about you."

I looked at my mother and all of a sudden I felt this wall of tears push through me. "You came at me with a *knife*!" I cried.

"What?" said my dad.

"Right here!" I said. "It was just like this! You were standing there and I told you. And you came at me with this knife . . ."

My mother hugged herself as if to keep herself from falling apart. "I was holding the knife when he came in," she muttered to my father. "I was upset . . . I forgot to put it down . . ."

I fell back in my chair and looked up at the ceiling. "For fifteen years," I said, "I've had this picture in my head of someone coming at me with a knife like they were going to attack me. And it's stuck with me, it's stuck in my head. Like they were going to attack me." I pitched forward and caught my head in my hands, staring down at the table. "It pops into my head at weird times. All of a sudden there they are, with this knife. Whenever I want to do something, there they are with this knife." I looked at my mother. "You scared the shit out of me that night. The knife, and then Dad. Then you called the cops. I never wanted all that to happen. I never wanted him to go to prison. I just wanted him to stop."

"What were we supposed to do?" she said.

"You made me feel like a *criminal*! When you chased him down the street, screaming at him. You may as well have been screaming at *me,* calling *me* a criminal!" I looked at my dad. His mouth hung open. I turned toward him and squared myself. "Jerry Houseman started it," I said, drilling it into him. "But I continued it. Don't you see? I went back for more." I leaned in still closer to him. "I was part of it," I whispered. "I was a part of it."

He stared at me as uncomprehending and curious as a dog. Then he took a step back, away from me. "That's ridiculous," he said. "You're telling me you wanted to do it? You're telling me he didn't coerce you? You're telling me he didn't deserve to be arrested and sent to prison?"

"I don't know what he deserved," I said. "He doesn't deserve to be dead."

"But he killed *himself.*"

"He did it because of this."

He turned to look at my mother, astonished, then looked back at me. "Rob," he said, "it wasn't *your* fault." He said it like he couldn't understand why I didn't see that.

"He did it because of *me,*" I cried. Why didn't he see *that*?

"No," said my mother. "That's not true."

"It *is.* If he hadn't been sent to prison . . ."

"Rob . . ." said my dad. He squatted by me and put his hand behind my neck as if to steady me. He waited for me to look him in the eye. Somehow I didn't want to. Somehow I didn't dare. But finally, slowly, I did. "Rob," he said, "it wasn't your fault." He bored the words right into me. "Whatever Jerry Houseman did, he did it on his own." I'd never seen him look at me like that. So steady, so full of intention. Then he stroked my head once like he used to do when I was little and his voice took on a gentler tone. "He wasn't the kid in this story, son."

That's when I started sobbing. "But he wasn't trying to hurt me . . ."

My dad pulled my head against his shoulder and wrapped his arm around me, then stroked my head as I cried.

"He wasn't trying to hurt me," I said.

I felt my mother's hand on my back, flat between my shoulders, rubbing. She knelt and whispered into my ear. "Neither were we," she said.

5

I got back to Chicago about ten-thirty that night. It was strange to be there, alone again, and surprising how small my apartment felt. And how quiet, and how still. Everything was exactly, just exactly the way I'd left it, as if the air had been sucked from the place while I was away. I turned on the light in the hall, the lights in the kitchen and the living room and checked my answering machine. There was just one call, from Nick, to remind me to bring him his magic tie when I came into work the next night: His parents were coming to town. I wrote myself a note, then erased the message and turned on the television. Beavis and Butt head were yukking it up over a Meat Loaf video. I left the television on while I went in to take a shower, and slowly the sound, the steam and the light made the place begin to feel like it was home again.

I stayed in the shower for quite a while, letting the water pummel me, then wrapped a towel around my waist and padded into the kitchen, leaving a trail of wet footprints. I noticed the guy across the alley was eating ice cream, talking on the phone. I finished off a box of crackers, then lay down on the couch with a beer and did some channel surfing, but didn't get into anything and finally turned the thing off. I thought about calling Nick or Phyllis but didn't really feel like talking. So I just lay there and looked at my stuff. The posters. The second-hand furniture. The books and discs and sound equipment. I listened to the traffic outside and felt the breeze waft through the window, trying to imagine how the place might look with different things, or how the things might look in a different place. Maybe I'd move the desk from under the window up against the wall, so when I looked up I'd see my books instead of someone else's life. And maybe it was finally time to replace that chair from my parents' attic, the one that Reuben always complained felt like it was stuffed with pomegranates.

It was funny. After that scene with my parents, this is what I'd done too. Just lay down and looked at things in my room, as if they could reveal something to me. My mom had stayed downstairs in the kitchen to finish fixing the shortcake. My dad had gone out to the garage, I think, or maybe down to the basement. And I had gone up to my room to pack. It didn't take me long to pack, all I had to do was throw some clothes into a bag, but I stayed in my room for quite a while, sort of adjusting to things. I felt like I needed to just be still, to try to get a sense of myself, the way I imagine somebody might try to do after an accident. Do I dare move? How much? How fast? And in what direction? So I lay down on my bed and stared at my turtle tank and posters and stuff and finally fell asleep. When I woke, I could smell the shortcake baking.

We had a kind of awkward dinner. Nobody knew quite how to act. My dad grilled burgers and we ate at the picnic table in the backyard. Potato salad and baked beans. We talked about the Sox a little, about my mom's geraniums and whether they ought to put a birdbath in the corner by the garage. My mom asked if I'd seen Patty at the reunion and wanted to know everything about what she was doing now. Then we talked about the trip to Chicago my folks had planned for the fall. It was all a little halting. While my mom was getting dessert, my dad brought out the cordless phone and we tried to get ahold of Danny and Janice in San Diego, but we only got their machine. Then we finished the meal with the strawberry shortcake, admiring my dad's mowing job, and listening to the crickets and the coo of the mourning doves.

I finally left around dusk. Both of them came to the car with me and told me to drive carefully and not to be in too big a hurry. Then my mom gave me a big long hug—too long, too tight, but I got the message—and when we broke I could see she was crying. Dad hugged me too, which he'd never done, and clapped me on the back. "You take good care of yourself," he said.

"I will," I said. Whatever that meant.

Then I pulled away. I decided to go through town instead of getting right on the highway. I took a roundabout tour through the park past the dirt bike hill, the old zoo, the rose garden and the picnic pavilion. I drove past my old grade school, then down past my junior high and the high school. I took a turn past Patty's house. It felt like I was searching for something but I didn't have any idea what, so I finally gave up and took West Avenue out to I-94.

Then I was on the road again, tunneling through the darkness again. I didn't listen to music at first, just drove along in silence, watching different images from the weekend float in and out of my mind. Mom and Dad at the picnic table. Patty by the pool. Me sitting in the sun on that rock by the brook where I used to go with Jerry. Mrs. Houseman standing in line behind me. Mrs. Houseman crossing the parking lot. Mrs. Houseman. The urge I had to kill her.

I imagined calling her up, or maybe writing her a letter. I tried to imagine what I would say. That I was sorry for all that had happened? Maybe that would be good, to say that. But once I said that, what else would I say? I didn't have a letter in me. So I thought about maybe just sending a card. But why would I want to do that? Then again, why shouldn't I do it? She looked so solo driving away in her car, like she didn't have a place in the world.

I thought about that day I rode by and stopped to talk with her while she was cleaning out her garage. That seemed to be from another lifetime. Not only because it was so long ago, but because it went Before. I wondered if Jerry was watching me, even then, from their bedroom window. I pictured his face looking down at me, pictured him pulling the curtain aside and peering around it, to see me. I pictured the trembling of his hand, and the fear in his eyes.

I pictured him in their bedroom. The frilly lampshades on the night tables. Their wedding picture on the dresser. The humming of the digital clock: four o'clock in the afternoon. The sound of a dog barking somewhere outside.

A screen door slamming.

Someone calling out.

I remembered the coolness of the sheets on my skin. Jerry coming out of the bathroom and sliding in beside me, naked. The way the gold chains slithered through the hair on his chest like snakes through grass. The smell of his cologne, just applied.

I thought about something else. About Linda in California. The bed, the tangled sheets, the milkiness of her skin. The way she glistened with sweat and stretched her neck like a cat, and the tickle of her fingernails tracing words on my back. The way we rolled around together, and laughed, and her hair fell in her face.

I slipped a tape into the deck. Philip Glass, *Dance Pieces*. Great for driving; it just keeps rolling.

Then the image again of Jerry in his bedroom, bending over to kiss me. The slithery feel of his tongue, so big. More complicated smells. The press of his dick against my leg. The press of mine against him, against all that bristly hair. His mouth on my skin. My mouth on his.

I found myself trying to swallow it back.

I turned the volume up, drove faster.

I remembered that guy in Oregon, the encyclopedia salesman. The top of his head as I looked down on him, the balding spot gone pink from the sun, pink as a baby's butt. The movement of his head, in and out. I wanted to hit him, to swat his head and see it split apart like a pumpkin. But I grabbed his ears instead, and pulled. "You fucker," I muttered to him. "You fucker." The defeat I felt, standing over him. The squalor of that moment.

The squalor of Linda, that tacky town.

Then the picture of Jerry in the courtroom, saying he was guilty. Saying he'd touched me. The judge looking down on him, the corners of his mouth pulled down. Jerry standing before him, made small, looking up like a little kid. Jerry, like a little kid. And me lifted high, up over him, looking down on him.

That was when I cried again. For Jerry. Myself. For everyone. My parents, my brother, Jerry's wife. Even Linda in California. Even Ted in Oregon. I had a pretty good cry for us all. But as quick as it came, it was gone.

I turned up the volume still more and drove on, thinking now of where I was going. Thinking about this life I had to live, the people I had to meet, all the things there were to try. I wanted to be an adventurer. I wanted to go exploring in life, the way I used to explore on my bike. I'd tethered myself to that bar at Charlie's, just like a dog on a leash, for years. I had this image of myself chained to a post in a field of snow. It was an image I'd had in a dream. There I was in this field of snow, in the park near where I grew up, and I was chained to this wooden post. I could only move in a circle around it, in and out and around; there were paths of footprints in the snow tracing my endless circles. There was no one else around, just me and the post and the field of snow. And then on closer look I saw that the chain was not attached. I could move away from the post if I wanted, but I didn't want to. In the dream, I didn't want to.

But now, in my life, could I do it? Could I go out into the world again? There wasn't any reason to think that anything should change just because I'd had that scene with my parents. Just because Jerry was dead. But I wanted it to change, I wanted everything to change. I wanted someone in my life, someone at the other end of this drive who would be waiting for me. Someone who would go traveling with me, who'd keep her toothbrush next to mine.

And I wanted to finish my college degree and then ignore it, or use it, whatever. I just wanted to be done with it, to free myself up for other things. Maybe I'd be a teacher, or not. Maybe I'd get married, or not. Have kids, or not. Relocate, or not. I wanted to have choices, and to have freedom in making choices. To be not afraid of the choices I'd make, not afraid of regret or mistakes. It seemed like I'd lost faith in myself, like I'd lost faith in my instincts. Could I get it back again? How do you come to believe in yourself again once you've forgotten how?

Does it require belief in something else?

Something bigger than yourself?

It started to rain when I hit Benton Harbor and continued all the way through Gary, but by the time I reached Chicago the storm was on its way out. You could see the clouds moving over. I slowed as I drove up Lakeshore Drive to pay my respects to the city again, my bustling, big-shouldered buddy. On the right, the dark void of the lake stretched out into infinity, a great black hole of nothingness. On the left, the towers of the city rose up and disappeared into the clouds, the extent of their upper reaches limited only by the imagination. I looked back and forth from one to the other. Then I opened the window, cranked up the music, stuck my head out into the wind and skated the edge between them, singing.

ACKNOWLEDGMENTS

I want to thank my writers' group and my friends and colleagues at Vermont College for their help in developing this book, especially Sena Jeter Naslund for the strength and depth of her support and the wisdom of her advice.

I also want to thank Stephen Holt and Carol Flynn for their thoughtful readings; John Darrell, Lisa Freije and George Pierce for their lessons in courtroom procedures; and Stephen Conley and Larry Finton for their instruction in the ways of lawyers and policemen.

My gratitude also to Richard Parks and to Jennifer Hershey for their vision, conviction, daring, and savvy: They continue to exceed my wildest dreams as agent and editor. And finally, for helping create a nurturing climate in which this thing could grow, and for helping me to grow with it, my deepest thanks to Richard MacMillan.